GILDED SAINT

ARROW TACTICAL SERIES
BOOK 7

ISABEL JOLIE

ISABEL JOLIE

Editor: Lori Whitwam

Proofreading: Karen Cimms

Cover Design: Damonza

❀ Created with Vellum

For the resilient souls of Western North Carolina, who turned Hurricane Helene's fury into a testament of community strength. My characters chose your mountains as their sanctuary; you've shown why that choice rings true. #AshevilleStrong

"Never forget that a saint is a sinner who keeps on trying."

-Nelson Mandela

PROLOGUE

SAM, AKA SAINT

"The deal's done."

"Any surprises?"

There was something about the way Jack Sullivan asked, the tilt of his head, or maybe it was the fact we were sitting in a high-security location that led me to believe he already knew the answer to the question.

"I didn't meet with Yuri Petrov. The man I met sounded British, but his name is Russian. Nick Ivanov. He said Petrov was indisposed."

"What did you think of Ivanov?"

The syndicate representative wasn't what I expected. Intelligent. Well-spoken. My gut read him as trustworthy, even though our intel argued otherwise. "Came across like a respectable business executive. My hunch is the project got dumped in his lap."

"Did you spend time with him?"

"Dinner. He didn't share anything relevant, if that's what you're asking."

"For our purposes, everything is relevant."

"I'll detail the conversation in my report."

Jack studied me, and an unwarranted uneasiness struck. Jack Sullivan asked me to handle this for him as a favor on an off-the-record project. But it was a test. Subconsciously, I knew it. And I reacted the same way I reacted to all tests, determined to ace it.

"He liked you." Jack's statement came across like an accusation.

"You spoke to Ivanov?"

"He called and asked if he could hire you. You sure there's nothing you want to share about what happened in London?"

I crossed my arms, not liking what Jack insinuated one bit. "It was a straightforward deal. Handguns and rifles. Upsold him on suppressors and the new mini-explosive device. Told him it works well on doors, gates, and the like. Got you another twenty million on top of the original deal."

"You're a natural."

"I like the product. Did what you said. Played it real. But I don't understand why you're selling to these guys. Delivery will occur over international waters. If you choose to deliver. Now you know how they skirt the system." And that was the point of this op.

Jack rapped his knuckles against the conference room table. I sensed indecision, but if he had any, he resolved it in a split second.

"If we don't sell to them, someone will. Information is

power. The syndicate owns government leaders. Not only in the United States. The entire G8. We need to know who."

"I didn't get that kind of intel. But for the delivery of this order, he'll send coordinates next week with detailed instructions. I'm telling you, I learned nothing of value."

"He wants to bring you onto his team. He's looking for an arms dealer to negotiate on behalf of the syndicate. But he doesn't want to offer you the position if we'll be offended."

"Seriously?" Nick and I got along fine over dinner, but not let-me-steal-you-away-from-your-company level fine.

"We're surprised too."

"And he asked you?"

"They take family seriously. You went out there posing as my cousin's kid. To them, that's family. Our sources say that Yuri Petrov picked up a nasty heroin habit. Explains Ivanov stepping in. Petrov is, coincidentally, his cousin. But from what we've gathered, Nikolai Ivanov doesn't party."

"Nick," I corrected, but regretted it when Jack looked at me the way an officer looks at a recruit. "He goes by Nick. And drugs may not be his thing, but women are. After dinner, half a dozen joined us. He offered me first choice. They never said they were prostitutes, but I assumed they were all on the payroll. I declined. Figured he wouldn't like me after I turned him down, but since the deal was inked, and this is a one-off, it didn't matter."

Jack smiled slightly, like I gave him the information he'd been seeking.

"You turning him down showed him you won't bow down to him. Foremost, he's a businessman. He's looking to replace Petrov with someone he can trust. He wants you to return to London and discuss the job. Says he wants an industry expert, someone with negotiation and interpersonal skills. He says you fit the bill. And I think he likes that it strengthens ties to Sullivan Arms. The syndicate values connections."

"You said these guys have expansive and uninterrupted global reach. Wouldn't they be privy to Sullivan Arms's role in taking down a Mexican cartel?"

Jack Sullivan ranked as a Navy legend. A naval academy graduate, he and his brother inherited their father's company only to learn his uncle cut deals with the cartels. A lot of shit happened some fifteen plus years ago, but if I'd heard the story, so had any criminal organization.

"They view it as family infighting. Something they might do themselves, given my daughter's abduction. The incident fits within their moral constructs."

I stared at him, wondering if that was exactly what had happened. In-fighting among family. But he answered the unspoken question.

"No. We didn't sell my uncle out for revenge. We've ended any connection with the drug trade. Yes, we sell weapons to unsavory organizations, but Liam and I stopped aiding all trafficking efforts. The syndicate profits from both legitimate and illegitimate businesses, like any modern-day criminal organization."

The Sullivan brothers split responsibility of Sullivan Arms after their uncle was removed from the corporation. Jack functions as the CEO, and Liam leads R&D.

Jack is also a partner in a black-ops organization called Arrow Tactical. They take on jobs for various government entities, like the CIA and NSA.

My gut told me I could trust Jack, just like it told me I could trust Nick. But I had difficulty grasping exactly what Jack wanted me to do. "You want me to go back out and meet with Nick again?"

"If your meeting goes well, we expect he'll offer you a job. It sounds like he's been itching to bring the role of negotiator into the corporate fold and away from the Russian mafia. He might not offer you a job. But if he does, we'd like for you to consider saying yes."

As a Navy SEAL, an active member of SEAL Team 8, I took Sullivan's off-books project and associated trip to London while on a short leave.

"You'd be coming into the CIA fold full-time, working deep undercover. We never thought we'd get a man on the inside of the syndicate. If they offer you a job, this is an enormous opportunity. We know they've bought US politicians and business leaders, but we don't know which ones. Possibly military leaders too. Leaders around the world. If you get a job with them, the intel would be invaluable."

"These guys are dangerous?"

He nodded his affirmation and confirmed, "Deadly."

"The kinds of guys who would go after a traitor's family members?"

"Yes." He didn't even blink.

"I have two sisters. I love my country, but I won't put them at risk."

"I understand. More than you know."

Legend said Jack Sullivan was an operative and sniper for the CIA for years. Rumors said he was a part of a group within the CIA that technically didn't exist. If any of that was true, I imagined the married man and father did understand. He stood at the head of the conference table, placed both hands firmly on the back of a chair, and looked me directly in the eye.

"If you get the job, we can make the world think Sam Watson died. It's probably an unnecessary step, but if you're worried, we can do it. Set up a scenario where you're missing in action. You can return when the op is over. There would be no risk your sisters would be retribution targets."

"That sounds…" I was at a loss for words. "What about your family?"

"You went in there as an employed distant cousin. There's plausible deniability. We'll make it look like you sold us out, too. We can fake prosecution or legal troubles to sell the story if we need to."

I continued staring at him in disbelief.

"Of course, if you get caught, your death will be painful. I won't sugarcoat it. If you agree to this, we'll train you. We'll provide every resource you need."

"You'll train me," I said, repeating those words, although that shouldn't have been the piece that stuck. As a SEAL, my life was a series of trainings.

"If Ivanov offers what I think he will, this will be an invaluable opportunity. The value of the intelligence is incalculable."

"I'll think about it." Yes, I walked into that room wanting to impress a legend and ace an imagined test, but I wasn't about to change careers without giving it some serious thought. And what about my sisters? How would that even work?

"The meeting with Ivanov isn't for another three months. He wants to meet after the delivery of the order. There's time for you to think about it and time for us to prepare. But the op starts the second you say yes. If I were Ivanov, I'd have people watching you, double-checking you are who you say you are. Which means if you visit your sisters, you'll need to take precautions. You should stay here in Houston, living life as Leo

Sullivan, and let us handle getting you places as Sam. We'll get a body double to stay in Houston when you need to leave."

"I have a job. I'm due back—" I flicked my wrist, checking the date.

"You're on indefinite leave, cleared by your commanding officer. While you think about it, in addition to your Navy salary, a private entity will triple match your base while you consider the opportunity. You decide against it, you go right back to your team."

"My CO signed off on this?"

"The Admiral did. No one else can know."

"If I do this, if I go to this meeting and accept the syndicate's job offer, how long will I stay in the role? How long does an op like that last?"

"Six months, a year tops. You say the word, we arrange an extraction. You'll be back home, free to resume your position in the Navy or to pursue any number of opportunities that arise."

"If I do this, it won't be for my career." Money didn't motivate me. "If I do this, it will be for my country."

CHAPTER 1

SIX YEARS LATER

SAM, AKA LEO, AKA SAINT

"Whiskey or cognac?"

Nick gestures between a bottle of Louis XIII by Rémy Martin and a crystal bottle of Macallan.

"Bringing out the crystal?"

"It's your fifth anniversary. Can't let that go without celebration."

"Whiskey all the way." I sling an ankle over my knee and swipe dust off my cowboy boot. I added boots to my wardrobe when I took this gig to emphasize my Texas origins, but now I wear them because they're a thousand times more comfortable than the shiny, pointy-ass dress shoes European men in my circle favor. "What's a bottle like that cost?"

Nick holds up the bottle with a proud expression. "This one is over two hundred thousand euros."

I raise my eyebrows in the expected show of appreciation. He hands over a crystal highball glass, because Nick likes all the finer things, and I swirl it, inhaling a mix of cedar, oak, possibly cinnamon and clove, and hints of vanilla and caramel.

"To five years."

Our glasses clink, and Nick settles against the front of his desk. One might expect breaking open a Macallan from the Six Pillar collection would mean the end of a workday. But Nick didn't choose the armchair across from me, which means he's still got projects to tick off his list.

"I need you in Italy next week."

I swirl my glass and watch the liquid gold cling to the crystal in a thin veil.

"Massimo De Luca wants to capitalize on our network as they look to, ah, beef up their arsenal. I've offered your negotiation services."

The Lupi Grigi was once the most powerful mafia organization in Italy, but about a year ago, they suffered a huge bust. Twenty-five million in product gone. The capo arrested. From the outside, it looked like the Italian authorities started doing their jobs. What really happened was Nick questioned their allegiance to the syndicate, and he cut them off at their knees. Massimo's uncle is serving a life sentence.

"Have they rebuilt?"

"Reportedly. I need you to get a read on the situation."

"They came to you. That's a good sign."

"Possibly. Here's the score. Alessio Gagliano's shipping business is running strong, a proper, tidy operation. If you ask me, he should've been the one wearing the big boy trousers.

Massimo…he's twisted." He exhales and waves a dismissive hand. "A right arsehole. His brother's worse. Anyways, Sara's sorted your travel bits. Alessio is hosting an engagement party and says it's prime time for you to pop down. All the power players in one place."

Over the years, I've learned that the mafia and cartel members of the syndicate are Nick's least favorite. From his perspective, they're a necessary tool. It's not the money they bring in that makes them indispensable. The syndicate earns plenty from their legitimate businesses. It's the manpower they deliver. They instill fear, and they do so with a disciplined culture not too different from militaries.

"Fun times." Nick hears the sarcasm and grins. "You've got the tech summit next week, right?"

"Tokyo. Love that city." He pushes off his desk and kicks back in the armchair, a sign the business portion of our meeting has concluded. "Lina asked about you."

I raise a single eyebrow. "You pushing me and your sister?"

That earns a chuckle. "Fuck, no. I have a hard enough time keeping her out of the business as is."

My read on his sister is she's a good one. I only ever see her on the rare occasions I meet Nick at his Yorkshire estate. She's clueless that her Oxford-educated brother is a leading member of the syndicate, a group that influences global policies through both legal and illegal means. For a few years, I thought Nick was the head, but the structure is cooperative. With all the egos in play, it's the only way the alliance survives.

As for Nick's sister, nothing will ever happen between the two of us. Leo Sullivan exists on paper only. I'd never bring a decent human into my fucked-up world.

"Spoken to Ivy?"

Ivy's a college classmate of Nick's. We ran into her at a bar a week ago. Nick went home with an escort, and he believes I went home with Ivy.

"No," I answer before sipping and savoring the most expensive whisky that's ever crossed my tongue. It's smooth and rich like butter. Worth two hundred thousand euros? Fuck, no.

A light flashes on his desk. Nick pinches the bridge of his nose and closes his eyes, wincing.

"Tick tock," I tease.

"Bloody fucking hell." He rises, highball glass in hand, and returns to his desk. He has several secure communication devices displayed on the credenza, and a security team ensures none are being traced. The flashing light translates to disaster. It's the only time someone would dial that number.

SAM, AKA LEO, AKA SAINT

St - Bkgrd on I Lupi Grigi

Pre-2023 Bust, Lupi Grigi owned 25% of the European heroin supply. Current estimate at 15% of mkt. The new leader, Massimo De Luca, is under pressure for growth but lost market share in Europe, and sources say he's working to break into the US market. As you're American, they may see you as a valuable contact. Play along. Alessio Gagliano, a Lupi Grigi member, owns Titan Shipping. Sources claim he is expanding into the shadow fleet, specifically doing business on unmarked carriers with Russia, Iran, North Korea, and Syria. Confirm.

I delete the file and the history. Remove and crush the SIM card. There's a deadness in the air. No, the weight isn't in the air. It's in the eyes staring back at me in the glass reflection.

I check the chamber in my Glock out of habit. A gun isn't required. These men would never fuck with the syndicate. They'll be schmoozing, throwing drugs and tits my way.

There's no thrill. Not one iota. That's the deadness. If playing the world's fiercest criminals no longer thrills, I'm truly fucked. Not even forty, and I'm bored with life.

I can't forget why I'm doing this. The mission is critical. But is it really? Five years on this damn op, and has anything changed?

I shuffle through the hotel lobby and climb into the waiting taxi. Two minutes later, the taxi stops in front of another hotel.

Shit. If I'd paid attention, I could've walked and gotten some fresh air.

Alessio Gagliano, the shipping titan, is hosting the weekend's engagement celebration festivities. Nick's assistant sent an engagement gift. I don't know who the fuck is getting married, nor do I care. With luck, we'll do the meet and greet tonight, negotiate tomorrow, and I'll be free Saturday evening.

The hotel lobby is as grand as the one I'm staying in. The woman behind check-in smiles, and I look away, sending a message that I don't need her help. There's a framed pedestal that in Italian reads the celebrated couple's names with the name of a terrace. My boots and shuffling gait grate against the marble floor. A man in a black suit carrying a tray of bubbly offers me one. I decline, step out onto the terrace, and take in a stunning view of the Mediterranean.

The stone railing, weathered through the centuries, cools my skin. The sense of permanence anchors me. The centuries-old structure underscores the fleeting nature of my life.

A sprawling lawn extends below the balcony, and a woman stands before a similar railing, looking across the sea. Her light blonde strands shimmer in the sunlight, and her sundress flutters around her calves in the breeze. Her slight frame, the wind-tousled waves in her hair, and maybe her dress's youthful floral pattern remind me of my youngest sister, and an ache pulses.

I squeeze my eyelids shut, burying the weakness. I have a mission. A purpose. Two deep breaths and I open my eyes.

A young man with black hair stands beside the woman. He tilts his head back, laughing. Perhaps they're the happy couple, although if he's the one getting married, I'm definitely getting old. The gangly kid looks like he's sixteen, tops, but my perception of age has been fucked for years. The blonde glances over her shoulder. She's young as fuck, too. She's got the curves of a woman, but she's young.

The Italian mafia families are infamous for marrying young. A few years back, I attended a wedding celebration where they hung the bloodied bridal sheets to prove she was a virgin. Nick said not too many families follow the old ways these days, but now, nothing surprises me. She could be fourteen and her groom fifteen and it would be another day in a fucked-up world.

"Leo Sullivan. Is that you? You don't have a drink. I need to fire someone," Massimo De Luca says in perfect English.

Italian conversations buzz all around me, but there's an understanding that unless an interpreter accompanies me, they should speak to me in English.

I force a chuckle and take Massimo's hand, then Italian-man-hug and arm slap him. I met him before he claimed the leadership position. Sources say he stepped into the position as capo with little opposition.

Massimo raises a hand, scanning the terrace for the waitstaff.

"They offered," I say.

He lowers his arm. "You don't drink. I forget."

I don't have an issue with alcohol, but it lowers my inhibitions, so I no longer imbibe at work events. Miraculously, refusing drink, drugs, and women garners more trust, at least within the syndicate. Pretty sure guys like Massimo assume I'm a recovered addict. They would be wrong.

"Still wearing those cowboy boots. It's how I knew it was you." He slaps me on the back then grows serious. "Now, we have business to discuss. Then no more business until morning. *Capisce?*"

"I'll follow your lead."

"Submersibles. Is that an area of yours, or do you have a contact?"

"Submarines?"

"Eh. Yes. Cargo capacity is the priority. As opposed to military designs."

This is swift confirmation Titan Shipping is indeed expanding into the shadow fleet. "If it's not on the market, we can have a custom model manufactured."

"That's what they say about you."

"What exactly would that be?"

"The cowboy delivers. Or, I should say, the lion cowboy delivers. Anyone ever call you that?"

"Can't say I've heard it before."

"Leo. Means lion."

I grin. Pretty sure the Sullivan brothers were inspired by Leonardo Di Caprio when they derived my name, but… "Yes, that much I know."

"Is it short for Leonardo?"

"No. Mom named me Leo." He's unimpressed. "American." I

shrug. What can I say? My paperwork says Leo. "So, should I meet with Alessio now or..."

"Let's take a stroll. Most of the men have needs. And I'd like for you to get a lay of the land, and then I'm interested in the discount the syndicate will offer."

Right. Discounts are a network benefit, along with distribution consulting and coordinated protection from the authorities. I'll determine his purchasing needs, and then Nick and I will determine which partner will reap the contracts. Everybody gets love. And the guys back home get intel on the latest scheme to skirt international law and traffic illegal commodities.

CHAPTER 3

WILLOW

Every cell in my body pleads to leave, to disappear somewhere far away. But leaving is not an option. My father is the host, and the important men in the family are present.

Goose bumps sprout, and I curl my arms around my waist, compensating for my dress's thin fabric. The breeze carries a chilly undertone. It's a direct contrast to the summery hues of the crystal blue Mediterranean.

A four-piece band plays a cheerful instrumental tune, and young, naive children laugh and dance along the lawn. The wives cluster in groups, sipping cocktails and gossiping. The men lurk somewhere indoors discussing business matters. This scene could have played out fifty years ago. Nothing has changed. There's no progress.

In an ideal world, my father would disassociate from the Lupi Grigi. Titan Shipping has grown exponentially under my father's guidance. He doesn't need blood money. A legitimate businessman, he's not like these men. But he's loyal. As much as I wish it otherwise, he'll never stand up against the family.

I should be grateful. That's what my mother says. I attended university, a rarity for women in our world. My father's success means that, unlike some of the other women, my marriage won't be crafted to deliver business connections or to rise in the ranks. My father is a billionaire—on paper, at least—and he has no interest in being an underboss. My cousin Scarlet told me there were rumors father's name had been bandied about for capo, but he declined consideration.

Unease coils through me so tightly I can't possibly mingle. There's no need for me to be anxious, but my anxiety doesn't listen to logic. It doesn't matter who approaches Papa. He won't barter me away to one of these monsters.

He's loyal, but he loves me. My mother says I've had him wrapped around my finger since I was two minutes old. There's no need to be nervous.

Orlando steps out from the shadows, and I jump. My younger brother grins, pleased with himself. At fifteen, he hasn't yet become a man, but Scarlet says his ceremony will be soon. I hope she's wrong. I hope Papa gives him the chance to go to university, so he's in the best position to lead Titan Shipping. My little brother admires the men for maintaining harmony throughout Italy, but they do that through fear. He wants to become a made man, but that's not what I want for him. He's not a killer.

"If we didn't sell drugs, someone else would." Orlando said that to me once, on the day I realized I could only guide him so far without risking my freedom. Of course, made man or not, Papa is grooming him for the shipping business. He'll follow in

Papa's footsteps, growing the legitimate business, and will hopefully skirt the darker corners of our world.

If I weren't so on edge, I'd return Orlando's boyish smile and suggest we find Scarlet.

"What're you doing by yourself?" Orlando asks, sidling up to me. The ill-fitting suit jacket he's wearing over his linen shirt crinkles around the shoulders.

"You should've gotten that taken in. It's too big." Mamma complains he's impossible to dress these days, and when she alters his clothes, he can only get one wear before he's grown more inches. But today, other than the shoulders of his jacket being too broad, his clothes fit well and he could almost be mistaken for a man.

"Did Mamma pick that dress out for you?"

Avoiding Orlando's ribbing, I hold the terrace railing and take in the expanse of sea. The breeze lifts my hair and circles my exposed décolletage. If the scooped neckline were any lower, my nipples would show, and yes, my mother purchased and forced me to wear this dress. It could be worse. Other than the neckline, the dress is demure, falling to my calves. In the mirror, I told myself the pastel floral pattern made me appear younger. It's the push-up bra she forced on me that undercuts my hope and feeds my anxiety.

"How're the meetings going?" I do not wish to discuss my dress.

"Eh, they're smoking cigars and drinking. If any business is getting done, it's behind closed doors."

"Is father mingling?" He's far too approachable at gatherings like this one.

"I haven't seen him in hours."

My stomach plunges like it does on the freefall ride at the Universal theme park in Spain.

"What's wrong?"

"Nothing," I answer.

"Dinner will be soon. Look, the meeting is breaking up."

Men, some in jackets, others in linen button-down shirts, all in trousers, filter onto the stone patio through the series of French doors that line the hotel exterior.

"Are you like this because of Scarlet?"

"What do you mean?"

"Afraid. Nervous. You don't need to be, you know? Papa would never choose a man like Vincent for you."

I cut an eye at Orlando. He's heard what happened, but that's not the same as seeing. He was too young, but I saw.

"Don't look now, but Leandro De Luca is headed over here."

The brother of our capo, Leandro De Luca, infamously quartered an enemy, and soaked with blood, sat down to dine. All the Grigi men are killers, but that one story will forever set him apart from the others. Papa disagreed with Massimo stepping in as capo because he believed Leandro would be a distraction for Massimo, as he'd always be cleaning up his messes. He believes Leandro's hotheaded and lacks impulse control. But Papa didn't fight the decision for Massimo to take over. He told Mamma it is best to choose your battles.

Black shades hide Leandro's cruel eyes, and gold necklaces glitter above curly white chest hairs that spill from his black linen button-down shirt. He steps close to me, and my unsettled stomach churns.

"Appreciating the view, *bella*?" he asks in Italian.

My brother and I speak English at home. My father insisted we both perfect the language, as in father's business English is important. Thanks to the booming tourism industry, his mandate felt quite normal growing up. Lots of children are expected to learn English, but it's more common in my generation than Leandro's.

I nod meekly, shifting to face the banister so my breasts aren't on direct display.

"Alessio didn't mention what a beauty you've become." He disregards Orlando, and my cheeks burn as he steps closer and his gaze lowers. I slouch, and the fabric dips, exposing my bra. I quickly straighten. *Damn this dress.*

The stench of cigars fills my nostrils. His fingers brush over my hips. Bile rises in my throat. I have to get away. If I don't, my upset stomach will release everything. I mumble in Italian as polite of an excuse as I can muster and clasp my jaw closed, breathing in my nose, one foot in front of the other, until I'm at the stone steps and I break out into a run.

Mamma will yell later. She'll say I must show respect, but her wrath is preferable to getting pawed by a dirty, creepy, old man with a serial killer vibe.

It's not until I reach the paved street below that I risk a glance over my shoulder at the railing above. Dark, circular shades stare down upon me, watching me above an unsettling grin. If you added clown make-up, he could be mistaken for the joker.

Heart racing, I don't stop running until I reach the shore and inhale the sea air. I remove my heels and let my toes sink into the sand.

CHAPTER 4

SAM, AKA LEO, AKA SAINT

My feet fucking throb, and my throat is sore from straining to talk above the quartet and the hum of the crowd. The cigar smoke probably doesn't help.

A full moon lights the stone stairs as I escape, head swimming with everything Massimo wants for his family.

The Lupi Grigi are looking to invest billions to shore up their defenses and enhance product delivery options. The guns and explosives will put them at an advantage over law enforcement all over Europe, and the submersibles Gagliano aims to add to his fleet will enhance the ships he's already converted to "stateless vessels," meaning they skirt international regulations.

When I'm back home, I'll convince Nick he's got to do something. The ever-growing expansion of the shadow fleet goes against the mission of the syndicate to maintain world order while promoting profits. The trouble is the balance of what's best for the world and what delivers profits is tricky. However, I stand a chance of convincing Nick this doesn't bode well. He's the one who engineered the mega bust on the Grigi family because they were too powerful. If we deliver everything Massimo is seeking, he might meet his goal of making them the most formidable in Europe once again, with growing clout in North and South America.

The flat sea laps at the shore, and I'm tempted to remove my boots and let the sand seep between my toes. High-end hotels line the cliff, but few wander this stretch of sand beneath the cliffs late at night. The steep trail deters the masses. The sandy beach makes Atrani a rarity along the Amalfi Coast, and if I were here for a different reason, it would be tempting to stay for a while.

A high-pitched cry breaks the peaceful ocean lull.

"*Stai zitto*!" the deep voice shouts in Italian.

It's the feminine, distressed cry that sends me running.

I charge up a dirt path and break into a run when I hit cobblestone.

The cries mellow, but high-pitch squeals escape every few seconds, as if a hand covers her mouth. And of course, I didn't bring my fucking gun.

In the shadows, the back of a man comes into view. His shoulders are wider than mine, but so is his waist. He has a woman's back pressed to his front. One hand covers her mouth. She kicks her leg back, but hits air.

He grunts in Italian, telling her to relax.

As I get closer, my eyes adjust, and I recognize the flower print dress.

I tap the man on the shoulder. He whips around, arm raised, defensive, forgetting all about the girl.

I haul off and deck him. His head slings back. I clock him with a right hook. He stumbles back against the stone wall, and I plant a fist head-on.

He holds a palm up to his face, and the whites of his eyes glow in the moonlight as he registers blood.

That's right, fucker.

"Do you know who I am?" he yells in accented English that's a spot-on match for all the Italians I hobnobbed with earlier in the day.

"No. Don't care to either."

"You're going to regret this, fucking American."

"Leave. Now." I point toward the street.

It's a steep climb to the town, but he can breathe through his mouth. Based on the spurting blood, I broke his nose. Good.

If he charges me, with one kick I'll break his leg and leave the fucker to crawl the incline.

He mutters, spewing Italian profanity. He raises a fist but pauses, looking between me and the girl. She's backed up to the wall, clutching her neck, which makes me think he throttled her.

I see red. Not the flowered dress. Not the blonde with wavy hair. I see my sisters. Rage overwhelms me. I raise my fist, and he drops his, wisely backing up.

"You'll pay," he grunts.

"For stopping an assault on a young girl? I don't think so. Get the fuck out of here."

I would've enjoyed cracking his leg, but the coward spins and heads off into the shadows.

There's no doubt he's in the Grigi clan. An older man, out-of-shape, with the ego to threaten. Probably the head of one of the smaller families, but I didn't meet him today, which means

Massimo doesn't see him as a player. Whatever the fuck. Everyone who knows me knows I won't stand for abusing women. Can't stomach it, so you don't fucking do it around me.

The girl backs away, hand on her neck, those gigantic eyes glowing in the moonlight.

"Did he hurt you?"

She sniffles.

"You don't need to be afraid. Not of me." The moon is the only light source in this area, and shadows abound. "Can I walk you home?" She's quiet, so I repeat myself in Italian.

"You don't need to," she answers in perfect English with a slight accent. Her fingers knead her throat.

"Did he strangle you?" I step closer, squinting to see better.

Child-like eyes glisten in the moonlight, full of tears. I'm not the police. I don't need to know the specifics, but I need to know she's okay.

"Let's walk," I say, backing up, giving her room, showing her I'm not another monster. "Where's home?"

"I'm fine. I live close."

She pushes off the wall and wraps her arms around her waist, head down. I follow from a distance. It's got to be statistically unlikely she'd be attacked twice in one night, but I can't help myself. It's in my DNA to protect. I won't sleep if I don't see her home. She stoops along the stairs near the sand and picks up a pair of heels.

The old man must've seen her on the beach and attempted to force her into the alley. Or hell, who knows what he was thinking. Maybe he was going to rape and kill. There are sick fucks the world over.

We walk in silence, her shooting me side glances that make it clear she doesn't trust me. I hang back, not wanting to frighten her, simply wanting to be sure she makes it home. About a mile up the shore, where the sand beneath the cliffs grows rocky, she turns onto a trail.

"Willow? Papa's looking for you." A teenage boy in shorts and a tee appears seconds later.

The boy, probably a young teenager, narrows his eyes and puffs out his chest ever so slightly when he sees me, as if warning me away. I nod my respect to the protective brother, and a glimmer of recognition crosses his expression. I don't recall meeting him, but I leave her, knowing the kid has her now, and she's safe.

CHAPTER 5

WILLOW

"What's wrong? What happened? Why are you crying?" Orlando asks.

He leads us up the steep incline, as his long legs are much faster than mine, but he continually glances back, worried. He doesn't need to know what happened. It's better if no one does.

"What does Papa want?" I ask.

"Massimo De Luca stopped by our house after the engagement party."

My calves and thighs burn, and I push into the familiar heat. No one climbs this path without paying the price.

Orlando jabbers on, but I shudder. I feel that man's pudgy hands. On my arm, gripping my throat. Over my lips, pressed hard against my nostrils. The bridge of my nose is sore. And my breasts. He grabbed them like they were toys. He said he came looking for me. Why?

"Mamma and Papa want to talk with you in the morning, but you can't. There are better men." I meet Orlando's dark brown eyes, nearly black in the moonlight, and there's something new there. The expression he's wearing adds years. He's shedding his youth. "Why were you with the American?"

"You know that man?"

"He's an arms dealer."

An arms dealer. I shudder. Saved from a monster by a monster.

"I don't know him. He..." Orlando is too young. If I tell him what happened, he'll get himself in trouble tomorrow, playing protective brother. "He saw me walking on the beach and wanted to be sure I got home safely."

"Willow..." Orlando's serious tone tears at my frayed nerves. He's never serious. "Massimo De Luca inquired about you."

"He's married." I spit the words.

"His brother...that old man who approached you at the engagement party. He's the one. It's sick. He's like old enough to be your grandfather."

"Papa said no." My heart ricochets. "Right?"

"I don't believe Leandro asked for your hand. But Papa was pissed you weren't around for him to introduce to the capo. He had me search everywhere for you, and when I couldn't find you, Massimo asked about your plans, and Papa dismissed me."

"You don't think..." Tendrils of fear climb my veins.

Was that why Leandro found me on the beach? To take possession early? He certainly didn't act like a man wooing a woman. But then again, I slapped him. He bent to kiss me, and I slapped him. And then it's all a blur.

"Did something happen to you?" His finger dabs my collarbone, and I shove it away.

"How long ago did Massimo leave? Did Papa say anything else?"

"Why were you crying?"

I grip my brother's bony shoulders and shake him. "What did Papa say?"

"Nothing has been agreed to, I don't think. Tomorrow, they want you to meet—"

"No." I break away, shaking my head.

"Papa can't say no to the capo."

"I'll run away. I'll pack a bag and go…" I have friends from university.

"No one leaves." Orlando's only saying what I know too well to be true. If I go to one of my friends, I endanger them.

"The American. You really don't know him?"

"What? No. Why?" I pace, attempting to quell the rising panic. There must be something I can do. Leandro De Luca has had four wives, and two of them committed suicide. After my run-in with him…the way he pawed me. Like I was an object. I just can't.

"Maybe you could strike a deal."

He's gone mad. "With who? Our father? What kind of deal could I possibly strike with him?"

"Not with Papa. With the American. His name is Leo Sullivan."

"The arms dealer? Orlando! This is not a game!"

"I know. I know. Just hear me out."

I have to find a way out of here. That's what I have to do.

"He's a good guy. At least, from what I've observed. I think he's gay, but…" I remember his punches, the glare. He stood up to Leandro De Luca with no hint of fear. "It's not like I have a problem with that," Orlando adds. "Not sure all the men feel the same way. Maybe that's why he hides it."

"What makes you think he's gay?" And what does this have to do with me?

"He never partakes with the ladies. I overheard a man talking about it today."

I clutch a chunk of my hair and tug, pulling until my scalp hurts. "Why are you talking about him, Orlando?"

"He lives in London. Doesn't drink or do drugs. He works closely with Nick Ivanov. In the syndicate. He's higher up than the De Lucas. Papa would benefit more from having you marry him than a De Luca."

"Are you out of your mind?" He's deranged.

Trade one devil for another. Orlando's lost his mind. Fuck all of that. This is the twenty-first century.

Papa wouldn't marry me to a man like Leandro. He wouldn't. And Massimo might be capo, but my father is a respected business leader.

"Willow. Willow!" Orlando blocks my path. "Listen to me. You could do each other favors. He could have a wife, so no one would question why he's never with women, and you could avoid a union with Leandro."

I blink. Breathe. Curl my fingers into my palms so hard the nails dig into the flesh. "Orlando. It's the twenty-first century. No one cares if he's gay."

"Think about it, Willow. He's an arms dealer. He deals with people in parts of the world where homosexuality is punishable by death. Listen to me. I know you think I'm too young to be taken seriously, but this is a good idea. It's way better than you running away, because there's nowhere you can go that they won't find you."

The man who threw punches scared me too. And I hadn't even known he was an arms dealer. But he had been patient with me. Kept his distance as I pulled myself together. He wore strange shoes.

"Orlando—"

"Willow."

"Papa wouldn't."

Orlando's sad eyes gut me. "Willow, he can't say no."

"Willow, where have you been?"

Mamma and Papa sit on the sofa, dressed in silk pajamas, the television frozen.

The frozen screen tells me everything. They've been up watching television, waiting for my return. Upon hearing us enter, Papa hit pause.

"I walked home along the beach."

"Willow, you are no longer a young girl. We expected you to spend the evening with us. Your absence was noticed and did not reflect well."

"You were at the event long enough to gain the interest of a prominent gentleman," Papa says, seemingly dismissing Mamma's reprimand with the worst insinuation.

Tears well in my eyes. "Papa." I want to sound strong, but my weak voice comes out like a plea.

"You brought this on yourself. You refuse to meet any of the men we recommend," he says.

"Papa, you don't need to do this. You don't need—"

"He's my capo." On the sofa, with his blue eyes veiled behind spectacles, his age shows. "We have sheltered you, but you are not ignorant. If you had been more amenable to the other men we found for you—"

"Papa!"

He hardens.

I still under his glare. I shouldn't have raised my voice.

His fingers clutch the armrest on the sofa so hard the nail beds whiten.

"We spoiled you. We gave you too much."

"Two of his wives committed suicide."

"Nonsense. Legends spread to instill fear. There's no truth to them. Tomorrow afternoon, we're hosting—"

"No." I capture Mamma's gaze and plead with my eyes. She can't. She knows what happens to women who marry men like Leandro. "Please—"

"*Tesoro mio…*" Papa's voice trails. He pushes off the sofa, and that's it. He's standing. It's done. "Massimo believes you could be good for his brother. You will calm him. Give him what he needs at home. His children are older, and they wouldn't be much work for you. He hires a full staff. You can still paint. You would want for nothing. He's second in line for capo. It's a good match."

Mamma's gaze drops to the ground, refusing to meet mine.

This is what Scarlet endured. Her mother, my mother's sister, forced her to marry a good match. She went through hell. She'd still be in hell if she hadn't killed Vincent, and now she's a pariah. So-called legend paints her as the monster.

I won't. There's no way.

"We're in the middle of a show. Why don't you get some rest, and in the morning, your mother and you can go shopping? You can buy something new. Shoes, handbag, jewelry, whatever your heart desires. We're breaking from the weekend's festivities and hosting Massimo's family on the piazza. Only for an hour or so, but you should look your best."

CHAPTER 6

SAM, AKA LEO, AKA SAINT

Back at the hotel, I stop at the bar and order a bourbon on the rocks. It's no Macallan, but it's needed. What a long fucking day.

Before Nick knocked them down a peg, the Lupi Grigi were the most formidable of the Italian mafia. The Russians, as a whole, are worse, but they've been preoccupied with war in recent years. They've also been forging alliances with China and Iran. Gagliano's expansion into the shadow fleet means the Russians are bolstering European alliances too.

There was a time when the mafia and cartels stayed in their own cities and most of their income was derived from alcohol or drugs. Now they hold influence across every political spectrum. In some countries, they are the leadership. Powerful leaders, the ones who influence events under the banner of maintaining a strong worldwide economy, will never eradicate them, because they serve as soldiers on the ground.

"Would you like another?" The bartender asks.

"*Si, grazi.*" I have another while catching up on the news. There's a television behind the bartender, but I don't watch it. I can't stand talking heads who dilute a complex issue into a thirty-second sound bite. In-depth articles, if written well, provide the details needed for any understanding of the reality of a situation.

"Would you like another?" the bartender asks. I've no idea how much time has passed.

"No. *Grazi.*" After scribbling out my room number, I push back, ready to call it a night. Three drinks are plenty. A headache in the morning would make tomorrow unbearable.

As I approach my room, I slow. The wire I laid out is broken. The Do Not Disturb sign dangles off kilter from the knob where I left it. And I don't have my fucking gun.

I knock on the door and announce in my best Italian, "Room service."

I give the intruder time to hide, press the plastic key to the door, stepping to the side should bullets fly, and push open the door with my foot. My SIG rests on the entry table where I left it.

No one is behind the door, no one down the hall. I step in, snatch the gun, check the chamber, and my muscles relax as my fingers wrap around the smooth grip.

If someone's in here, they're a novice. Would explain the broken wire. Maybe it's a common thief.

I'm in a suite, but since I'm by myself, my carry-on is open on the bed. I checked in this afternoon. Nothing appears out of place.

A rustle near the curtains has me flicking the lights. Behind the drapes. *Common thief.*

I whip the curtain back.

A blood curdling scream rips through the room.

Hands thrust sky high.

Blonde hair.

Floral dress.

It's the girl from earlier.

"Why are you in my room?" I lower my gun, but I'm not about to set it down.

"I need to talk to you." Fear ripples through those wide eyes.

She's pressed herself against the glass, as if I'm going to strike and she's trying to get as far away from me as possible.

"So you broke into my room?"

She tracks my gun. In the moonlight, earlier tonight, her irises had appeared black. Under the fluorescent lights, they're bright blue against flawless, milky skin.

She's young. What the hell is she doing breaking into my room?

She's too slight to be much of a risk. I stretch my fingers, holding the piece with my thumb and index finger, pointing it to the side of the room, a universal symbol for "I'm not looking to blow your brains out right now."

"Why are you in my room?" I step back, giving her space but still unwilling to set the gun down just yet. "And how'd you do it?"

"One of the hotel staff was doing turn down service. I asked if she'd open my room for me. I told her my father had a migraine, and I didn't want to wake him, but I'd lost my card."

"And she let you in?"

"He did."

Ah, a man. He'd probably been taken in by her innocence. "Why not call up to the room?"

"You didn't answer, and…I couldn't risk being seen."

I narrow my eyes. "By whom?"

She swallows. "Anyone." She pulls the drapes closed. When she turns, faint bruising along her neck shows. The bruising will likely be darker tomorrow.

"Are you hiding from that man?"

She tucks her hair behind her ear, then bites her thumbnail. I haven't seen anyone bite her nails since… ah, I can't think about them. I need to deal with this and get some shuteye.

"Are you gonna speak? Surely there's a reason you broke into my room. Which, how did you know where I'm staying?" Three drinks and my brain isn't as sharp. I'm getting too fucking old.

She drops her hand from her mouth and wipes her palms on the front of her dress. She turns, passes me, and sits on the end of the bed, feet flat on the floor, dress spilling over her legs, making her look like one of Sloane's china dolls stored on a shelf. Her hair is wild and uncombed, just like one of Sage's dolls. I should not be thinking of my sisters.

"I have a proposition for you."

I pause, unsure I heard her, and bite back a smirk. This, I did not see coming.

"Baby doll, this might surprise you after what happened out on the beach, but there are men in this world who believe you are too young for them."

Her cheeks flush. In this light, it's clear she dyes her hair blonde. Black roots deepen the color along her center part. There's something about the switcheroo, from blonde to black, that appeals to me. Or maybe it's simply the overall aesthetic.

She could shave her head, and her natural beauty would shine through.

"That's... What I'm going to propose might sound crazy. It is crazy." She fists the edge of the comforter, holding on as if she's at risk of falling off the bed. She's scared, but she's got balls. She's here. That deserves admiration and a second to hear her out.

"Go on." I hope my southern twang calms the girl. Sometimes it works, but I haven't tried the good ol' boy dialect in Italy. It might make it impossible to understand me.

"That man, the one from tonight, his name is Leandro, and he's a psychopath."

"Leandro De Luca. Massimo's brother?" I knew the fucker looked familiar.

"Yes. He's cruel. To animals, to women." I nod, as he probably would've raped her if I hadn't come along, but I need her to get to the reason for breaking into my room. Does she want me to kill him? Did someone tell her I'm an assassin?

"And, well, I know it's crazy, and I don't know why, but apparently, he wants to marry me, and my brother, Orlando—you met him—he thinks Papa will agree, which is crazy because these are modern times, and I should have choices. I am college educated. I should have options, but I don't. If I leave, they'll find me."

Who told her I'm an assassin? How did I go from arms dealer to assassin?

"And, well, it's my understanding that you are a homosexual."

Come again? She's staring at the ground and keeps rambling.

"I could be your beard. You could save me from having to marry him, and I could make you more presentable around the world. You know. When you go out there selling bombs and guns and whatever arms dealers sell."

Her words blur together, and I swear I get a little dizzy. How many glasses did I drink down at the bar?

A fist pounds on the door to my suite, and Willow jumps.

"You expecting anyone?"

She shakes her head. The terror in those eyes…Fuck, I hate seeing that in a girl so young.

"Leo. Open up." Whoever is at the door sounds pissed. "I know my daughter's in there."

You have got to be fucking kidding me. I twist my head, perplexed.

There's a gold locket around her neck, and it all clicks.

"Is that necklace a tracker?"

Her fingers clutch the locket and her eyes widen. I'd tell her to hide in the bathroom, but there's really no fucking point. Her father clearly knows she's here, either because she's got a tracker on her or she purposefully led him here.

The pounding gets louder.

I narrow my eyes at her. *What the fuck have I gotten myself into?*

"How old are you?" If she says anything lower than eighteen… I grit my teeth, waiting.

"Twenty-one. Twenty-two in a week."

"Willow. I know you're in there."

I glance at the door. "I've got to let him in."

"Please." Her plea is breathy, filled with desperation.

"I'm around two decades older than you." But as I say it, I realize it's all relative because Leandro must be forty years older.

The pounding at the door halts and other male voices mix in. The hotel staff must've been called.

I feel for the girl, but she's latched on to the wrong guy to get her out of a shit situation. Technically, I don't exist.

My boots pound on the floor as I approach the door, much like my fucking mood. All I wanted was to get a little buzzed and crash.

I sling the door open. Sweat beads across Alessio's forehead and red tinges his flesh. A skinny kid in shorts and a t-shirt stands at his side with a sheepish expression. It's the kid from earlier on the beach.

Two uniformed hotel employees stand on the other side of Alessio. "Sir, Mr. Gagliano needs to see you. I would appreciate it if you could keep the noise down out of consideration for our guests—"

My phone rings in my back pocket. When I reach for it, the hotel employee glimpses the gun in my other hand.

"We don't want any issues," the employee stammers.

Alessio pushes past me, ignoring the men.

"It's fine. I promise you, there won't be any issues." I hold the door for Orlando, who appears far too pale for a teenager living in the Mediterranean. "Come on in. I've got to take this."

I hold up my phone and slide to answer before it goes to voice mail. It's Nick, and he doesn't do well if his call isn't answered.

"Can I call you back?" I mutter as Orlando slinks past me into the room. I shut the door on the two bewildered employees.

"What is this?" Alessio shouts.

"Mate?" Nick asks, clearly confused as fuck.

"You have my daughter in your hotel room?" Alessio's livid.

Possibly rightfully so, but if she's twenty-two…or almost twenty-two…Jesus I hope she told me the truth about her age.

"I have a situation," I say to the phone.

"Sounds like it."

I hold up a hand and add a stern glare. This man will not intimidate me. I am not at fault here. He can handle his daughter.

"I'm going to take this call. Your daughter can explain what's she's doing here." I pointedly scowl at the two of them and slip into the en suite bathroom where I can close the door.

"Sleeping with a mafia member's daughter isn't the smartest move, mate."

"I didn't sleep with anyone," I bite out, loud enough I hope Alessio hears me. "What's up?"

"Got your note about submersible manufacturers. Does he want nukes?"

"Not on the wish list. He's looking to move sanctioned products."

"For the Russians?"

"Yes." I stare at the closed door. Alessio isn't yelling anymore, and the silence distracts me. "When I'm back, I'll share my thoughts."

"No need. We don't want that connection to strengthen."

"Precisely." I step closer to the door, listening.

"Can they hear you?"

"Possibly." Although, based on the mishmash of angry tones reverberating through the panel door, I don't think Alessio particularly cares about my conversation. "Hey, are the Grigis one of those conservative mafia groups? Like do they arrange marriages?"

"They're one step above Neanderthal." Over the years, I've

learned Nick doesn't think much of the mafias or cartels. "Why?"

"What is this? Hiding in the bathroom?" Alessio's booming voice comes through clearly, so articulate he must be standing by the door.

"Do you need help?" Nick asks.

"Hold." I open the door, and sure enough, Alessio blocks the doorway with his broad shoulders and extended midriff. But I'm taller than him, and I can take him. The guy's in decent shape for his age, but he's got to have twenty years on me, and he doesn't have my training.

"Business. Can you give me a minute?"

"No man is going to want her if she's seen coming out of hotel rooms. You stain my daughter, and you dare to tell me to wait while you do business?"

I open my mouth, ready to lay the truth out there, but glassy, tear-filled, terror-stricken eyes stop me.

Behind him, Willow mouths, "Please."

The thing is, I don't see the young girl I saved earlier today. In that moment, I see my youngest sister in a hospital bed, and I would've done anything to help her.

"What wasp nest did you kick?" Nick asks in my ear.

"Can you give me a moment? This is the syndicate. You can help yourself to a drink." I gesture to the open bar in the sitting area and half-expect the angry old man to spit in my face, but I slam the door before he can.

"What, exactly, have you done?" The wanker sounds thoroughly entertained.

"Alessio Gagliano's daughter broke into my room and asked me to marry her."

"Don't play tickle fuck with me."

I bark out a laugh. "I couldn't make this shit up. She's pegged me as a better match than Massimo's brother...what's his name?"

"Leandro?"

"Yeah. He was about to rape her on the beach, and I intervened."

"Of course you did."

"Didn't know who he was." Truth is, I still would've stopped him. There are lines I will not cross, and allowing a woman to be assaulted is one of them. "What am I dealing with here? I mean, I'm not Italian. I don't believe in their shit. He wouldn't even want me to marry her, would he?"

"You're in the syndicate. Leandro has a reputation. No sane man would want his daughter marrying her. You might be the best option. Hell, maybe he put her up to it. She broke into your room?" The bastard chuckles.

"Be serious. I don't have all day. I'm locked in the loo."

He sobers up, and I scan the ceiling, seeking calm.

"You're a member of the syndicate. They won't fuck with you. Sort it however you want. To them, you're untouchable. If they do anything to you, the wrath of the gods will rain down. Those guys aren't the highest educated, but they understand world order."

I scratch my forehead, envisioning those watery blue eyes pleading. "If I were to marry her, if we got divorced or I died, what would happen to her?"

"God damn. You are such a noble bloke. You're thinking you'll marry her, bring her to London, and set her up to live on her own. Playing the knight in shining armor once isn't enough, so you'll do it twice?"

"What happens to her?" There are no sounds through the

door, and I'm on edge. I crack the door and relax when I see her sitting on the bed. Crying. She's so fucking young.

"You bring her to London, and if you set her up financially, there will be no reason for her to return."

"The same protections afforded to me would extend to her?"

"You're planning on marrying her and divorcing her, aren't you? So bloody noble. You haven't even fucked her either, have you? What a fucking saint you are."

"I'll call you."

"If you need a best man, say the word."

I end the call and open the door.

Orlando sits on a velvet bench, head down as if in prayer. Alessio holds a highball glass, and there's so much anger soaking his glower I half expect I'll need to duck.

"Are you going to do the right thing?"

"I haven't touched her. You can't force me to marry her. I'm not Italian." This probably isn't the best way to go about negotiating for her hand, but I won't be cornered.

"You want me to call your boss?"

"Be my guest."

He mutters a string of expletives in Italian. He steps up to Willow and slams his palm against the back of her head. She cries out in pain, and a second later, I have the fuck up against the wall.

What is it with these men?

"Where I'm from, you don't hit women." My forearm jams his neck. If he fights me, the pressure will crush his windpipe. Through gritted teeth, I repeat, "You don't hit women. *Capisce?*"

Fury blazes in his eyes.

I lift my arm and make a show of straightening his shirt. He brushes my hand away and his lips curl into a snarl. If he was a dog, he'd be growling, and his hackles would be straight up.

"You have my daughter in a hotel room. And you dare to touch me?"

"Papa, let's go." A single tear falls down Willow's cheek, and I look to the heavens for strength.

I've lived a lie for five years. What's one more in the mix?

"Willow, if you will have me, I would be honored to be your husband."

Hope radiates from her big baby blues, and I don't want to think about how good that feels, so I look away. Orlando's head lifts and beams like he hit the jackpot.

A shove to my shoulder knocks me back. "You think that's the way you win my daughter's hand? With your hand on my throat? She's a Gagliano. You don't ask her. You ask me. I am the father." He rubs his neck and his face wrinkles. "And no. After what you just did—"

"Papa," Willow exclaims, "I love him. Please."

"Love," he scoffs.

Yeah, she's not a talented actress, and he's not buying her show, but at least I'm pretty sure this wasn't some complicated scheme he put her up to. He opens his mouth, catches my warning gaze, and shuts it.

"If I give you my daughter's hand, I want wholesale rates. Better than network pricing. You understand? The best pricing anyone in the world gets. None of this percentage to the syndicate. Nothing on top." He glares at me. "*Capisce?*"

I nod, incredulous that I'm in this situation. She peers up at me like I'm her savior. Will she be of the same opinion when I disappear? How she views me doesn't matter. This insane action saves her from a fuckwad, and I'll leave her in a better place.

"When should we set the date?" Alessio has his phone out, checking his calendar.

Fuck me. "What's a normal engagement period?"

If he says six months or a year, then it won't be any use to Willow, as I plan to be long gone. My exit is overdue.

"When are you returning to London?"

"Sunday."

"Let's do it Sunday. We'll make it a small affair, immediate family only."

The shock on Orlando's and Willow's faces tells me this isn't normal, and skepticism stirs. "Is Massimo going to have an issue with our arrangement?"

"No." Her father smiles, but it's more of a nasty leer. "Because you're going to promise that the connection will prove lucrative to our family. By the time Leandro finds out, it will be a done deal."

I could be reading my young fiancée wrong, but she looks as shell-shocked as I feel. She sidles up to me, giving me an eyeful of her breasts, thanks to the low-cut top she's wearing. Fantastic tits. Perfectly shaped. Natural. Her bra must be pushing them up, holding them just so, as if on an offering plate. She has no business wearing such a low-cut dress.

Her father emits a guttural noise, reminding me of the present predicament. A young woman pleaded with me to help her, and bringing her back to London with me is an easy enough fix. I'll set her up well before I split, and she'll be safe. If it were one of my sisters in this fucked up situation, I'd want someone to step up for them.

"All right. Sunday it is."

CHAPTER 7

WILLOW

Scarlet tugs on my braid. Her lips are downturned, her eyes despondent and dark. Even her brilliant red strands appear dull in the evening light.

"This is a good thing," I reassure her, though not quite believing it. But if my parents planned on marrying me to a made man, a man who killed for initiation, then this indeed presents my best chance for escaping this world.

A puffy white concoction hangs on the garment rack in the middle of the room. The dress is one of several my mother had sent by courier from Milan, and the only one that required minimal alterations. It's too tight in the ribcage and transforms my average breasts into bountiful mounds, an attribute my mother values. I look like a swirl of meringue in the dress, but it's what Mamma wants, and I have no preference.

My future groom prefers men. If I'm lucky, we'll foster a

strong friendship. He's a good man, with kind brown eyes, and courage. He fought off both Leandro and my father. He's a fierce man, but his expression softens around me. There's every reason to be optimistic we can spawn a supportive partnership.

"I don't have a good feeling about this." Scarlet's voice is soft and meek. Her fears stem from experience, a horrible one.

I take my cousin's hands and squeeze.

"He's not a Lupi Grigi."

"He's in the syndicate, Willow. For all we know, that could be worse. And London. If you need help..." Her eyes glaze with unshed tears. "How would I know?"

"If I tell you something, will you promise not to tell anyone?"

"Who would I tell?"

She's right. She doesn't like anyone here, and I can't blame her. They stood by and did nothing, and now they have the audacity to judge her for protecting herself. "Promise."

"I promise." She forms a swift cross over her heart.

"He's gay. That's why he's willing to do this."

Her eyes narrow. "How do you know?"

"Orlando told me. And think about it. He travels to the Middle East. Places where it's frowned upon or even criminalized. That's what he gets out of it." I reach for her hand, but she pulls it back, distrust evident in her frown.

"You don't know...Vincent wasn't motivated by sex."

"He saved me. I...Scarlet, please. He's better than Leandro."

She sinks onto the mattress.

"You'll come to visit. Often. He travels frequently." Her eyes narrow, fully aware I met the man yesterday. "He told me. I promise you'll come and visit me, and we'll find a reason for you to stay. I don't think he'll mind."

"You're so young." Scarlet's six years older than I am, but she and Aunt Caterina lived with us after her father died. She's my cousin, but she's more like a sister.

"I'm three years older than you were when you got married."

Moving to London means I can pursue a career. For the first time since returning home from Florence, excitement thrums from possibility.

"But you're naive." She won't drop it.

There's a truth to her observation that stings. Days ago, I thought Papa wouldn't force me into marriage. I was naive. He may run one of the legitimate businesses, but he's a Lupi Grigi member. And to serve his business, he contemplated selling me to the worst of all the men.

Spread out along the table is the lingerie my mother hand-selected, and trunks are open, brimming with my clothes. Mamma has the staff working overtime today, preparing to ship me off, cheerful because Papa told her it was a good liaison. My union took priority over this weekend's engagement celebration, so much so she and I both missed today's festivities. But we'd been productive.

"I need air."

"Where are you going?" Scarlet's miffed, but the portrait is painted, so to speak, so there's no point in hearing her negativity.

"To the beach."

"Willow," she wails. "That's such a steep hike."

My brother stands in the doorway, and I sense he wants to talk, but I'm done talking. I want this to be over. I want it all behind me. The next stage awaits.

"I want some time alone." I pass Orlando's bewildered gaze

and leave for the sandy strip of beach that has served as my haven.

Orlando believes he saved me by suggesting this match, and perhaps he did. But it's infuriating that I needed saving. That I was born into a world where some men think my purpose in life is to serve their needs.

When I reach solitude, I open my arms, letting the breeze cool my skin and swirl my hair. I won't have this in London. Of course, I don't have any idea where I'll be living. He might live outside of London and simply tell people he lives in London.

"I'd expect after yesterday you might think twice about wandering around by yourself." His deep voice comes from behind me, blending with the soothing sea.

I lower my arms, wrap them around myself, and angle my body to face my future partner. "All the men are at a celebration tonight. Why aren't you with them?"

"I've played my role. If it weren't for you, I'd be on a flight to London."

"I'll be a good wife."

Amusement flashes across his face in the form of a slight smile and crinkles around the corners of his eyes. He's wearing casual clothes, shorts and a button-down shirt with the sleeves rolled midway up his forearms. He's barefoot, and his leather sandals dangle from two fingers. His mocha brown hair whips around, and, drizzled with salt air, curls spring around his brow. He told me he's older, but like this, it doesn't seem so. He looks like he would have been my friend at university, more handsome than any of my friends actually were, but...once again, I'm struck by the feeling he's a good person, syndicate member or not, and all the fears Scarlet attempted to instill in me dissipate.

He scans the beach, then his gaze cascades over me. "Are you wearing any necklaces? Carrying a phone?"

My fingers trace my clavicle. I removed the locket earlier today when trying on dresses and jewelry and forgot to put it back on.

"No."

"If you're going to walk around by yourself, carry a phone. So you can call someone if needed."

I don't carry my phone because I'm fully aware my parents track my every move with it. Last night I didn't have it, but… "You truly think there's a tracking device in my locket?""

He gives me a knowing look, which reminds me of Scarlet. I'm naive. He gestures to the shore. It's low tide, so the stretch of sand is wide. "Shall we walk?"

I loved that locket, a gold heart, a gift from my father on my sixteenth birthday, but I shall leave it behind.

"This marriage, tomorrow. You understand it's an arrangement? I'll do this to protect you, to get you away from here, but all we have is an arrangement."

"But we'll make it look real, so people believe you're, well…" I let him fill in the blanks, but I need to remind him this isn't just about me. He benefits, too. I learned that from Father. Both sides benefit in a prosperous arrangement.

"I'm not really gay, you know." I side-eye him, and he's grinning.

"But if you're not… Why would you agree?"

"I'm a sucker for a damsel in distress." He's still grinning, but my stomach sinks. If Orlando's theory is wrong, what is he getting out of this?

"You know, I'm not a virgin." It's customary in our world to expect a bride to be one, and if that's what he thinks he's getting…

He smiles so wide the moonlight glimmers across his teeth.

"I'm serious. If that's—"

"I'm not a virgin, either. At twenty-two, I didn't expect you would be. And it doesn't matter. What's between us…" He gestures back and forth over the space between us. "It's for show. I'd never—" He smooths his fingers over his lips, and the effect is of wiping his smile away. "No woman should be forced to marry a man like Leandro De Luca. You'll come back with me to London, and we'll get you set up. What do you do?"

I blink, unsure I understand the question.

"You went to university. A man I was speaking to earlier today mentioned it. What'd you go for?"

"Art. I'm a painter."

"Ah. Well, good. We'll find a studio for you to work in. I have a friend with connections in the art world. You'll pursue your art. That's what you'll do."

My heart vibrates in my chest, flittering like a bird about to be released from a cage. Naive. Scarlet's word haunts me. "And what do you get out of it?"

"Oh, I get to feel good about myself." He shoves one hand in his pocket and kicks a foot through the water, sending rivulets splashing.

It's hard to trust him because that doesn't mesh with what I know of men. It doesn't matter what they do. The crueler they are, the better they feel about themselves.

"And a stronger allegiance with your father's business is helpful."

Ah, there it is. He's looking to either get into the shipping business or inherit my father's business. "Orlando will inherit Titan Shipping."

"I've no interest in shipping."

Again, amusement. "This isn't funny."

His pace slows. "It's the strangest situation I've ever been in. Sometimes you've just gotta laugh. Anyway, I think you'll like London."

"I'm confused. Do you want me to act like your wife or not?"

"I suppose you'll need to act like you're my wife. But not because of your father, but because of Massimo. Your father and I spoke earlier today. His one fear is that Massimo will see through this as a manipulation to avoid giving you to his brother. It's a lovely family you have."

The dig is deserved. "What's your family like?"

The question sparks something I can't put my finger on—sadness, I think. His smile disappears. "They're good people."

"Will I meet them tomorrow?"

"No, they couldn't make it in time. And, as you know, this is an arrangement. I wouldn't ask them to drop everything for this."

"Right. Of course." That was a stupid question. Even from my side, only immediate family will be present. Rumors will probably fly that he took my virginity and father forced him to marry me.

"But you'll tell me if there's anything I can do for you, right?" My words feel suggestive, and that's not what I intended. "You're doing so much for me. I want to return the favor, if I can."

"I'll need for you to be smart, stay safe, and build a life that makes you happy. You do that, and it's favor enough for me."

CHAPTER 8

SAM, AKA LEO, AKA SAINT

"Satellite imagery confirmed the shipment is en route."

"Should be around the Horn of Africa tomorrow. This file includes every item in the shipment. The names are those who financially benefitted when the US administration declined to authorize the sales."

Nomad released a long-winded sigh I identified as weary of this game. We dedicated too much of our careers to passing information with no sign our efforts were paying off.

A cardinal's high-pitched tune eclipsed the thrumming forest, a reminder that light thrives, even in the shadows.

"Any plans this weekend?" I didn't expect Nomad to answer me. I asked to wind up our covert meeting and to force an end to the growing apprehension that my efforts were futile and my sacrifices in vain.

"You won't believe me if I tell you, mate."

Nomad smiled and stood, brushing off his pants and adjusting his cufflinks.

"Try me." Hell, entertain me.

"I'm getting married."

"No shit. For real?"

"Before God in a church. I'm not a particularly religious chap, as you may have gathered over the years." He paused, raised an eyebrow.

We'd both killed and been responsible for killings. We'd never waxed poetic over philosophical matters, so I assumed he referred to the killings.

"But her family is. Her aunt and uncle. It's happening tomorrow."

Friends of mine, in my former life, had had the same beam to them. "Congrats, mate." I bounced the British friendship term back at him and clapped him on the back. "Your family excited?"

He stiffened and said, "It'll just be her family."

"Don't be an ass. When you get married, you need the important people there."

That's what I'd said. The brief conversation from years ago with Nomad, my Interpol contact, comes out of nowhere. It's obvious why that memory would surface on my wedding day, but this one's an arrangement. It's not a real wedding. I'm helping a young woman. She's a mafia princess who could become a mafia queen, but she wants more for herself, and I'm assisting. I'm doing something good, something that's within my power to do.

That day in the woods, when Nomad talked about his wedding, marked the day a true friendship sparked between us. After that day, along with sharing photos of my sisters, he started sharing photos of his wife and then later, his daughter, breaking every rule in the book.

Will I tell Nomad about my little arrangement? I might as well. There's no way other sources won't inform him. And if I can't trust a contact willing to show me photos of his daughter, who the fuck can I trust?

"Papa sent me to get you." Orlando approaches, wearing what I'd bet is the same suit from Friday. The sunlight reflects on a path of sparse dark hairs the kid missed when shaving.

"How old are you?" He's tall but gangly and baby-faced.

"Fifteen." His back straightens. "Almost sixteen." He's nearly up to my chin, but at fifteen, he's likely got some inches in front of him. "Why?"

"I'm shit at pegging ages."

His eyes narrow, and I guess that means he doesn't understand my American vernacular, but he doesn't need to.

"So, is it time to get the show on the road?" I ask.

"Five minutes. Willow will be arriving soon, and they want you inside, so you don't see her until she enters the church."

I can't believe this shit. "Everyone knows this isn't..." I exhale both amusement and frustration.

Orlando bites on the corner of his lip, looking more prepubescent than teen. His hands fall to his waist and he blows out his lips. "You have my eternal gratitude. I didn't want to see her with..." He hesitates, and I sense he's been told to not speak badly about the men in his outfit. "If there's ever anything, if you ever need anything, I owe you."

I understand him more than he knows. If someone saved one of my sisters, I'd be all kinds of grateful, too.

"Brothers?" He offers his hand, and I take it, and a load of shame threatens to take me under. It's one thing to fake friendships when in deep cover. It's a requirement. But faking family falls into questionable integrity territory.

If I act like I like someone, either he's a criminal I might kill one day or turn over evidence on, or I genuinely like the guy. Most of the time, it's a mix of both situations. Faking family is a whole 'nother level I've gotta wrap my head around.

His grip is firm, belying his youth.

The heavy church door opens, and a woman's voice calls, "She's close. You need to get in here."

The church the Gagliano family secured for our nuptials is centuries old and comprises one room with pews. Stained glass windows adorn the front of the church and along the aisles. A modern architect would have positioned the church so the stunning view of the Mediterranean benefited the congregation, but in this church, those exiting the damp, cloistered room profit.

My dress shoes rasp against the dusting of sand covering the pavers. My heart rate rises, and I swipe my palms against my trousers. None of this is real. The situation incites the physical reactions. It's the church. It's the day. A day that, as a boy, I assumed would one day come, and as a man following a select path, believed impossible. It's my past coming to haunt me. My mother, my father, my sisters, my teammates. Shadows from my past that I carry in my soul.

I shake my head as I walk, pissed at emotions and thoughts that should be tamped down.

A black Mercedes with tinted windows spins dust behind it.

Orlando pauses, watching the approaching Mercedes. The woman in the door well shades her eyes with a hand.

"Is that Willow?" I ask.

Orlando gives a quick shake. Negative.

I reach for the Glock tucked in my waistband, a last-minute wardrobe addition when I considered the potential for a Red Wedding. It's my understanding Alessio took a coward's approach, canceled some cocked-up cocktail hour with Massimo and Leandro, and didn't mention the arrangement to Massimo until sometime last night.

From what I've heard of this Leandro character, I wouldn't put it past him to use force to stop the wedding. With men like Leandro, it's a matter of pride and ego. He wants something, and if he doesn't get it, it's an insult.

And these are the people I'm negotiating arms deals for in order to gain intelligence. It's sickening.

The car slows to a stop.

I unlatch the snap on my holster, readying the gun.

A uniformed driver exits.

The back passenger door opens well before the driver reaches it.

Nick steps out, grinning from ear to ear. "Word on the street is you need a best man."

He says something to the driver, who goes to the trunk of the car as Nick waltzes over like he's saving the day in a freaking tux.

"What the hell are you doing here?" I'm grinning, too, but it's because this guy is such an oaf.

The driver lifts a garment bag from the trunk.

"Brought you a wardrobe change. If I'm your best man, you're getting married in an outfit befitting a gentleman. Those boots of yours…disaster." His face crinkles in disgust, and I snort.

"*Ciao,*" he says, greeting Orlando. "I'm his best mate, and his best man, Nikolai Ivanov. Is there a place he can change?"

"Orlando," a woman's voice calls, "call your mamma. Tell her to have the driver wait a few minutes." An attractive older woman steps out from the shadows. "I'm Caterina Gagliano, Willow's aunt. *Andiamo*. There's not much time."

Caterina leads us to a small building that from the outside might be mistaken for a crypt, but it's a marble building the local church uses to store items, and it apparently doubles as a small office. She leaves us, but not without admonishing us to hurry with a tap on her wrist for emphasis.

Nick grins as his driver passes over the garment bag. A shoe bag dangles in front. The driver brushes his hands over the front of his uniform, scanning the area. Based on how he positions himself outside the door, the driver doubles as security.

When the door closes, I unzip the garment bag, marveling that Nick acquired a tuxedo in my size on tight notice.

"You know this isn't real, right?" I spare him a glance, and he just grins his maniacal grin. "This is going overboard."

"Everybody needs a best man." He shrugs like it's no sweat to drop everything, find me a tux, and fly to another country. "Besides, you're too good a soul. If you're doing this, it's real." I stop, one leg in a trouser, one out, ready to set him straight. "Don't argue. You'll honor her more than men who marry for love. It's in your genes. It's why you're one of the few I trust with my life."

Long-buried guilt threatens to erupt. If he knew me for who I am, Nick, known in my covert communications as Falcon, would have me killed in the most inhumane and excruciatingly painful manner known to assassins.

"Unless she's a hag." His nose crinkles in disgust. "Is she ghastly?"

"Nick." My tone is meant as a warning, but he cackles.

"My money says she's–"

I glare at him, and he wisely shuts the fuck up.

Silence mixes with the dust as I dress, and Nick feigns interest in the clergy's papers. I fumble with the buttons, and he pushes my hands away and finishes buttoning my shirt and ties the bow tie. There's no mirror in the room, but I trust his skill. I don't need a mirror to know he's tied it better than I could.

"You, my mate, look like a man about to shackle his ball sack."

"Thanks for that."

There's a knock at the door, and Willow's cousin, the redhead, peers in. "Are you ready?"

"I am."

"No, you're not." Nick says and shifts his coat, withdrawing a velvet bag. "Rings."

"I'm sure the Gaglianos—"

"They don't know your ring size. And you don't want a bride with some tasteless ring on her finger." His gaze travels to the redhead, and, for once, Nick appears apologetic. "No offense, love."

"None taken," she says. "My name is Scarlet." She holds the door open, waiting for us to exit.

"How do you know my ring size?" Inside the velvet bag there are indeed two rings.

Nick's transfixed on Scarlet, but casually says, "I know everything about you, mate."

If that were true, I wouldn't be alive.

"Let's go." Scarlet, tired of waiting, returns to the church with long strides, leaving us to catch up. She completely disregarded Nick.

That might be the first time I've ever seen a woman ignore

Nick. He's flustered by it, too, looking at me as if he wants to ask if I saw that.

"She married?" he asks.

"Don't believe so."

"Fascinating."

"Are you two coming?" she calls, halfway to the church.

All I can do is grin and rush to catch up.

Grinning like a lunatic has never been a more apt fit. My alias is marrying an Italian mafia princess, and a leader in an international criminal syndicate will stand by my side as my best man. And he's eye-fucking my bride's cousin as if she's a woman he can select from a menu board. If I live to tell the tale, no one will ever believe me.

CHAPTER 9

WILLOW

As a child, I daydreamed of a wedding in the Collegiate Church of Santa Maria Maddalena, a historic church with views of the coast. In my dream, I wore a splendid, ornate gown with a long train befitting royalty. In my childhood fantasy, friends and family packed the pews.

Five family members are present for our nuptials. My father, mother, brother, Scarlet, and my aunt. One person is present for my groom, a man I've never met.

When I pitched Orlando's crazy idea, desperation drove me. I believed the arrangement would be mutually beneficial. But what if there is no benefit for my groom? He claims he's straight. He's not a politician. No one cares that he's not married. And if he wanted to marry for love, he's handsome. He could easily find someone to marry for love, which begs the question: At his age, why is he single? Has he been married before? I don't have any idea. I didn't even think of asking when we walked along the beach because "have you ever been married before" isn't something my friends and I ask each other.

My nerves are haywire over the unknown. If growing up in the Lupi Grigi *famiglia* has taught me anything, it's that in every negotiation, each party gains. Otherwise, it's a poor deal. *Pessimo affare*. Not to be trusted. He gets nothing from our arrangement.

The twinkling of piano keys breaks through the quiet, my legs tremble, and light-headedness forces me to lean on my father.

My heart thumps so hard my ribs vibrate and light perspiration coats my skin. I risk a glance at Papa, wondering if he can hear my heart thundering. Does he care?

"*Tesoro mio,* are you ready?"

No.

My feet are lead, rooted to the spot. I should've asked more questions last night. I shouldn't have done this. My father shouldn't have put me in this position. He should have stood up to the *famiglia* and said his daughter would not be forced to marry, tradition be damned.

My papa's palm smothers the back of my hand, and I'm tugged forward. A fog blankets me as I am handed off to an American I barely know, and the nuptial mass begins. Words spoken by a priest I've known my whole life echo against the ancient walls. Father Francisco never asked if I wanted this. He never inquired if I'm prepared to take on this commitment because he knows I have no choice. He understands our world. This is my destiny.

Scarlet stands to my back, holding my flowers. There is no

train, but the gown Mamma chose skims the floor and Scarlet adjusted it with the care one would give to a lengthy train. If I need her, Scarlet will help me.

"Do you promise to be faithful, in good times and bad, in sickness and in health, to love and to honor him, all the days of your life?"

This is what the priest asks me. My throat closes, and my tongue thickens in my dry mouth.

Pressure on my hands calms my erratic heartbeat, and I lift my gaze to soothing, golden, deep-set brown eyes. Kindness. That's what I see. A gentle kindness beneath a fierce, predatory exterior.

"I do." Because this is my best option. I have no choice.

He hears my unspoken words.

As we stand before the Father, Son, and Holy Spirit, I don't comprehend my groom's unspoken words. He has a choice. By virtue of being a member of the syndicate, he already possesses connections to Titan Shipping. Why is he helping me? Why is he being kind? What does he want?

"Are you tired?"

He's being nice, or at least his tone sounds amiable, but I can't bear to look at the man I married, so I keep my gaze focused on the passing scenery. "Where are we going?"

We're in the back of a limousine, and the dress digs into my hips and itches.

The car turned onto the *autostrada* a while ago, leaving my town and life behind.

"Rome. Flying home tomorrow."

"Your best man, what was his name?"

"Nick."

"He refused my father's limousine. Nick had him move my luggage into the car he provided. Why? Does he not trust my father?"

The man I am contractually bound to glances away from his phone. From what I glimpsed, he's reading a news article. "Honestly, I'm not sure what that was about. The next time I speak to Nick, I'll ask him. It might've been his insistence that he perform his best man duties, or there might've been something more to it."

His eyes narrow and he pushes a button that raises a felt divider between us and the uniformed driver. I had assumed the driver could hear anything we said, but perhaps that's not how the syndicate operates. My father trusts the men in the family. Growing up, it was assumed he trusted anyone, man or woman, he employed.

After the divider meets the ceiling, sealing us in privacy, Leo adds, "This car features bulletproof glass. That might have been a reason he insisted we take it. We've got several hours' drive in front of us. If you want to get some sleep, you're safe."

"Why wouldn't I be safe?"

He lifts a glass water bottle and twists the top off. A chilled champagne bottle, crystal champagne flutes, chocolate-covered strawberries, and an assortment of petite sandwiches are set out on a small table with a recessed center, presumably to prevent the items from sliding. The champagne holder is built into the table.

"Were you surprised when your father rushed your ceremony and held it without others in attendance, on a weekend when all those who matter in the Lupi Grigi were in town?"

"We didn't want to take away from Carlos and Maria's engagement weekend."

The censure in his expression tells me he expects more of me. Reality hits in a flash, like a lightning strike.

"Leandro. Father's worried he'd... Massimo blessed our union, right? Father wouldn't go against the capo." That would be unheard of. Orlando said Father would never...

"I was told Massimo is aware." He sighs and tips the water bottle back and, after swallowing, wipes his mouth with the back of his hand. In a tux, he's breathtakingly handsome, but add in his aloof demeanor, and he's intriguing. "I believe the concern is Leandro feels slighted. I've heard nothing specifically to that effect, but I'm reading between the lines."

That thought is unsettling. Wouldn't Leandro obey the capo, like we all do? If Massimo blessed the union, it should be a done deal.

"Don't worry. Leandro De Luca might be pathological, but he's not suicidal. Nick's cautious. If Leandro planned on tracking us, Nick thwarted his plan by switching cars. There won't be time for him to find you in Rome, and he won't come after you in London. Such a move would be suicide."

"Why wouldn't it be suicide in Rome?"

"Because..." His gaze travels to the passing scenery. "It's his territory. Who knows? His logic doesn't matter. Word is Leandro De Luca suffers from extreme rage, but he'll burn it off long before he finds you. Give it a day or two, and he'll accept that you're my wife."

One corner of his lips rises in a half-smile, and he winks. I feel that wink all over, from my itchy shoulders down to my cramped, sore toes.

He opens a black bag and removes a silver laptop. With the

push of a button on the side rest, a desk slowly rises and extends in front of his lap. He puts on a pair of black-framed glasses that shave years. Wearing them, he could be mistaken for a graduate student or professor. An extremely handsome, polished, intelligent man.

He quickly becomes engrossed in whatever he's reading, so I study him. His hair is a deep brown, and sprinkles of gray dapple his crown. Thick brown eyebrows, shades darker than milk chocolate, curve over deep-set brown eyes. A well-defined jawline tapers to a full chin. While a tux hides all manner of sins, I've seen him in only a dress shirt, and he's fit, with broad shoulders. Judging from how he manhandled Leandro and Papa, he's strong and capable.

I relax into the seat. Why would this handsome man agree to help me? And is Papa afraid of Leandro? Is that the real reason we held a swift, secretive ceremony? Was that why he was willing to marry me to Leandro in the first place, because Papa was intimidated by Leandro? Did Papa place himself and my family in danger by marrying me off to someone other than Leandro? How badly have I overestimated Papa's position within the Lupi Grigi?

There are so many questions, and I want to ask Leo, but he's engrossed in whatever he's reading. And given how he's treating me, he's probably like my father and the other men in that he doesn't believe the women need to know the details. And what right do I have to ask anything of him? He's helping me, and he's getting nothing in return.

He lifts his gaze from the screen. He must feel me watching him. That's never a good feeling. So I shift, giving him privacy, and zone out, letting the passing landscape blur into a haze of muted, calming colors.

"Willow, we're here."

The car door clicks open, and a uniformed man wearing white gloves steps back, holding the door for me.

Familiar marble columns below a series of flags greet me. Yes, I know this place. The black awnings with the striking font and the statement title Le Grand Hotel perch high above. It's The St. Regis. My mother brought me here for afternoon tea more than once. It's never been a hotel Papa favored, but it's beautiful, and I've often wondered what the suites and the infamous butler service would be like.

I rub my face, settling into my situation and smile up at the patient porter. I must've fallen asleep. A car door slams. The desk is put away, the black bag is missing, and the champagne and food remain untouched.

Leo appears at the side of the car, offering his hand. "Ready?"

I take it, and as he helps me out of the back of the vehicle, a couple standing to the side smile.

Of course they do. I'm in a wedding dress.

The woman says, "*Sei bellissima.*"

Once we're in front of the grand entrance, Leo releases my hand and leads the way into the lobby. I speed walk, struggling to keep up in my heels and cumbersome dress.

We should've changed before taking this drive, but I didn't know where we were going. No one bothered to share the plans with me. I doubt anyone shared our plans with Mamma, or she would have purchased a travel suit for me to change into.

I focus on the detached tuxedo-wearing man at my side, far too aware that my dress has attracted the attention of every single person in the lobby. It's a wedding dress in Rome, and all the visitors are thinking of love.

Or maybe they're wondering why the groom isn't doting on his wife. They might envision an argument occurred.

They might observe our age difference and cast judgment. Perhaps they assume I married for money and deserve to be left behind. Could others tell with one glance at us that two decades separate us? I'm not certain. The make-up artist Mamma hired created a mature, elegant persona. I'm guessing most would assume I'm in my late twenties, and passing by so quickly, Leo appears to be in his thirties at most.

In the elevator, the porter accompanying us says, "Did you come straight here from your reception?"

"Straight here from—"

"Milan," Leo interrupts.

I let Leo carry the rest of the conversation. He lied about where we came from, because he doesn't want people to talk. Word might spread about a bride from Atrani who rode hours in a limousine in her dress.

"You're staying in the Bottega Veneta suite. It's my favorite suite." The uniformed employee beams, pride oozing, as if this is his personal space and he's allowed us entry into his private haven. "May I give you a tour?"

"No, thank you, *grazi*," Leo answers.

I flinch at the rudeness of his response. Even Papa would have been gracious and allowed the man five minutes.

Leo locks the door behind him and turns to me. "We'll order room service. I'm assuming you'd prefer to change into something comfortable?"

"I would love to get out of this dress." I'm not hungry, but he might be.

"Luggage should be in the bedroom."

The suite is done in a belle epoque style with a mix of modern and classic Roman elegance. The sitting area overlooks the piazza high above the city, and sepia leather sofas sit atop a white marble floor. Eighteenth century landscape art adorns the walls.

I step into the bedroom and take in the king size bed with what I suspect are Rubelli fabrics. The door to the ensuite bathroom is open, but I barely glance at the black marble and soaking tub. I'm stuck on one aspect of this suite.

"There's one bed," I announce to Leo, who has taken residence on one of the leather sofas. "I didn't think—"

"I didn't make the arrangements, remember? Nick's aware of the arrangement. He's just fucking with us. Don't twist your knickers. There's an ensuite study with a fold-out sofa. I'll take that." He sounds annoyed and tired. I didn't mean to insult him. I'm simply confused. And I'm uneasy because there are so many unknowns, the biggest being is why he agreed to this arrangement.

He toes off a black tuxedo shoe and looks up, one shoe on, one off. "What?"

"Can you help me with my dress?" There's a zipper, but there are a million tiny buttons over it, and they all must be undone.

"Oh, right."

He removes his other shoe and, in black trouser socks, steps up behind me, kicking the hem out of the way.

He jerks my body, fumbling with the back.

"Damn. These buttons are small." One goes flying across the room. "Fuck."

Another button pops, but this one must fall directly to the ground.

"Fuck it."

There's a ripping sound, and the tightness around my ribcage loosens.

The dress falls in a pile around my knees. I stand there, shocked. He ripped my dress. From the top to the bottom, he ripped it.

"Why are you wearing that?"

I turn to him, dazed. My dress is a pile of fabric around my feet. My sore feet are packed into too tight heels, and he destroyed a dress that cost over twenty thousand euros.

He holds up his palm and steps back, clearing a view of my reflection in the framed mirror.

Pure white sheer thigh highs, a garter, a lace bra, and a barely there thong. This is the lingerie Mamma picked, and it's too revealing. My hands fly to my lace covered breasts.

I'm mostly covered, yet I am bared, and still very itchy.

"Go change."

His expression and tone strip me of confidence.

My heel catches on to the taffeta, and I crash to the ground. A sharp pain stabs my knees.

"You okay?"

I'm on my hands and knees, in a ridiculous get-up I would've never picked, straddling my ripped wedding gown, the most expensive garment I've ever owned, and probably will ever own.

Tears burn my eyes, threatening to break the dam. I'm tired, ashamed, and far too confused. The only thing I have to hang onto is anger because I am not to blame for this fucked-up world. These are modern times, and I shouldn't be in this situation.

"I'm fine."

My palms flatten over silk, cooled by the underlying marble. I lower my head and dig deep for inner strength. Shame flames my cheeks and chest.

A strong, masculine hand with short, clean nails extends into my line of sight. I take it, using it for balance as I rise. He steps on the dress, and I step out of the heap of silk and tulle.

My heels click on the marble, and I struggle to ignore the breeze over my tush. In a mirror, I glimpse Leo, standing in his socks on my dress, watching me with an unsettling intensity. Disgust? Hatred?

I'm too overloaded. I can't think about what he must be thinking.

The door clicks closed, and I sit on the edge of the bed to remove the painful shoes.

He probably regrets helping me. My fingers tremble. Goosebumps climb my arms, but my palms are clammy. Undefinable emotions swirl.

Breathe. Think.

He doesn't hate me. That's my emotions playing with reason. Unreasonable emotions are bubbling up, and I don't know what to do with them. Feeling sorry for myself won't get me anywhere. I need a shower. I need to remove the make-up, rid my hair of pins, wash away the hairspray, change into comfortable clothes, and calm down.

CHAPTER 10

SAM, AKA LEO, AKA SAINT

My back aches from a night on a sofa, an annoying reminder of my age and my predicament. What the hell have I done?

When her dress fell to her calves with one harsh rip, the stupidity of what I'd done hit with the force of a grenade. One glance at her lacy white lingerie and my dick went rock fucking hard.

Those sheer white thigh highs burned into my retinas, along with the lace garter belt and the most perfectly fitting lace thong I've ever seen.

Jesus, I wasn't expecting any of that. It wasn't a real wedding. I wasn't expecting her to be dressed like a Victoria's Secret Angel underneath that fluffy dress. More like a *Penthouse* pin-up. She surpassed every erotic dream I've ever had and all the porn stars I've watched too.

She struck me speechless, and my view had been of her

back. My fingers itched to touch the smooth slope of her neck, on display as her hair was still pinned in an elaborate twist. With one flick of my fingers, her strapless white lace bra would have fallen to the floor. Thinking of the lines of her waist, the dip in her lower back, and those two perfect ass cheeks tightens my throat.

I ached to push her up against a wall, to do things with her I had no business doing to a woman younger than my sisters. And who am I kidding? I still ache like a madman to do it to her now.

And I'm supposed to take her home with me? To my flat? Contrary to everyone's notions, I am not a saint. And she's already shared she's not a virgin.

I tossed and turned all fucking night. One, because I'm on a goddamn sofa. And two, because I fucked up royally. When I close my eyes, I see her body, her curves. God, those thigh highs. When she turned around and I glimpsed her breasts, bound by lace and pushed into tempting pillows, I almost came right there like a fifteen-year-old. And if I had, who could blame me? It's been five fucking years since I've had sex.

Over the years, as a syndicate member, I've had plenty of prostitutes offered to me, in countries where it's legal, but I just couldn't bring myself to do it. And I haven't let myself explore anything real because I'm not real and it wouldn't be fair to the woman.

And here I go and play hero to a woman younger than my sisters with a plan to bring her into my home. Not, of course, to my real home. I don't have a real home. I'm in a never-ending job assignment where I'm playing so many sides you'd think I was a politician. I'm bringing the temptation wrapped in lace to my flat, and I'll have to keep her at a distance because I'm so deep undercover doing anything else would be cruel.

I'm not a saint, but I'm not cruel either. Given how I can't get her out of my head, I'm definitely not a saint, but apparently, I am a masochist.

Knock. Knock.

The sound is faint. I rub my tired eyes and glare at the narrow stream of light between the drapes.

Room service? What the fuck time is it?

I swing my legs off the sofa and reach for my watch on the coffee table.

Pound. Pound.

The soft knocks now resemble a hammer.

Room service wouldn't knock that hard. *Fuck.*

The bedroom door is cracked. I pull it closed without looking inside the dark chamber, find my bag, unzip it, and remove my SIG.

My mobile vibrates on the coffee table.

What the fuck is going on?

"Who is it?" I ask, gun raised, standing to the side of the door should someone decide to blister it with bullets.

"Leo. It's me. Open up."

Nick?

I swing open the door, and Nick's gaze drops to my briefs.

"What're you doing here?"

"Didn't want to call. Our lines might be compromised."

I glance past him to an empty hall. He's alone.

Nick strides into the suite like he owns it, and given he paid for the suite, I suppose he does. I lock the door and flick on the lights.

"You slept on the sofa?" He's smirking and, mother of all things holy, I need coffee.

"What're you doing here?" He's fully aware that this marriage is a sham, and I'm not in the mood to deal with bullshit.

He strides over to the window, taking in the city view.

I ruffle through my bag, pull out a pair of jeans, and ask, "Can you order us some coffee? You hungry?"

"I won't be here long." He looks at the closed door. "Is she sleeping?"

"She was." There's no light beneath the door. I slide on the jeans and don't bother with a shirt. "She grew up in the Italian mafia. I think you're cleared to say most things. What's up?"

If he's knocking on my honeymoon suite, shit's going down.

"If you turned on the news, you'd see."

A darkened screen hangs on the far wall. I scan the room for a remote, but Nick waves his hand.

"Don't bother. There's another bust. Shipment through the Red Sea. But that's not all. One of our shell companies was hacked and liquidated. Two hundred mil gone. We're under attack."

"What can I do?"

"Nothing about the hack. My tech team is on it."

I've got a good idea how it all came down with the bust. But hacking syndicate financial accounts is a death wish. We've got the best in the world, and when they trace it, the guilty parties will die a slow and gruesome death, after their loved one's die in front of them.

"When do you plan to introduce your new bride to your family?"

His question startles me out of my sleep-deprived fog. The first image I have is of my sisters, and they can't ever know about the life I'm leading, or else they too might end up on a firing line.

"Did you tell your relatives about your marriage yet?"

I blink, and it slowly dawns on me he's talking about my cover family, the Sullivans, back in Texas. I really need coffee.

"Haven't gotten around to it yet." His expression is unreadable. "It's a sham, Nick. You fucking know that."

"Right. Well, I propose you play it like it's real."

"Why?"

"One, it's better if Massimo De Luca believes the love story. If he thinks he got played because someone didn't want to give his brother what he wants, he'll see it as a sign of disrespect. It won't play out well for the Gaglianos, and I don't want issues for Titan Shipping."

"I don't plan on returning to Italy anytime soon." Therefore, Massimo can believe whatever line Willow's family feeds him.

"A trip to Texas to introduce her would give you some time to talk shop with your family. Face to face, no risk of breach."

"You think someone's monitoring us?"

"They're always trying. Either they were successful, or we've got a leak. I want to know what deals the Sullivans have struck and with whom. I want to know who, outside of our circle, is buying right now. Your wedding is the perfect excuse for one-on-one time."

The bedroom door opens, and Willow stands in the doorway. She's no longer wearing virginal white thigh highs, and the garter belt is gone, but she's wearing a see-through white gown that falls mid-thigh, and her breasts are on full display. The way the light filters through the gauzy fabric, she might as well be nude, and I'm instantly hard.

Fuck me. One more image burned into my retinas.

"Get back in the room."

She spins, giving us a clear view of her bare, fine ass, and the door closes. Fucking hell. Could she not hear our voices?

"You slept on the sofa instead of with that?" I glare at Nick, and he chuckles. "She's your bride. It might not be love, but it's legal. You might as well fuck her." He pushes off the armchair and stares at the closed door. "I certainly would."

I faked a marriage with her to protect her, not to use her.

"You silly cunt."

I want to smack that irritating grin right off his face.

"Right, then. I'll be getting out of your bridal suite. Call me when you're back at your flat. Let me know when you'll be returning to Texas."

The door closes with a loud click, the sound emphasized by the heavy weight of the hotel door. I scrub the back of my head with my hands furiously. *Coffee or shower?*

Fuck it. I'll go with a shower. Maybe after I jack off, I won't be so pissy. I need to meet with Nomad, but I'll have to be careful. With a battle brewing, eyes will be everywhere.

When I sling open the bedroom door, she's sitting on the bed, a pillow pulled over her stomach, knees bent up to her chest, timid and impossibly younger looking. Christ.

"Why in the devil did you come out dressed like that?"

Glassy, innocent blue eyes peer up at me.

Tears. I fucking hate tears.

"I didn't know he was here."

"And you thought it was okay to walk around in that around me?"

Does she think I'm so old I'm not affected? She's a fucking walking pin-up. Jesus fucking Christ.

"It's what my mother packed for my wedding night. The trunks aren't here."

She's right. They shipped the trunks straight to London.

She sniffles, and I just don't have the patience. I head to the bathroom and catch myself in the mirror. I am a better man than this. Sexual frustration is clouding my judgment. I pause in the doorway, head bowed, back to her, an apology on the tip of my tongue, but it'll never pass.

"Look. I get that we have an arrangement. I'm older, but I'm still a man. Unless you plan on throwing sex on the table, cover up."

With that, I close the door, turn on the shower, and take care of business.

CHAPTER 11

WILLOW

We have an arrangement.

Those words continue nonstop in my head like an intrusive melody. I itch to combine shades of red on a palette, drench my brush, and flick the paint for a blood spatter effect. What does it say about my mindset that I am aching to mimic blood spatter?

I didn't pack my clothes, nor did I know anyone was in the suite when I opened the bedroom door. How could I have expected he would rip my wedding dress to shreds when unbuttoning the back? If he'd taken his time, the strapless dress wouldn't have fallen to my knees.

The light pink Chanel skirt suit hanging in the closet taunts me. It belongs on a dignified, proper woman twice my age. The outfit symbolizes the woman my mother wishes for me to be.

I'll donate it after we arrive in London, since it's nothing I would choose to wear. My mother packed it, but I packed the trunks with my clothes that were shipped to England.

Yes, this is an arrangement, and an odd one. But I need to focus on the positive. I am officially independent. The good news about the airport outfit is that it shouldn't be a problem for Leo. The sleeveless silk top is demure and the skirt skims my knees.

Leo did me a favor, and I'll do him one. I'll do everything I can to stay out of his way, focus on my art, and build a career for myself. With luck, the arrangement will continue until I'm financially independent and have distanced myself enough from the family that when Leo and I separate, there will be no talk of my returning to Italy.

I always believed my father would look out for me, and with this arrangement, he did. It's not the ideal scenario, but everything will work out. Day in and day out, perseverance is my friend. With perseverance, the snail made it to the ark. Are there any other truisms to call upon? Things could be much worse. That's another one.

The iron has cooled, and I wrap the cord and stow it away. I exit the bathroom to dress in my travel suit…which, by the way, Mamma, no one wears travel suits anymore. My toes squeeze into the front of the heels, and I have to suck in my breath to button the skirt, but this is the last time I'll be required to squeeze into an outfit. Come to think of it, I should toss the wedding dress in the rubbish. It's ripped, and it made me look like a doll wrapped in meringue.

Dressed, I press my ear to the bedroom door. There are no sounds, so I crack it open and peer into the living area of the suite.

"Leo?"

A folded blanket lies on one end of the rumpled sofa where he slept. I would've been willing to sleep there, but he'd insisted.

Intellectually, I recognize he's a good man. He agreed to help me, after all. But he'd been furious. His brown eyes darkened and his lips pressed together, and I feared he would lash out to teach me a lesson. Of course, he's never given me a reason to fear him. Scarlet's stories are in my head. I barely know Leo Sullivan. He's not in the Lupi Grigi, but people say the syndicate is worse.

His reaction last night terrified and mortified me. He made me feel repulsive and dirty.

I press my palms over the front of my Chanel jacket, smoothing it.

"Leo?" I call again.

A piece of paper catches my eye at the same time there's a knock on the door. I read the scrap of paper on the way to answer the hotel room door.

Willow,

I have some business to take care of out of town. Matthew will pick you up from the hotel at ten, will fly with you to London, and deliver you to my flat. Judy, the housekeeper, can assist with any of your needs.

Leo

I check my watch. It's five minutes after ten.

He couldn't knock and tell me?

I open the door and explain I'm running behind, then rush to gather everything. Matthew waits patiently by the hotel room door, arms folded in front of him, like an obedient security detail. He's tall with dark hair and an olive complexion.

"I'm sorry," I say as I approach the door with my suitcase and handbag. His gaze flits to the pile of white draping over the circular trash can by the decorative desk.

He takes the handle of my suitcase and wordlessly holds the door for me.

In case he doesn't understand English—although that's doubtful, given his occupation—I repeat myself in Italian. He remains mute.

At the airport, he scans the crowd at all times, at least, that is, until our flight departs. We're flying first class, but it's a short flight and not particularly decadent. He insists I take the window seat, not with words, but with gestures.

There are buds in his ears, and I'm not sure if they are hearing aids or communication devices. He's not carrying a weapon that I can see, but based on his build and the way his arms never quite rest until we sit, I suspect his hands legally qualify as weapons.

Security isn't a new concept for me. His dark trousers, white Oxford with the top button undone, and a black suit coat remind me of the wardrobe choice of the security team my father employs. Given it's clear he has no intention of carrying on a conversation, I recline my seat and close my eyes. I didn't sleep well last night, too startled and undone by Leo's reaction to me in undergarments. I had more clothes on than if we'd met up at the beach to go swimming.

My brother assumed he was gay, but he said he's not. If he's attracted to women, or if he has sexual needs, he clearly has no intention of sating those needs with me. When he saw me, his nostrils flared and he looked almost feral.

Still, there's no denying that he's handsome, fit, and when he's not angry, he's approachable. If I hadn't been so absorbed in my problems when we met, I would've noticed him. Heat and vitality come off him in waves. Golden brown eyes beneath straight dark brows. Glints of silver and gold in trimmed nut-brown hair, an angular, commanding jaw and broad shoulders. His skeletal structure would make him a pleasure to sketch.

When he'd been in only jeans and barefoot, I hadn't been prepared for my body's reaction to the sight of his taut chest and defined abdomen. My breathing slowed, and I couldn't tear my gaze away. There's no way he didn't notice. My ex, Jules, had been skin over bones compared to Leo. Even Leo's pale, bare feet extending beyond the denim held sex appeal.

Of course, if Leo's like the Grigi men, he has girlfriends all over the world, and girlfriends is a kind descriptor.

It's absolutely fine if he dates women all over the world. "Date" is probably another kind word. "Sexual relations" is more accurate. What he does isn't my business, as we have an arrangement, one he agreed to out of kindness. *Unless you plan to throw sex on the table.* Obviously, I'm not. He didn't sound like he wanted me to, either. He'd been angry.

But even angry, he didn't threaten or belittle me. If Leo was like Vincent, Scarlet's husband, he wouldn't have ever offered to help me. He would've walked right by Leandro in the alley, or maybe stopped to watch.

But the nagging voice reminds me Vincent was polite and gracious when we first met him. Muscular, he filled out a suit well, and aside from his front gold tooth, his appearance didn't match one of a mafia enforcer. When I first met him, I'd thought Scarlet's mother had made her a desirable match. I'd believed Scarlet to be fortunate.

It's a disturbing thought. The silent security guard beside me does nothing to settle my nerves.

If I arrive at Leo's flat and it's clear Leo suffers from a perverse nature, I'll leave. I'll call Scarlet, and she'll help me. Unlike me, she trained with a fighter. She's skilled. I should train.

If there's a room in his house with chains or whips, or if there are body parts in the refrigerator, I'll leave. I won't call Scarlet unless he traps me. I'll wait a suitable amount of time before returning to Italy so I'm not forced into a union with Leandro, but I will listen to my gut. If I don't feel safe, I'll leave. I packed jewelry I can sell. I have a credit card in my name and euros in my wallet.

Solitude leaves me with nothing but my thoughts. While my nerves become a live wire of uncertainty and determination, Matthew says nothing.

At a young age, I learned the security team puts their lives on the line to protect us, and I shouldn't do anything to distract them or lessen their effectiveness. Therefore, I don't talk to him, although conversation would be a welcome distraction from the thoughts whirling through my head.

When we land, Matthew escorts me through the airport to a black sedan with tinted windows. He opens the back door and, as I take my seat, the driver says, "Good day, miss."

The driver pulls away, leaving Matthew at the curb. The driver's focus remains on the road, and, like Matthew, he doesn't say or do anything to invite conversation, so I follow his cue.

Traffic from the airport merges into a slow, stop-and-go

stream. The passing buildings appear especially gray, as is the sky. If I were to paint the scenery, I would use a monotone palette with a mix of white and black, one marked by a complete absence of color, and the other scored by a saturation of all colors. Yin and yang.

Today is my first day officially free from the Lupi Grigi clan. How ironic the sky is bleak and I'm alone. Oh, and let's not forget…safety remains a question.

The sedan meanders through city streets. It slows in front of a gate that slowly rises. The car dips down into a covered garage. I wasn't paying close enough attention, but it appears we are in a covered area for an apartment building for multiple units. The spots are marked with unit numbers.

The car door opens, and an older woman with a splendid mix of white, steel gray, and black hair holds the door for me.

"Welcome to Stratford, dear. I'm Judy. Unfortunately, you're arriving later than I expected, and I must rush off, but before I do, I'll give you a quick tour of your new home."

When I stand, I tower over Judy. The top of her head doesn't reach my shoulder. Her gaze falls to my heels.

"We won't have far to walk. The elevator is up ahead." She leads the way, and I glance back at the sedan.

"Should I get my—"

"John will get your luggage, dear. Your trunks have already arrived. I hope you don't mind, but I took the liberty of unpacking for you. A few items were a little worse for the journey and I sent them off to be pressed."

Judy's steps are tight and quick. Even with my longer legs, I scurry to keep up.

"This building has twenty-four-hour concierge service. Your name and photograph have been added to the registry. Mr.

Sullivan said you're an artist. The building includes co-working spaces, and at Mr. Sullivan's request, I have inquired about obtaining one for you to use as an artist's studio. Mr. Sullivan's flat is a three-bedroom unit. He said to give you the two smaller bedrooms and to remove the furniture from the room if you'd like to create a studio in the apartment. I'll need a list of the supplies you will require." She presses the elevator button. "The kitchen is fully stocked. Cleaning service arrives every other day at present, but if you wish for a daily cleaning, simply let me know. There is a rooftop garden that you have access to."

The elevator slides open. She places a plastic card against a pad and presses the number forty-one. The doors close, and my stomach freefalls as the elevator ascends.

"I'm trying to think what else you will need to know. The bathroom is fully stocked, but if there is anything you need, please let me know. Message me, and I'll have items delivered as quickly as possible. I'm Mr. Sullivan's home manager, but I also manage the properties for four others in this building, so if you need anything, don't hesitate to message me. In all likelihood, I'll be close by." She peruses my body, and my spine straightens.

The lift stops and the doors slide open. Light reflects off a polished concrete floor. Wide metal stairs lead up, and glass walls with an expansive view of the city line two walls.

"I take it Mr. Sullivan doesn't suffer from fear of heights."

"Oh, dear. Do you?"

"No," I answer, but a slight dizziness takes hold. It feels like I could step to the edge of the concrete and fall to my death.

There's a bike with thick wheels to one side, propped so perfectly it could be part of the decoration. A pot with a plant with green fronds sits on the far side against a concrete wall. The bike and the plant are the only two items in the entry.

"If those spikes are hurting your feet, please feel free to take them off. This is your home now, love."

Judy has removed her black leather shoes and holds them in one hand. She's wearing thick wool socks that jut out below her loose-fitting trousers and a pale pink blouse. A gold cross dangles from a short chain around her neck.

I bend my leg and remove one heel, then the other. Judy charges up the stairs without a backward glance.

The concrete is cool against the bottoms of my bare feet. My dizziness increases as I climb the stairs.

"If you're afraid of heights, they say it helps to focus on either the floor or the inner part of the building."

We arrive at what I presume is the main floor. It's smartly decorated. In fact, it's so perfectly decorated that it doesn't feel lived in. There are rooms like this in our family's home. Formal rooms that no one spends time in, but to the far side of this room is a kitchen. The design, like the rest of the flat, is modern with slate gray panel cabinets and a heavily streaked marble inset behind the stovetop and matching countertop. Twelve mid-century modern chairs surround the long, narrow wooden table below gold-rimmed circular lights.

The mid-century modern decor incorporated into the mix of contemporary furnishing infuses a touch of warmth. The white pine floor offsets the dark elements, and crisp white walls lend a Scandinavian aesthetic.

Monochrome art evoking Picasso, Ritcher, and Degas adorns the walls. Two black sculptures perched on pedestals catch my eye. Veils cover the women's faces, but their breasts are exposed. It's an interesting choice, and I can't help but wonder how Leo interprets his art. What does his attachment to monochrome mean? What kind of human prefers a world void of color?

"Down this hall are two bedrooms. I placed your wardrobe in the bedroom closest to the primary suite. If you wish for anything to be moved, simply let me know. Okay, love?"

I nod.

"The closed door at the end of the corridor is Mr. Sullivan's suite. Through the galley in the kitchen is Mr. Sullivan's office, and the door remains locked."

She steps into a bedroom, and I follow. The floor-to-ceiling glass wall is too much from this height. As if reading my mind, Judy sets about pulling the cream floor-to-ceiling drapes closed, narrowing the view outside to a thin strip of horizon.

"The mobile charging on the side table is yours. My number, John's, and Mr. Sullivan's, are pre-programmed. If you need to leave, you can call John and he'll ensure a driver is readied." She claps her hands. "I believe that's it. Remember, anything you need, simply message me. Are you quite all right, love?"

I open my mouth, and she says, "Oh, and food. I don't currently have a chef scheduled, but if you would like one, simply let me know."

"No, I'm good…I can cook for myself."

"Oh. The menu drawer. Follow me."

I do so, and she pulls a drawer filled with menus.

"These all do take away, and some do delivery. I'm sure as you get settled in, you can figure out what you'll be needing."

"Yes."

"Have a goodnight, dear. I hate to rush but must be off."

It's midafternoon, but I don't correct her as I watch her leave. The faint swish of the lift doors wafts up from the entry below.

I wander back down the hall to the bedrooms. Lightheadedness has replaced the dizziness. I sit back on the bed, hungry but not hungry enough to do anything about it. I was curious about unpacked clothes, but too stunned with this turn of events to open the closet door.

The mobile vibrates. I startle and stare. The screen lights with a bright gray, then dims to black.

I stretch across the bed, reaching for the device.

Leo Sullivan
If you leave the flat, take John with you.
It's not safe for you to go out alone.

CHAPTER 12

SAM, AKA LEO, AKA SAINT

The clay disk hurtles through the air, and a shot shatters the quiet a second before the ceramic explodes into fragments.

The subtle purr of an engine passes down the trail. I lift my binoculars and peer through the trees, confirming the occupant.

I've spent the last week at Tristan Voignier's private estate, out of the public eye. Needing a place to decompress, Tristan, or Nomad on covert channels, offered a place off the beaten path and far away from surveillance. The official story is that I'm ensconced in my flat in a state of matrimonial bliss.

Nick spent the past week in Greece shoring up relationships with a couple of syndicate power players. He believes I'm following up with the journalist who broke the story about the drug bust before anyone else. The story hit the wire too early for her to have not had an inside source. Of course, I'm not following up with the journalist because I already know exactly how she ended up with her intel.

The vehicle stops in front of the nearby guesthouse. The door to the Land Rover opens, and Tristan steps out of the vehicle as I pull up on my ATV.

"Dapper as ever," I comment, smiling. He's my Interpol contact, and technically he's my handler, but he's a friend by lieu of being the only person outside of the States who knows my true identity.

If it weren't for the situation, we'd probably never hit it off. The Brit dresses like a tool. Tapered trousers, glossy pointed dress shoes, three-piece toppers. Today he's wearing plaid tapered trousers, a turtleneck sweater, and hunting boots. It's about as casual as I've ever seen him.

"How's married life?"

I ignore his dig and lead the way inside the guesthouse, a cabin on his gated estate.

"Care for a drink?" I counter.

"Lucia's back at the main house. Told her I needed to check on the property. She'll suspect something if I come back smelling like alcohol."

"Right." I set the crystal lid on the decanter.

"Do the accommodations meet your needs?"

"Yes. I appreciate the breather."

"Not a problem. By my count, you haven't had a holiday in close to five years. I'd say you're due." He shoves his hand in his pockets. "So, what've you got for me?"

"Nothing new."

"You spent a weekend partying so hard with the mafia that you came home with a wife and nothing else?"

"I didn't say I got nothing. I said nothing new." Fuckwad.

"Titan Shipping is legit, but they are transitioning into the gray."

"Transitioning how? Siding with Russia?"

"I don't know about siding. I'd say profiting from. It's the same old story. The Lupi Grigi have a complex mix of legitimate and illegitimate businesses. Real estate, supermarkets, hotels. The normal mix. I heard them talk about all of it. Drugs and arms are their two illegal businesses. That and corruption… If you want to catch them, I'd say accounting is the way to go, but…these guys are expert money launderers." Not that any of this is news to him. "One guy, a mouthy foot soldier type, told me there's a new guy who's pissing them off. An Italian man of Argentinian descent who mostly lives in Spain. He imports bananas from Ecuador and owns sports centers in Marbella and Granada. Plus bars and restaurants all over. He's infringing on their territory."

"He's infringing on the Lupi Grigi?"

"That's the story."

"He won't live long enough for us to look into him. What's his name?"

"Fernando Cavenaghi. You going to pursue him?"

"Me? Unlikely. But the Europol commissioner is on record saying that organized crime is the biggest threat to the European Union. I'll pass it on. Someone will do something."

There's nothing to act on. I've been doing this for five years. If the powers that be find the relay of intel valuable, so be it.

"You got the update with their exploration into submersibles?" I ask.

He nods. "Longer we carry sanctions, the more attractive profiting from them becomes. What does Ivanov believe you've been doing for this past week?"

"Nick thinks I'm looking for the BBC journalist. Which I have been doing remotely. She hasn't shown up in the London feed. She didn't go missing, did she?" He tilts his head thoughtfully in a way that doesn't sit well. "We fed her that story to catch those fucks. For fucking sure, we protected her. Right?"

"Haven't heard anything, but I'll check around." Tristan pulls out his mobile and taps away on it, likely adding something like *check the morgues for journalist* to his to-do list. "In other news, sources say Leandro went ballistic when he discovered you snapped up the young bird he had an eye on."

"Ballistic?"

"Lost it. Set loose an assault rifle at the hotel. Two employees died. I'm not clear if that was intentional or if they caught stray fire."

The memory of him holding Lucia against a wall flashes, as does my anger.

"Piece of work, that one. Quite mad," Tristan says.

"Assume he's still on the loose? Didn't get into any trouble?"

"You mean with the authorities?" Tristan scoffs. "Massimo owns them. The fact a suite at the Regis getting shot to bits isn't all over the telly is proof he owns the journalists too. But, bright spot, my source says Massimo is calming Leandro."

"How?"

"Drugs?" He shrugs. "Your guess is as good as mine. My money is on anything other than the psychiatrist he needs."

"I suppose every family needs a member who will kill, no questions asked."

"Kill and derive enjoyment from it. He's a sick fuck. I recommend you stay away from Italy."

"No plans to return. But now you see why I helped her out."

Tristan places his weight on the back of the sofa, leaning

onto it. From his perch, he looks down at me, and I know damn well he's about to dig.

"There's nothing to it." I hold up a hand before he can start. "She was being forced to marry Leandro, and that hotel incident is not an outlier."

"How did you end up—"

"It's a crazy story." He folds his hands, waiting. "She reminded me of…" I stop myself from saying my sisters, because while Tristan knows my real name, mentioning my family out loud is an unnecessary risk. You never know who's listening. The risk is minimal, but it's never nonexistent.

"A little birdy you wanted to shag?" he supplies.

"Fuck off." My grip on the glass tightens and I have half a mind to hurl it at Tristan's head.

The pisser is, he's not far off. I can't get that vision of her in her skimpy sexy-as-fuck white lingerie out of my head, and that's problematic. She's way too young, and aside from the matter of age, she doesn't know who I am and never will.

Tristan's right. I want to fuck her and walk away. But I can't fuck her and walk away because she lives with me now. When she reminded me of my sisters, the attraction was negligible. Throw in lingerie and put her on the no-touch list, and suddenly I'm fucking obsessed.

"Eye-opening news. Your betrothal, that is. Doesn't seem having her move in with you was the brightest. To do so, I assumed there had to be something…"

"There's nothing." I slam the bourbon back and lean into the burn. "Bad decision making at its finest."

"You may end up caring for her." I give him a sharp look that informs him exactly how wrong he is. "Never know. I didn't anticipate Lucia…and look at us now."

"Parents? Well, you see, when you don't use a condom—"

"Sod off." He rubs his hand briskly over the back of his head and mutters, "She's the best thing that ever happened to me. It's a miracle I haven't cocked it up."

"I won't bother asking how you think you'd do that." You never really know someone, but what I know of the man I called Nomad for years, and more recently Tristan, he's a decent guy. I expect he's a devoted husband and father.

"Well, as long as she trusts me, I suppose I won't. It's a fine line to walk. Deciding what I can tell her and what I can't."

"And I'm on the side of the no-tell line?" I study him, hoping he's smart enough to keep his loved ones out of the bullshit world we live in. Sure, we mostly interact with educated, affluent business executives. But those men met success by leveraging a subcurrent of thugs and killers.

I'm way past giving a shit about my life. It's a fucking miracle I haven't been burned yet. But I take seriously the risk of burning the innocent.

"That you are. You shan't meet Lucia."

"Good. Keep your loved ones safe."

"She works for us. She's aware enough." His expression goes blank. Unreadable.

"Why the hell—"

"Not in my group. We have employees who are free to talk about what they do. That's most of them, you know."

"Those exist on our end, too." Of course, when I get burned —and I often think in terms of when, not if—the CIA will claim I don't work for them. There will be no star on a wall for me. Which is fine. The Navy already honored my memory. "Keep her safe."

I look him straight in the eyes, but the women I'm thinking of are my sisters, Sage and Sloane.

"What about your new wife? You keeping her safe?"

"She's got security." He nods, judgment clear. "For the last fucking time, it's an arrangement." I married the woman with my cover name. Tristan the wandering nomad should be very much aware of that fact.

"I'll keep you apprised of any further developments with your in-laws."

"For fuck's sake. They won't come after her. Her father blessed the fucking union." The subtle, disagreeing eyebrow raise irks me. "What else do you have?"

"Are you going to the tech conference in Abu Dhabi?"

"Leave tomorrow." I'd like to connect with the journalist before I go, but that's looking unlikely.

"When you go, I'd be interested in a list of attendees. Specifically, in the back rooms."

"I'm there to cut some off-the-book arms deals. I won't recognize any new players in the cybercrime arena. It's not my area." I let out a sigh and stare wistfully at my almost empty crystal glass. "When I return, I'll be heading to the States."

"Oh? Bringing the bride home?"

"Nick's interested in what's happening in the US market."

"Huh. So, you're going to bring your arrangement home to meet the family? And she's going to live in your home, and never pick up that you're not exactly who you say you are? Is that wise?"

"No." It's dumb as all fuck. But we'll make it work.

"You're done, aren't you? You've got no more fucks to give."

"That's about the truth of it." I knock back my drink.

"What's the exit strategy?"

"That's an excellent question. When in Texas, I plan on telling them it's time to hatch the plan. Overdue, actually." The week away did nothing to ease my shit mood. Tristan's right. I'm disengaged and apathetic. That gets dangerous quick.

"I'll get a jump on it."

"Much appreciated." Of course, the Interpol officer who's become my friend has no issues with ending the op. But my gut tells me the guys back home may push for more. *What we're getting from you is invaluable. Something's afoot. We still need you in place. Just a little longer.* I can hear Jack now.

CHAPTER 13

WILLOW

Moody, dark shades swirl on the canvas. It's not as structured as a Mark Rothko piece, but melancholy is undeniably present in the hues. Long gone are the reds, oranges, and yellows. My mood, and my art, contrast with the bright blue sky I'm told I should take advantage of outside.

A rapping on the wall snags my attention. A young man with shaggy, loose, dark curls and a paint-splattered smock stands in the doorway.

"Sorry to disturb you. I work a couple of rooms down. Thought I'd stop by and introduce myself. I'm Geoff."

I'm in the co-op space, in the small room Leo rented. I've been working here for almost two weeks but have yet to meet anyone. Most tenants work with their doors closed, or perhaps the others use their space at odd hours.

"Oh, hi. I'm Willow. You're an artist in the co-op, too?"

Saying the word *too* thrills, because yes, I am an artist. It would be better if I were an artist earning an income, but baby steps.

"Landscapes."

"Why are you inside on a day like today?"

"I was out this morning. The light changed. I'll spend the afternoon working from the studio. What do you paint? Can I see?"

I hesitate, only because it's a work in progress and, if I'm honest, it's a reflection of my state of mind as opposed to a piece with strategic direction.

"It's okay," he says, sensing my hesitation. "I get not wanting to show a piece in progress." His timid smile sets me at ease, and I take in the youthful man with angular cheekbones and long, bony fingers. His aesthetic strikes me as more French than British, but his accent is unmistakably British. "I was going to go grab lunch. Would you care to join me?"

A shortened acoustic version of "Strawberry Fields Forever" by the Beatles blares, and I scan the floor for my mobile. It's my ringtone for Scarlet.

When I find the mobile, I tap it quickly and answer, "Hey, hold on a minute."

"Another time?" Geoff asks, backing away like I've already turned him down. I wouldn't have, as I'd love to get to know others in the London area, especially artists.

But he's gone before my brain kicks in with a counter response to keep him here. When I look back to my mobile, my gaze snags on my fingers. Ringless fingers.

When I come across Geoff again, I'll make it clear I'm married but welcome the friendship. I don't know what the syndicate is like, but I know no woman in the Grigi family would dare cheat on her husband. Retribution could be painful for both the wife and her extracurricular.

"Hey, I'm here," I answer, stepping up to the window to peer over the green quad.

"Is Leo back?"

"No." Scarlet's aware I haven't heard from Leo since departing Rome. We've had countless conversations debating what that means. Should I expect to live a solitary life from here on out? Does he not live in London? Did he place me in one of his properties to keep me safe with no intention of more? What rules should I live by? What are his expectations?

Yes, we have an arrangement, but most of the unions in our world are arrangements. What rules am I bound by? He disappeared without any discussion, or at least, after scolding me for my attire. For all I know, he could have a different lover in his bed every night. Just because Orlando never saw him with anyone doesn't mean he's celibate. He may choose discretion.

"Willow. I wish I could reach through this phone line and give you a hug. You sound sad, but you barely know the man. You should be grateful. The men in our world would've demanded sex."

"I am grateful." My high-pitched response earns a well-deserved annoyed groan from Scarlet. Is it wrong I'm disappointed? Is it weird I keep asking myself what's wrong with me? Why doesn't he want to have sex with me? He's beyond distant. He's not here.

"I, for one, am relieved for you. The fact he's not coming around means he's sleeping with someone else somewhere. Give thanks to the heavens."

I try not to think about him with someone else. But she's truthful. I don't like the queasy feeling in my belly when I think about it. It's completely illogical. I suppose I'm too traditional or…confused. It's an arrangement. He's helping me out. That's all.

"Willow?"

"I'm fine," I snap.

"It could be so much worse." She's speaking from experience. The pad of my thumb roves over a clump of dried paint on my smock. There's no good response to Scarlet. "You can't trust the men in our world," she says in Italian.

"I know," I respond in Italian.

"Tell me something good," I say in English, forcing a brightness in my tone I don't feel. "What's going on at home?"

"Leandro came to visit."

"You?" He can't possibly want to marry Scarlet. If my leaving saddled Scarlet with that— "You're a widow. He can't—"

"He wasn't here for me." She snorts. "Trust me. He's too much of a coward."

Scarlet killed her husband in self-defense. Rumors abound she killed him by divesting him of his manly body parts and letting him bleed out. It's one reason no one has asked for Scarlet's hand, and, according to Mamma, they never shall. She'll be the Scarlet Widow of the Lupi Grigi for the rest of her life.

"If he didn't visit with an interest in you, then why? What did he want?" I don't particularly want to hear her answer.

"He asked about you."

"Me?" My stomach twists and my hand falls over my unsettled tummy.

"Wanted to know how you were getting on in London and if I had any plans to visit you."

"What did you tell him?"

"That you are happy and in love. I repeated everything Aunt Ludie spouts to anyone who will listen."

"Why would he ask you?"

"I've no idea. But that's the reason I called. Be careful, Willow. The man gives me the creeps by simply being, but his questions…I get the feeling he doesn't know where you live. He's trying to find you."

"Why?" My twisty stomach sinks. "He wouldn't go up against the syndicate."

"A sane man wouldn't. A narcissistic, egotistical monster might."

"And Leandro checks all the boxes."

"Do you have security?"

"Yes," I say automatically.

"Do you?" There's an insistence to her tone that makes her sound like a mother.

"John doesn't accompany me to the studio. I technically haven't left the grounds. Our building is in a complex, and I stay within the perimeter. What are the chances Leandro could…" Why would he want to find me is the question I want to ask, but Scarlet's right. Asking why assumes rational thought. "What else? Tell me something good."

I don't want to hear about the capo's psycho brother. I left that world behind.

"How's Orlando? Have you seen him?"

"Have I ever. I'm his newfound best friend since you've been gone."

"He doesn't call me."

"Does he call anyone?"

"Probably not. Maybe I should learn how to play one of those games he plays."

She snorts. "Good luck with that. I suspect he has a bit of a crush—"

"On who?"

"One of his classmates. I saw him walking with her along the beach."

"Not alone?" Orlando's on the young side for a marriage, but there are plenty of families within the Grigi who would love to marry into Titan Shipping. "He's got to be careful."

"I don't think she's one of ours."

"Oh." Sadness falls over me. That's not any better. He's probably too young to fall in love, but someone Father doesn't approve of will never be an option for Orlando. Not if he wants to run Titan Shipping one day, which he does.

"Don't worry. He's probably just ogling her tits."

"Ah, she's endowed?"

"She might be a grade or two older. She's got a set."

"Oh, Orlando."

"You don't need to worry about your little brother. He's got a bright future as a heartbreaker."

"Until he's forced to marry."

"Please. You think he'll be any different from the others?"

"Papa doesn't cheat on Mamma."

A pointed silence falls across the line.

"Scarlet. Stop it. He doesn't."

"Don't be a fool, Willow. Of course, he does."

She's wrong. My father adores my mother. They have one of the good marriages. They are the reason I thought Papa would never force me to marry for any reason other than love.

"I need to run," I say to Scarlet. It's been a short call, but I don't want to talk to her anymore.

"Where are you off to?"

"Lunch. The chef made a salad that's on its last day."

"You're eating at home?"

"That's what I've been doing. I don't like asking John to follow me around."

"John is your bodyguard?"

"Yes. Well, he's employed by Leo. I've been instructed to have him with me if I leave the premise." John's the only security I've met, and he works a full day, so I guess Leo assumes I won't leave the flat at night.

"You need to get used to having security around. You're not in Italy. It's important."

"I will." I love Scarlet, but I hate that she sometimes acts like my mother. She's not that much older. "I'll call you later. I'm meeting with a man who is going to examine my art. He might be willing to be my agent."

"That's awesome, Willow!"

I grin. It really is. Leo honored his word and is helping me to get my feet on the ground as an income-earning artist.

I head down the hall and out onto the quad. The paved path to the apartment building turns onto Olympic Park.

Geoff rambles down the street in the opposite direction, and I smile and wave. He holds a white paper bag smeared with grease.

"What'd you get?" I ask when he reaches me.

"Sandwich and chips."

"I'm going home for lunch today, but I'd love to grab lunch one of these days."

"Really?"

His upbeat response has me grinning. It's obviously early days, but my gut says we'll be friends. He falls into step beside me.

"You live near here?" he asks.

"I do. You must also live near here? You work in the co-op." It's one of the benefits of Manhattan Loft Gardens. Based on the real estate literature I saw, it's a highly sought-after East London residence.

"Ah, no. I don't live here. A friend got me access. So, you live in one of the loft apartments?"

I nod.

"Quite posh," he says.

"It is." I can't deny it. The real estate value of Leo's apartment must be north of twenty million pounds, at least based on some of the postings at the realty. "Where do you live?"

"Putney. You've probably never been there, have you?"

"Can't say that I have. But I'm new to London. I mean, I've been here before as a tourist, but I'm a new resident."

"Well, why didn't you say? I'll have to show you about. I've lived here my whole life. Resident expert at your service."

There's a man standing outside the lobby entrance, and I zero in on the shadowy figure as we approach. He's tall, with short, dark hair, a blazer over a white Oxford, and weathered tan boots. It's the heeled boots that kick my heart into pitter patter overdrive. It's Leo. He's back.

CHAPTER 14

SAM, AKA LEO, AKA SAINT

The young guy walking up the path with Willow looks like a fucking kid. An enamored, gooey-eyed kid who aims to win her over. His shoulder-length hair and paint-splattered clothes tell me he's nothing like me, but I knew plenty of girls back in the day who fawned over artsy types.

I stretch my fingers, alleviating the tension tightening my spine and shoulders. She's not mine. She's far too young for me. I'm not even who she thinks I am. Yet the caveman deep within roars to bludgeon the horny adolescent.

I wasn't always like this. There was a time I didn't have a need to resort to violence when angry. But years of watching men die for lesser crimes, orchestrating the delivery of guns to monsters who kill and thrive, it's all changed me. And I can't say I like who I've become. All this anger. The vitriol twirling about inside makes throwing a fist or pulling a trigger far too welcome.

When you kill and you feel nothing, you've lost your soul.

Those words from a friend come to mind, and oddly enough, they deliver peace. I still feel. I recognize what I'm becoming, and I don't like it. I haven't given up. Not yet.

Willow laughs at something the long-haired pansy says. I bet the jackoff plays the guitar. He looks like that kind of guy. A total fuckwad.

The mass of wavy blonde hair bounces with her steps. Military-style boots peek out from her long white skirt. She's wearing a thick cardigan that falls below her hips, but it's undone, and beneath it she's wearing a white tank top with scalloped edges that leads the eye straight to her perfect, youthful, pillowy breasts.

In truth, the two of them look like a picture-perfect couple. And a better man would step into the shadows and let nature take its course.

The second she spots me, awareness sparks. Those bright blue eyes widen and her steps falter. Her rose-pink lips spread into a timid smile, but lover boy doesn't notice as he simply slows his pace, his attention solely on my wife. My gaze drops to her ringless fingers, where she's fiddling with the edge of her sweater.

My teeth grind, and the chilly day permeates my clothes. Seeing her with another man shouldn't piss me off. There's nothing real between us. I helped her out because she was in a hard place. She's way too young for there to be anything between us, even a fleeting thing.

I haven't spoken to her in two weeks. But I have ensured her safety. Expanded security. Hired a goddamn chef. Watched each night to ensure she was safe inside before going to bed.

"Leo." She says the name with an air of awe.

It's not my name, and I'm not her husband, and we're not real.

But unfortunately for this punk, I've got a role to play, and in that role, a syndicate leader wouldn't be at all okay with his wife—even if it's arranged as fuck—messing around.

"Wife," I answer. I must be sporting a killer glare, because lover boy stumbles, nearly crashing to his knees.

"Oh…um…" He glances between us, speechless and totally out of his fucking league.

"Leo, this is Geoff. Geoff, this is my…" Those big blues question, as if uncertain. What the fuck is she uncertain of?

"Husband," I answer for her.

She swallows, blinks, and places a hand on the motherfucker's arm. My blood pressure might go through the roof.

"Geoff and I work near each other. He was out and about and was walking me home. He paints landscapes."

He'll find that very difficult without hands.

The thought comes unbidden, and I close my eyes. Jesus, the monster within is running rampant.

"Oh, well, you're home now, love." He flinches at his word choice, as he should. He holds up a white paper bag. "I'm gonna head on back now. Have lunch before I get back to it. Lovely to meet you both."

"Nice to meet you," I say, then place a palm on Willow's ass and pull her against me, crushing my lips down over hers.

She tenses. Her lips are soft and unresponsive. I pin her to me so the fuckwad can't see whatever shock is playing against her features. When I lift my head, I avoid her eyes and watch the fuckwad retreat.

"Thanks for walking her home," I say to his withdrawing figure over her head.

"Right. Right. I'll see you. Nice to see you."

Willow wisely stands still, close to me. Her hot breath warms a spot of skin on my chest, but her muscles are tight and wound like a coil. He turns the corner, and the sound of his steps on cobblestone disappears into the mix of birdsong and city din.

She flattens a palm against my chest and presses. "I can explain."

The heat from her palm radiates across my chest, and I take a beat to process what she just said. I expected a slap on my cheek or a solid reprimand for being an ass. Because I was out of line. But she's expecting me to be worse than the men in her family. I suppose if I'd been Leandro, a cleaner would've been required.

"Let's go inside," I say, releasing some of the irrational rage with a change in direction.

"When did you get back?" She sounds chirpy, so I suppose she's not going to rip into me for being a tool. She should. I deserve it.

"About an hour ago. I was going to come down and check out your studio."

"You were?"

No, that's a lie. I came down when I saw on camera that she left her studio. I wanted to see where she was going without John, her daytime security.

"Is the studio sufficient?"

"It's fantastic. I really, truly can't thank you enough."

We pass through the lobby and to the elevator. The doors close on the two of us, and my gaze catches on her fingers.

"But you don't wear your rings." I absentmindedly twirl the gold band on my finger. I've been wearing mine because anyone I meet might have heard I got married. The ring supports my story. It's now a part of my cover.

"I don't want to get paint on them."

That's a flimsy excuse, but there's no point in arguing. The elevator shoots us up to the forty-first floor, and I resist the urge to hold on to the rail. No matter how many times I ride upward, I still feel the burden of rising above the Earth's hold.

Natural light pours in as the elevator door slides open, and I push forward to the stairs into the showplace. There's nothing in the entry other than a staggering London view, suspended black stairs above a gleaming polished concrete floor, and some decorative crap.

Nick's sister, Lina, found this flat for me when I moved to work for him. A friend of hers decorated it. Then a special team hired by Jack's firm came in and outfitted the place according to my specific needs.

I've watched Willow on the camera feed over the last two weeks while I've been away. She hasn't snooped around. But there's no denying bringing her into this flat bears risk. If she discovers a cache of weapons, identification, or a stash of bills, I'm betting it will feel normal to her, given the family she was raised in. In that regard, she's a safe bet, but perhaps a bet I shouldn't make. She might look too closely.

I shouldn't be putting my cover at risk. The fake marriage ploy is a bad idea. She's a bad idea. But I've always struggled with protective urges. Even as a kid with my younger sisters. Maybe if they hadn't both needed protecting at times, I wouldn't be like this. One sister bedridden, the other socially awkward. So what is it about Willow? Perhaps the protective urge arose because I saved her from being mauled. I have an undeniable soft spot for young women who need protection.

Upstairs, I stride to the windows and peer across the horizon. I don't need to watch her because I sense her. The swish of her skirt, the soft pad of her boots. Through the glass, her reflection shows as a blur in the window, hovering at a distance.

"I won't bite," I say to her, although given my recent conduct, I can't exactly blame her for wanting to distance herself from me. Still, her fear is not only unnecessary, it will drive me nuts to have someone afraid of me living under my roof.

"Maybe I want you to."

That gets my attention. I turn and study the young woman. She's backed up against the island, wide blue eyes filled with what? Fear? No. Challenge? Yes, that's it. I suppose that fits. Something tells me if I hadn't agreed to this arrangement, the wily woman would have found another way of circumventing her father's plans to marry her to Leandro. Which means I put my cover at risk needlessly.

Brilliant.

"Have you had lunch?" The second the question crosses the room, I recognize it as a stupid one. She was walking home for lunch, and she just said she might want me to bite. I'll disregard that remark. Nothing to be won with that exploration.

With a few brisk steps, I'm at the paneled refrigerator, scanning the contents. "Would you like a sandwich? Looks like there are three panini. Split one?"

"Sure. Do you want me to—"

"No." I gesture for her to back away. "I've got this. Heating panini is something I can do. Hence the reason I ask for them to be stocked."

"When you're home?"

The panini press clatters on the counter. She startles at the sharp sound. "Sorry," I mutter. The cabinet door slams loudly. Everything I'm doing is too loud. "Can you pick some music?"

We need something to soften the quiet. Up here on the forty-first floor, there are no city sounds. No birds. The thick glass walls and metal support beams muffle the occasional jet that roars past.

"What kind of music do you like?"

I suppose her question is harmless. Can't recall Nick ever asking about my music choice, although I'd bet he assumes I have a thing for country, given my theoretical Texas roots.

"Alternative rock. You?"

"Indie. World."

She's perched on the island like a big-eyed bird, inquisitive but on edge. I have the sense that if I stepped up to her too quickly, she'd flee.

"Play something you like," she says.

I pull out my phone, set it on the counter, and select a recent playlist. Death Cab for Cutie falls into the first rotation. Ben Gibbard croons on about taking a picture to remember this by and a déjà vu sensation hits. Or maybe that's not the right term. The sensation I feel is of playing a role in a film that will be over all too soon.

The cheese sizzles on the pan, breaking me from my somber thoughts. I go to pull out a knife and notice two walnut cutting boards propped against the counter. Those are new. I take one and place the panini on it.

"I like this song," she says.

"It's a good one. One of the band's best."

"What's it called?"

"'Pepper.'"

"I'm going to write it down," she says. "Great lyrics." I slide a plate with half a melted meat and cheese panini over to her. "Is that how you listen to all music? On your phone?"

The flat is wired with a sound system. I could easily hook up a service and speak out loud to an Alexa or Siri and have music playing through every room. But I'd rather not open myself up to a hack.

"You lived with your parents before me, right?"

Her lashes flutter, and I get the sense my topic change threw her, but she settles and smiles. It's a soft smile, one that highlights her innocence and youth.

"I did. Well, I lived in Florence for four years. But yes, after I finished my art program, my father…he expected me to return home."

"By the ocean?"

"Well, where we met was one of our seaside homes. The house I grew up in is farther north."

I recall seeing the Gagliano estate on a map. The satellite view shows mostly trees, roads, and some significant buildings. The secure compound rests on a higher elevation with a cliff bordering the ocean.

"How is London treating you? Missing Italy yet?"

She loops a golden curl behind her ear. Sitting on the stool beside her, I'm higher than she is. She parts her hair down the middle of her scalp, leaving a clear dark line on both sides of her dyed blonde strands. But the smile on her face, it's genuine.

As she talks about the differences between London and Italy, I can't help but wonder why she's smiling. What lights her up from the inside? Is it that she's been lonely here for two weeks and she's relieved to have someone to converse with? Does her excitement brim from living in a new city, or from living on her own?

"What brought you to London?" I have a mouthful of panini when she asks, which buys me time.

"Job," I answer. Anyone she asks will corroborate, as it's the truth.

"And how does London compare to America?"

Oh… My first thought is of California. The Pacific. But then I think of Asheville, where my sisters are. And Rocky Mount, the small town I grew up in. It's a different place these days. All the places I've spent time in keep changing.

"That's not an apples-to-apples comparison. You'd need to pick a city within America and almost any city other than New York City is big-time smaller. London's energy, the variety of neighborhoods, the history, there's nothing in the United States that's comparable. New York, perhaps. But London beats it on the history front by centuries." Of course, I like it as a base for pragmatic reasons. "London is convenient for travel."

"You travel a lot?"

I have this urge to brush my finger across her nose. To tease out that smile that fell behind a cloud. "I do. Nature of the beast."

She brushes her hands off. She only ate the top bread and cheese and left the meat behind.

"Are you a vegetarian?"

"Pescetarian."

"Interesting." Sloane, my sister, once attempted veganism. Didn't work out well for her.

"Well, I suppose I should get back to the studio. Unless..." She pauses, plate suspended, "Did you want to do something today?"

"No." It's a weekday. Email is piling up as we speak. The job Nick hired me for is quite real.

"I'm not sure. I just...what do you want from this arrangement?" She sets the plate down on the stool and faces me with one arm crossed over her belly. The cardigan gapes open, and my gaze drifts to the silhouette of a perky nipple beneath the outline of the flimsy tank.

Jesus, I'm a pervert.

I push off from the barstool, lift my plate, and collect hers.

"Nothing." I'm one step past her when I realize I lied. "No, that's not true." I set the plates down on the island. "This business of going around town without security has to stop. You need to be safe. I expect you to coordinate with John."

"I know how to be safe." Her spine straightens, and her hands fall to her side.

"You're in a new city." Nick sends regular updates on Leandro. The fact he's made it into our status file doesn't sit right, but there's no point in scaring her. "Just be smart."

Her chin tilts up, defiant.

"What's that look for? I can't imagine your father let you walk around without security."

"I absolutely did."

Ah, fuck. She probably did. If anyone laid a hand on her, they knew they'd die shortly after. Everyone except the capo's brother.

"Well, you're not in Italy anymore, sweetheart. You chose to come here."

"You're right. I did. And I'm appreciative. But I'm also confused. Why won't you tell me what you want in return?"

A grin breaks out. This version of Willow is much better. The strong-willed version who will go toe to toe is much more to my liking. I'm about to tell her to get back to her art when a vision of lover boy strikes. "What's with that kid?"

"Kid?" she asks with enough petulance I half-expect her to stomp her boot. "You know, I'm in my twenties. So is he."

"Barely," I counter.

She's too fucking young, which is one more reason this farce is a bad idea.

"Just say what you want. You don't want me to date? Wasn't planning on it. Although…have you been celibate these past two weeks? Because what's sauce for the goose is sauce for the gander. Isn't that the saying?"

I rub my jaw, hiding my smirk. "What's good," I correct.

"Excuse me?"

"The saying. It's what's good for the goose is good for the gander." I scrub my fingers through my scalp. What we've got going on is an ill-conceived arrangement, and this conversation is pointless because I will not promise my fidelity. It sets expectations. But then I think about that kid. Jesus. "If you care for your little friend, watch yourself with him."

"What's that supposed to mean?"

I'm talking like a thug, but what the fuck? It's the role I'm playing, and it's a language she should comprehend. "It's exactly what you think it means."

She huffs and stomps off to the stairs, her pale hands balled into tight little fists at her sides. Her boots thump against the concrete.

"You should really take your shoes off inside," I call after her.

Am I taunting her? Yes, I am. There needs to be some benefit to this fucked up role-playing.

She doesn't slow down but raises an arm and lifts her middle finger. I bark out a laugh. This reminds me of fighting with Sloane.

"I'll have dinner for us. Be home by six," I call to her retreating back.

"Yes, dear."

She never looks back as she descends the stairs, and I just grin. Yeah, it's stupid, and I'm out of my mind taunting a Gen Zer that I will never, ever touch, no matter how tempting she is, but it's fun. She's fun.

CHAPTER 15

WILLOW

"Honey, I'm home."

My voice echoes through the stairwell, and I hope it drips with sarcasm.

I spent a few hours splattering paint against blank canvases, blaring music as loud as I dared, but after a while the indie songs in my playlist calmed me enough that I lowered the volume and called Scarlet.

She listened to me rant and interrupted me with an exasperated, "What does this all mean? You aren't in a relationship. He's been away for weeks. Why is he jealous?"

Scarlet asks good questions.

"Has he hit you?"

This is Scarlet's worst fear, and in our world, it's reasonable. Not to mention, her personal experience contributes to her worry.

"No," I assured her.

"Did he ever tell you who he was with these past two weeks?"

"I never asked."

Was I supposed to? Our conversation skirted it, but did it matter?

"Are you falling for him?"

"What?" I'd sputtered. "How? I've seen him collectively for less than twenty-four hours."

"You're idyllic. You grew up dreaming of love."

"I gave up on that ages ago."

"Did you? Didn't you believe you would be allowed to marry for love?"

She didn't spend time with me when I was in Florence. She didn't get to know the independent Willow. The one who dared to have a serious boyfriend by opening her heart to someone she could never have. I didn't share that part of myself with her because it would worry her, and just like now, she would've doubted me and worried I'd make the wrong decision. But I didn't. I ended things before it got dangerous.

"Scarlet, you don't need to worry." That's what I'd told her.

"If you're telling me the truth, he's respectful and decent." Finally, she heard me. "And if you are sharing the truth, it's not what you're used to. He's handsome. You're going to fall for him."

"You say it like that's a bad thing. If I'm in this arrangement already, why exactly would that be bad? Isn't it better to like the person I'm supposed to spend time with?"

I'd argued with Scarlet in my mind, disagreeing with her because he's not just handsome, he's gorgeous. I want to draw him. Maybe even paint him.

"You'll fall, but he's not going to," she'd said. "He's already told you this is temporary. He's doing this as a favor, biding his time. You can't lose sight of reality. Trust me on this. Because if you do, reality might break you."

Her answer stayed with me into the condominium lobby.

Reality might break you.

Her words stay with me until I step into the living area and find lit candles on a table and Leo's sleeves rolled three-quarters up his arms, with socked feet peering out beneath his worn Levi's, standing over the grill.

My heart pitter-patters and my knees wobble. And suddenly, I'm not thinking, I'm feeling. It's not love, but it is an undeniable attraction. It's lust. Undeniable lust.

I entered this flat ready to throw down snark, but apparently rolled-up sleeves in a kitchen softens me into the consistency of warm gelato.

"You lit candles." Paint-splattered and flustered, I say the first thing that comes to mind and immediately regret it.

"Don't read into it." With tongs, he flips a piece of meat and the pan sizzles. "Saw you put out candles. So I lit them. Saw the flowers too. And the cutting boards. Nice touches. Sit. I've got this."

Uncertainty washes over me. Is this him apologizing for being an arse? Or does he like to cook? *Don't read into it*. That's what he said.

With his back to me, I place my fingers over my mouth and breathe out. My breath is stale. "I'm going to go take off my smock."

"Sure thing. Get comfortable. Maybe take off those heavy boots."

I glance down at my Doc Martins. Mamma hates these

boots, and for that reason, I own six pairs of them in different styles and colors.

After sitting on the edge of the bed, unlacing the boots, and letting them fall to the floor, I step into my bathroom and take stock. Frizzy flyaways surround my scalp. A streak of dark paint crosses my cheek, and my hands are stained blue from the paint I washed off back in the studio. The faint smell of paint thinner wafts off my skin.

Don't read into it.

We have an arrangement. Chances are he's spent the past two weeks with someone else, or many someone elses. He's in the syndicate, and while I know little about the syndicate, I've gathered the Lupi Grigi respect them. Which means he's probably not a good man.

Scarlet told me Vincent had been attentive and loving until he wasn't.

I pull back my hair, taking care to capture the flyaways, splash water on my face, dry it, and add a little blush and mascara.

It's our first dinner, just the two of us. I should listen to his words. Don't read into it and don't expect too much. What I need is to better understand what he wants from this arrangement. It's like the business professor at university said, I need to understand what he wants. And Scarlet's wrong. I won't fall for him. I'll simply do my best to ensure I remain in good standing so I can pursue my art career. If the marriage lasts long enough, I'll be like Scarlet, and no one will force me to remarry.

I swap out my tank top for a fresh one, exchange the heavy cardigan for a lightweight one, spritz perfume, brush my teeth, and examine my reflection.

I'm twenty-two. I'm too young to give up on life. For many

my age, I'm too young to hope for forever. I'm the exact right age to live for the moment.

There's nothing to be nervous about. This isn't a date. Best to go see what's what.

When I return to the room, he's sitting at the long kitchen table that seats twelve in the chair closest to the living room. Two place settings are set at one end of the table, opposite each other. Neither of us is placed at the head of the table. An optimist would take that as a good sign.

I swipe my palms on my skirt and sit. He has a steak on his plate and a baked potato split open with cubes of butter melting inside. On my plate, there's a baked potato, and there are dishes of vegetables, sour cream, and shredded cheeses.

"Since you don't like meat," his shoulders lift, "I had Chef create several options for you to add to your potato. Tomorrow night, you can tell the chef to create your favorite dinner, but tonight, I was in the mood for steak."

He lifts his fork and a knife and pauses, suspending the utensils mid-air. "Is that okay for you? If you want something else…" He glances over his shoulder toward the refrigerator.

"No, this is great," I tell him. "Thank you for taking care of dinner. I can handle it tomorrow night."

"You can put that in your potato." He points with this fork. "If you like. This is supposed to be like a baked potato bar."

I spoon sauteed mushrooms onto my plate, then lift a bowl of sauteed spinach.

"It's a jacket potato," I say. "I typically would add arugula, tomatoes, and burrata, but I'm sure these toppings will be delicious."

He sets his fork down, picks up a bowl of sour cream, and spoons a dollop into his baked potato.

He poured two glasses of red wine for dinner, and I lift one and offer a "*Salut*."

He's chewing but sets his fork down, swallows, and lifts his glass. Our glasses clink, and his gaze softens. I swirl the wine and breathe in notes of blackberries and plums, with a hint of cinnamon and nutmeg. It's a full-bodied vintage, and I hope it will calm my nerves. Outside the windows, the sun is setting, casting hues of gold across the skyline. Soon, the horizon will flicker with a million twinkling lights.

He's halfway done with his steak, and I have yet to slice the potato.

"You had a good business trip?" It's a conversational question. I hope it sounds normal.

In the candlelight, his brown irises merge with his pupils, forming unreadable black orbs.

"You going to eat?" The end of his steak knife points at my potato.

"Yes." I set the glass down. "I'm not particularly hungry." It's the truth, especially since we're eating so early and he's being dismissive. "Can we talk about your expectations? If you don't want to talk about your business, I understand. My father didn't talk about business with my mother." I spoon butter and sour cream into the potato. "Although, if I had an interest in the shipping business, I would've pushed him." I risk a glance up and find him intently watching me. "I am a woman, but I am capable. I disagree with…" I set my fork down and regroup. I don't want to argue. "It's time for tradition to evolve."

"I hear you." He lifts his glass as if he's toasting me. "Blows my mind pockets of the world still do arranged marriages."

"Right?" In some cultures, the family is adept at finding prosperous love matches. But in some, like mine, the marriages are about prestige and business. Women are assets to be leveraged. I never believed my father would see me as an asset he needed to exploit. He's wealthy and powerful in his own right. Yet, if I hadn't taken matters into my hands, I'd be betrothed to Leandro De Luca. An uncontrollable shudder rips through me. "Thank you, by the way." He sets his knife across his plate and leans back in the chair. "For helping me avoid what would have been…" I shake my head, at a loss for words. He saved me from Scarlet's path. I would have either killed Leandro, or he would've killed me.

Leo's expression is unreadable, but his persistent gaze quickens the pulsing through my extremities, my brain, my lungs, my heart.

"There has to be something I can do for you," I say.

His lips purse, his jaw flexes, and his gaze lowers. "There are some things I need." He's stretched out in the chair, pushed back slightly from the table. One hand rests on his thigh, and one forearm rests on the table's edge. His index finger taps the napkin. "One, I need for you to be smart. As a mafia princess, you're used to security. You might feel safe in London, but you still need security. Don't blow off John like you did today."

I haven't blown off John, and I'm not a mafia princess. I open my mouth to argue, but his cold stare closes it. I focus on the base of the wineglass, fingering the smooth glass, and concede. "Didn't I agree with that earlier?"

"Two, I have a reputation to uphold. You should wear your wedding rings. If you don't like the engagement ring, we can get you another one. Or really, you don't have to wear one. But you should wear the band. People need to know you're married, and my wife would not cheat on me. Do you understand what I'm saying?" His eyebrows nearly join above his nose and his brow furrows. "This is an arrangement, a temporary one, but we need to play the assigned roles."

Assigned roles. Those two words bandy about in my head.

"Will that be a problem?"

"No." I suppose this conversation settles whether he was jealous. It's a matter of reputation. The men in the mafia world are the same. "And you? I suppose for you, playing the assigned role means you'll sleep with whoever you want?"

His molten gaze centers on me once more. "Do you remember how your brother told you he didn't see me with women at the parties?"

His behavior struck my brother as so odd he'd assumed he was gay.

"That's the reputation I have. If I sleep with someone, no one will know. I am a private person, and my affairs remain private."

"But you plan on having them?" He's doing me a favor, but the inequitable plan doesn't sit well with me. "Affairs?"

"I define affair as a business of any kind, commercial or professional. I didn't mean to imply..." He rubs his forehead. "You understand you're too young for me, right?"

"Why? I'm twenty-two. Most women are married by the time they're my age."

"In Italy, you mean? In your family?" I nod, and he scoffs. "I'm almost twenty years older than you. You're too young for me."

I open my mouth to protest. Leandro is older than him by decades.

"You're too young to know what you're saying. Or what you want."

He balls up his napkin and drops it on his plate like the matter is settled.

"I'm young, but I'm not naive. And I'm not a mafia princess." The look on his face says he clearly disagrees. I'm in the mafia, but I'm not the capo's daughter, but it's splitting hairs and a pointless argument.

"How long do you see us playing this role?" I push back the chair and cross my arms. "How long do I have to get my feet under me, so when the dissolution of our marriage occurs, I won't have to return to Italy?"

"You won't need to worry about finances."

"I'm the daughter of a shipping titan. I'm well aware I don't need to be concerned with finances. How long do I have before the end of our arrangement?" He keeps talking about it and throwing it in my face. He must have a timeline in mind.

"I don't know." His answer comes across as distinctly honest. "I hear you have an agent interested in your work?"

"Yes. The shipment with some of my older work should arrive in a day or two, and he's going to come by next week to see it."

"Who is shipping it?"

"Scarlet handled it for me."

"You trust her?"

"Yes. Completely."

"Be careful who you give your address to. I don't share my address broadly. Do you understand?"

"I gave Scarlet the studio address."

"That's a trail anyone could follow."

I feel scolded, and annoyance seeps through my skin. "Understood. Are those all the rules?"

"Yes." I expect him to push up from the table, but he lifts the wine bottle and refills his glass. "Would you like more?"

"No, thank you." I've lost what little appetite I had. I should be ecstatic, yet I'm not. "Security, rings, and all my orgasms come from my fingers or a battery-operated device. Got it."

He does not look amused. I don't really care. I'm annoyed. I'm probably also acting like a brat. Getting worked up is nonsensical.

This arrangement couldn't be more ideal, yet I'm let down. I shouldn't be. I have no right to be. He did this as a favor. We're temporary, and that's what I should remember. This is not my life forever.

CHAPTER 16

SAM, AKA LEO, AKA SAINT

Willow's clearly upset, but damned if I know why or what to do about it. She clears the table and cleans the kitchen as if she's a reprimanded kid. Only, for all my talk about her being too young, she's nothing like a child. As if I could forget her tempting figure wrapped in lace on our so-called wedding night. She's all woman.

I have half a mind to tell her to leave everything, that the staff will clean it. But, if I do that, she'll leave and either go to her room or to the studio, leaving me alone.

As she cleans, like a horny jerk, I watch her backside closely, perusing her curves, remembering those sexy-as-fuck globes in a thong. By the time she folds the cloth and hangs it below the cabinet, I'm uncomfortably hard.

"Goodnight."

Her blonde waves swish with her pissed off steps as she departs for her bedroom.

I could've asked her to stay and talk, but what are we going to talk about? I can't talk to her about my business. I know jack shit about art. What I know of her family, I can't stand. I can't breathe a word to her about mine. And around her my body falls completely out of line.

Beyond the glass walls, London twinkles with a deceptive purity and promise. A closer examination, if one hits street level, reveals the grit, the homeless, and the grind. But up here in the tower, from a distance, the night shines beautifully. Sure, the stars are few and far between, but who needs stars with a luminous horizon?

On the way to my bedroom, I pause at Willow's open bedroom door. She's closed the drapes, and she sits on the edge of her bed. There's not much to do in here. There's no television. It's her forlorn expression that tears at me. It's like stumbling on a grenade on base. Unexpected, but in this case, it shouldn't be. This is a safe space, but it's not a home—for either of us, it seems.

"What's wrong?"

She startles, as if she hadn't heard me approach. Maybe she didn't. After all, she hasn't been through awareness training.

"Nothing," she answers.

I half chuckle. Yeah, that's bullshit. I've got sisters to thank for being able to grasp that much.

I step into her room and pick up a framed photograph of Willow and Scarlet taken on a yacht with the Amalfi Coast as the backdrop. She's younger in the photo, and her blue eyes sparkle.

"Do you find me attractive?"

I could not have heard that question correctly. I breathe deeply, set the photo down, and turn to face her. "What?"

"I find you attractive. I'm just curious—"

"Willow." I shove my hands in my pockets. "Where is this coming from?"

"Our arrangement is temporary, but it could last for months, even years, right?"

If I'm still in this role years from now, I'll lose my mind. I might've already lost it.

"Right?" She wants an answer.

Tread carefully.

"Impossible to say." I rock back on my heels, assessing her. She is a truly beautiful young woman. A delicate bone structure, high cheekbones, full, rosy lips, and bright blue trusting eyes, crowned with wavy golden strands and raven roots.

She's an artist who simply wants to pursue her art and sidestep the destiny crafted by her heritage. The CIA didn't tell me to help her. Doing so didn't move me up any ladder or prove my skills to anyone. It doesn't help my country or my family. Helping this young woman might be the one selfless thing I've done.

"Regardless of our age difference, we are married." Her cheeks flush with what I take to be embarrassment. Thin straps cross her shoulders, holding up the flimsy cotton top that hugs her breasts and does nothing to conceal the shadowy silhouette of her nipples.

Proving I'm not a saint, my body reacts, my cock stiffening with desire like it always does when I take her in for too long. But she's too young, and regardless of what she might think, we're not married. Not legally. I didn't use my real name, and soon enough, she'll be a widow to the identity I used in the ceremony.

Entering her bedroom was a mistake. I step past her. It's early, but I'll go to bed. Or take a shower. Her big blue eyes shine with hope and maybe…lust?

"I'd have to be blind not to be attracted to you. You're gorgeous. I want you, but that doesn't make it right. Desire is not justification." *Nothing good can come from this.* That's what I want to say. Her expression is unreadable. Sloane, my middle sister, would rail at me right about now. Sage, my youngest sister, would never question me. And why am I thinking about my sisters? Willow's younger than both of them and nothing like them. I need to put distance between us.

"Night, Willow."

Back in my bedroom, I breathe with purpose to calm the fuck down. My dick throbs. And she's a fucking kid. I'm a monster. That's what this job has turned me into. I was supposed to stop the monsters, and yet I added to their numbers.

With careful steps, I enter the bathroom and flick on the shower. Steam billows, clouding the ceiling. I remove my shirt and let my jeans and briefs fall to the floor. I grip my erection and stroke up once, then twice.

I tighten my grip, close my eyes, and envision her. That white lace corset pushing her breasts into perfect pillows, the pale pink points of her nipples pushing against the fabric. The smooth lines of her ass that my fingers ache to touch. That slip of lace I'd give anything to slide to the side, to explore her folds with my finger, my mouth, my dick.

Jesus, I am one sick fuck. I remove my socks and step into the stream of water. I close my eyes and submit. Hot water flows from my crown, over my eyes, through my hair, over my body.

The vision that's taunted me for weeks surrounds me. Willow in lace. I've given myself permission, I've opened the box, and she's everywhere. My grip tightens up and down my shaft, teasing the tip. God, what I wouldn't give to drag my tip through her wet folds, to tease her clit. To lift her breasts out of that corset and suck her nipple, to tease her mercilessly. Why the hell did I have to see her like that? My palm flattens against the marble, and my speed increases. I'm going to rub myself raw fighting this urge.

If I had touched her that night, if I had removed those lace panties, or slipped them to the side, would she have been wet? Does she feel this lust, too? Is that what she meant by attractive?

The shower door creaks, and I spin, arms out, ready to fight blind. Blinking away water, my stance spreads, seeking balance.

"I…"

It's Willow, standing in the doorway of my shower. There's no lace. No. She's a vision. She's not wearing anything at all.

Dizziness strikes first, and my palm flattens once again against the marble. I swipe my eyes, blinking to confirm she's not a hallucination.

"What're…" I can't get the words out. A sharp intake of air doesn't clear a damn thing up.

"Men have needs. That's what I've always been told. And women have needs too. I would prefer that you come to me, instead of to other lovers. If you…"

Her gaze falls and I can only guess she's taking in my protruding erection.

"Willow. You should leave." My dick fucking weeps. I deserve sainthood. I force myself to turn back to the shower stream because, otherwise, I would stare at her perfect, svelte body with her pert breasts and wide, smooth hipbones and what I'd bet is a perfect fucking pussy, and my willpower would crumble. As it is, I have one more image to add to my spank bank.

One more temptation to deny myself.

My fingers itch to grip myself again, to jerk off a release, but I refrain, straining to hear the creak of the door. She'll leave. I told her to leave.

Warmth covers my backside. Her warm body, skin on skin, presses from my ass up my back. Fingers lightly mix with water, tracing my ribcage, sucking out all the oxygen. Black and white dots mar my vision.

I blink back water, watching as long, graceful fingers travel down my abdomen. The light flickers on a narrow gold band. She reaches the base of my shaft, and then those fingers gently wrap around me.

All that is holy.

"What're you doing?" I grit out as my hips involuntarily buck. Her grip tightens, and fuck if my knees don't threaten to snap.

"I'm going to prove to you I'm not too young."

She moves up and down with one hand, while her other flattens on my chest, holding me in place. Her soft breasts press against my back and her hips mold to my ass.

Jesus.

"Why?"

I have done nothing to bring this on. I've been good.

"Why not?" She strokes me, up and down. Her pressure is lighter than I like, lighter than I apply, but her touch still feels fucking amazing. The moment is more fever dream than real. "You've done me a favor. I want to return it."

"You don't owe me anything." Of course, as I say the words, I'm watching her fingers on my dick and the nails on her other hand scratch my nipple.

"Maybe this is for me. You said I can't have sex with other men. Is it so bad if I want sex? Or are women not supposed to enjoy sex?"

She did tell me she's not a virgin. Jesus, I'm so fucking lightheaded. Steam clouds the ceiling, and water rivulets cascade down the walls.

She's twenty-two. When I was twenty-two, I slept around. I spent my twenties dating sporadically. Going from bed to bed.

"I don't have a condom."

Her grip tightens, as do my balls.

"I have an IUD."

Fuck, I want her.

My mind blanks. Why am I resisting?

"That's what you want? Sex?" Her thumb circles the pooling pre-cum in a tempting, erotic rotation. I blink back the fog. "Meaningless sex? That's what you want?"

"Yes." The streaming water drowns out her answer, but I heard it, and the permission releases a dam.

I push off the wall, and she stumbles back. I fist her hair, angling her head. Her mouth opens slightly, and with hooded, tempting pools of blue, she gazes up at me. Her pale skin pinks from the hot water. I flick a thumb over her nipple and bend, allowing my fingers to roam her stomach, down to her glistening, pink folds masked by black, trimmed curls. I slip a finger inside, and my eyelids close in gratitude. She's hot, wet, and ready.

"God, I'm a sinner."

"We're all sinners." Twisted blonde strands veil her face as she shares her wisdom. Her gaze lifts from my finger and her pussy, the veil falls away, and those lust-filled baby blues are my ruin.

I crash my mouth over hers, brutally claiming her lips, her tongue. She tastes like heaven.

My dick presses into her belly, and my balls tighten. *Christ.*

I break away and take in her swollen, ruby lips as my chest heaves.

I spin her around and place her hands on the wall, palms flat, fingers spread.

"Keep them there."

She looks over her shoulder at me, hair soaked and darker with hot water, a smear of mascara tainting her angelic face.

"This is what you want?"

She nods. Maybe she speaks. The shower roars. Too loud to hear, to think.

"Spread your legs."

She does as I command. I drag my tip between her ass cheeks and bend my knees for a lower swipe.

"Flatten your back. Stick out your ass."

She does as commanded, and her movement shifts my tip to where I need to be. I grip her hips and surge forward. She's tight, wet, hot velvet.

"Oh, fuck, you feel good."

I slam into her, over and over. She feels better wrapped around my cock than I ever fucking imagined.

My balls tighten. Same with my lower back. I force myself to slow and reach around, searching for those dark curls, for her mound, for her clit. My fingers circle and pulse. The position is awkward, and I'm not as deep as I want to be, but her walls clench around me and she moans.

"That's it," I tell her. "How do you like it? Soft like this? Firm pressure? Or do you like it like a hammer?" I piston my fingers and she moans, pushing against me, her pussy tightening around me in a vice.

Guess she answered me. I still behind her, reveling as her body comes undone. Her knees give, and I pull out and lift her.

"Wrap your legs around me." Her eyelids flutter, and I lift her higher so her thighs hug my hips. She tilts her head back, and for some ungodly reason, my lips find hers again.

Bad decision.

It's too much. Too intimate.

I stumble until her back flattens against the wall of the shower.

I shouldn't.

The thought flees. I kiss her like a man possessed. Plundering her sweet mouth, savoring honey and mint and vice. Her nails scratch my back and the nape of my neck.

I break our kiss, needing oxygen, and needing more. "Hold on."

Her arms rise over my shoulders, and she presses down as her legs dig into my hips. With one hand on her ass, and one on my dick, I find her entrance and slide back into her heat.

"Jesus." It's all I can say in this heaven.

My muscles strain as I lift her and position her just right on the wall. Her tight channel grips me, so fucking right. Water cascades around us as I pound into her. She convulses around me, milking me for all I'm worth, and I explode, pulsing so hard inside her my legs weaken and I stumble to the ground.

We crash in a tangle of limbs on the floor of the shower. I

rest my back against the shower wall, settling her against me, and press a kiss to the top of her head. My hand wraps around her front, and I fondle her breast. I daydreamed about tasting these breasts, and I didn't even touch them.

She bends her neck, looking up at me, and I press my lips over hers. She smiles, and her fingers tenderly trace my jaw. "There. That wasn't so bad, was it?"

I laugh. A full-throttled laugh. I don't know where it's coming from. Possibly I've been way too sexually frustrated, or possibly it's the ludicrousness of the situation. Me, on the floor of the shower with my twenty-two-year-old fake bride.

I help her off the floor, turn off the shower, and reach for a towel to wrap around her.

"This shower has two showerheads," I muse. "We could've used both of them, I guess."

"We only needed one." The coy smile playing across her lips is one that says she won. She turns to leave, but I grab her waist, spin her around, pop her ass playfully, and smack my lips against hers.

"Go to bed," I tell her.

She clutches the towel and bows her head, but I catch the self-satisfied smile. She steps past the bed, as if she's leaving my bedroom, and in a flash, I'm in the doorway. "My bed."

It's wrong of me. So wrong. But she is the one who entered my shower. And now that we've done that once, we'll definitely be doing it again. If not tonight, in the morning.

If you're headed to hell, you might as well enjoy the ride.

CHAPTER 17

WILLOW

"My bed."

His deep, commanding growl ripples down my spine, eliciting euphoria. This arrangement of ours will deliver for both of us. All I needed to do was to force him to see me as a woman worthy of partnership.

"I'll be back," I say, daring a glance over my shoulder to observe his reaction.

There's no hint of anger or annoyance. No, he's turned on. It's clear in his hungry, heated gaze and the semi he's sporting.

When I return to his bedroom, teeth and hair brushed, in a nightgown, he's in bed resting against stacked pillows with the comforter draped across his waist. He's wearing glasses, and I'm taken aback by how handsome he is in the black frames. The glasses knock him into the Grecian God realm. His chest and abdomen are muscular and lean. His showered hair has rippled into unruly waves, and the black-framed glasses bring another dimension to his personality. Instead of the intimidating, mysterious man from the formidable syndicate, with those glasses, he rocks a hot professor vibe. Like this, he's approachable and impossibly sexier.

He looks up from his book, and I toy with my fingers, unsure what to do.

"You braided your hair."

I braid my hair every night when it's wet. It's what gives my otherwise straight hair definition.

He pats the mattress beside him. "Join me. And take off that nightgown."

It's a silk chemise, and I've always thought of it as sexy. Jules liked it, but he liked everything, including my T-shirts.

The primary suite is about four times larger than my bedroom, and the windows surround two walls. The dizzying heights of the forty-first-floor place London on full, sparkling display.

"Would you like me to shut the drapes?"

The side of the bed he wishes for me to approach is mere feet from the wall of windows.

"No one can see in, you know." He pushes a button on a remote, and a mechanical sound whirs as the drapes slowly wind closed. "You weren't exactly bashful in the shower," he continues.

I pad toward the far side of the bed. If a mutually beneficial arrangement is what I wish for, openness is required.

"I'm not a fan of heights." His book falls flat against his abdomen, just above a path of dark spirals leading lower. "I mean, I'm fine in most situations. Elevators. Stairs. But I get queasy if I'm too close to a window in a tall building." Or on a Ferris wheel. Rollercoasters are out.

"Did something happen?"

"What do you mean?" I come around to the far side of the bed, facing Leo, my back to the drapes.

"A fear of heights in someone your age often stems from experience."

The cliffs near our home come to mind. The constant warnings to beware. "No experience, simply a healthy awareness of danger."

"No falls?"

In my mind's eye, a familiar scene plays out. A man in dark clothes, screaming, terror-stricken, flailing while falling, and then his broken form in the sand below, limbs twisted in unnatural directions. It's a recurring dream. I don't believe it actually happened, but the more I learn about my family, I sometimes wonder.

I climb into bed, lift the hem of my chemise over my head, pull the sheet over my breasts, and drape the chemise carefully over the end of the comforter at the foot of the bed.

He closes the book, sets it on the bedside table, and places his glasses on top. Lying on the flat pillows, I'm lower than he is. He must have four pillows stacked behind his back.

He lifts one of my long braids and twists it between his thumb and index finger, drops it like it's bothersome, rests his head back on the bedframe, and closes his eyes.

I roll onto my side, studying him. This part of what a man and a woman do is new to me.

When Jules and I dated, we never spent the entire night together. That wouldn't have been possible without risking his life. The lenient security team let me live a normal life, but they would have drawn the line at sleeping over with a man. Virginity is valued above all else.

When I approached Leo in the shower, I didn't anticipate he would ask me to join him in bed afterward. I don't know what I expected. Perhaps I expected nothing because I didn't think it through. I acted on instinct and determination.

"Who was your first?"

His question is so unexpected, I doubt he actually said it. But when his eyelids flutter open, I'm met with serious, dark eyes.

"His name was Jules. What about you? Who was your first?"

His lips contort, lightening his intensity. "I'm asking the questions."

"You don't want to talk about your first?" Surely, he's not like the Italian men I grew up with, believing only the woman's first matters. But then again, I know nothing about him. Not really.

"It was a long time ago. What happened to Jules?"

"The relationship ran its course."

"I meant how did he die?"

"He's alive." He's alive because I ended things with him, but it wasn't an epic tragedy.

"You said 'was.'"

"When?"

"You said his name was Jules."

"Oh, no…I suppose I used the wrong tense. He's still alive and well in Paris. He's a sculptor. We met at university." My fingers trace the crisp, smooth sheets. "Why?"

"Did you love him?"

"Yes…I think." He shifts the pillows and lies down on his side, so we're facing one another on an equal plane.

He traces my cheek with his index finger, the touch soft, his expression thoughtful. "Why didn't you marry him?"

"That would've never been an option." He pulls his hand back and mirrors my position in the bed, hands near his face.

"Your father?"

"Jules was an artist, like me. He was my rebellion. It was selfish of me to be with him." I hate admitting that out loud.

"Why?"

"I believed my father would never force me into an arranged marriage, but losing my virginity was a precaution, just in case. As it turns out, it wasn't the power play I assumed." I focus my gaze on his chest and the rhythmic rise and fall. "I cared about Jules. And that's why I ended things with him. My father never found out about him, but if he had…well, it would be risky." I sigh with the weight of the truth.

"It's confusing, isn't it? When we have different objectives?"

I'm not sure I understand.

"You wanted a life on your terms, but in the end, you cared about him and valued his life above yours. It must've been a confusing time for you."

I think back to those days that were up and down like a rollercoaster. At the peak, I thrilled to the freedom, and in the trough, terror haunted me. "If father found out, I would've been pulled out of university. He wasn't Italian, and he wasn't a member of the Lupi Grigi—or any family, for that matter—so no, there was no future." I was selfish, there's truly no other way to explain it. I'm lucky Jules escaped unscathed. Or at least, Scarlet says I am.

"I'm not Italian." I meet his thoughtful gaze. Is the syndicate's world different than ours?

"You're a part of the syndicate. My father respects the syndicate."

"I'm American."

"Yes, you are." I reach out and finger the curls on his chest. He grasps my wrist and presses his lips to my pulse point.

"Tell me about your first."

He lowers my wrist but doesn't let go. "Her name was Susannah."

"That's a pretty name."

"I didn't love her. It wasn't rebellion. I was horny." His expression is cocky, and I snort in amusement. "But I'm curious," he adds. "I thought mafia girls were supposed to be virgins. Weren't you risking a lot? Like, virginity is a big deal with mafia families, right? Hanging the sheets and—"

I break out laughing. "Not many families still do that. But yes, my father believed he provided you with a virgin." It's my turn to grow serious. "But you know, my father, he's a businessman. He knew this was an arrangement." That part still stings.

Leo strokes his thumb back and forth over the back of my wrist.

"It's true that many of the marriages in my family are more practical, solidifying connections and order. But I always thought that because my father is who he is, it wouldn't apply to me." How foolish. "I'm lucky you agreed to this."

"But you know, this is an arrangement." He says the words cautiously, like he's worried I might have different expectations now that I'm lying in his bed.

"True. But now that *this* is a part of our arrangement, there's no need for you to go to the brothels, right?" My cheeks grow annoyingly warm.

"Brothel?" He sounds…amused.

I lift my gaze to find him smirking. "What? You've spent the past two weeks—"

His fingers cover my mouth, and he shakes his head, smiling. "Brothel isn't a modern term. I'm more discreet and—"

I glare at him, and he snorts. "That's why you did this? Came to me in the shower? You're possessive?" He taps my nose with his finger. "Are you a jealous little minx?"

"So are you. You point blank told me I couldn't be with Geoff."

That wipes the smirk right off his face. "Were you planning to be with Geoff?"

"No, I'm simply making a point."

"How many men have you been with?"

"One." I smooth a finger over his cheek, surprised by the velvety smoothness. He shaved after the shower. "Now two. How many women have you been with?"

"I lost count." My throat constricts. "I'm a lot older than you."

"How old are you?"

He pauses, like he's trying to remember. "Forty-two."

He's said nearly twenty years older, but that's a full twenty years older.

"What was it like? Growing up in a mafia family?"

"Normal?"

His dark eyebrows come together as his eyes narrow, questioning my veracity.

"I didn't know." His eyebrows lift higher. "Really. We were sheltered. Titan Shipping is a legitimate business. When we visited my father at work, he had staff who greeted us with smiles, and his secretary had a jar of candy on her desk. We'd go out on the docks to watch the enormous ships sometimes. We knew we were lucky. Our home was larger than many of our friends' homes, and we had more land on the coast than many. But it wasn't..." I let out a sigh, thinking about the time I first realized the Lupi Grigi might not be the protective heroes I believed them to be. "It wasn't until I was sixteen that I had any idea that...well, our family participated in..."

"Drug trafficking?" he supplies.

"I wasn't sure what they did, exactly, but when Scarlet was first attacked, I told her she should go to the *polizia*, and she said that they owned them. I asked her what she meant, and she told me not to be so naive. I felt...foolish. That was when I started listening more, observing more. Orlando is seven years younger than me, and he seemed more aware."

"I always expected they would tell you at a young age."

"No." I shake my head. "I went to a small school in my first years, filled with other kids, and none of us talked about it. Then father brought in tutors. The school I would have gone to was nearly an hour away, and he didn't want us to spend so much time traveling. That's what they said. By the time I went to university, I knew. When Scarlet killed Vincent...I pieced more together. And I knew I didn't want to be a part of that. I had believed father wouldn't make me. He told me I didn't have to worry."

"And you thought that meant he wouldn't expect you to marry?"

"I assumed too much," I admit.

I lived a storybook life until the fairytale darkened.

"It's natural for children to believe their parents are heroes. We always want to see the best in our family."

"What about you? What are your parents like?"

His lips turn up on the corners, and there's warmth in his

expression. "They were great. They were heroes. True-to-life heroes. My mom and my dad."

"Were?"

"Yeah." He swallows as if he's reining in emotion. "They passed away a long time ago."

"I'm so sorry."

"It was a long time ago."

"What happened? Did they die together?"

"I'd rather not talk about it, if you don't mind."

I study him, wondering if they really died long ago. "Were you raised in the syndicate?"

He grins. "What do you think the syndicate is? You married into it, but you haven't asked any questions."

"I just…" Once again, I've been foolish. And complicit, behaving like father would have wanted and assuming the business wouldn't be discussed with a woman. "I assumed it was… is…a group like the Lupi Grigi."

"It's more of an alliance of powerful individuals with influence around the world. It's a collective, if you will."

"And you weren't born into it?"

"No." He grins. "I was hired into it. I negotiate deals. Get good prices."

"You're the arms dealer."

"That's right. So you do know what I do."

"I heard, but…"

"Do you have an issue with criminal organizations?"

"What do you mean?"

"Morally. Did you have a problem with your family when you discovered what they do?"

"They're not all bad," I say, but I can't meet his gaze when I say it. "They help keep peace and order. And the drugs and whatever else…" I risk a glance up. "I'm really not sure what else they do. But I hated how they treated Scarlet. How they treat women. Like we're a commodity. I can't stand that. I don't want to go back to that."

"You won't have to." He says it with conviction. "But I find it interesting you jumped to another situation without knowing much at all about it."

I exhale, considering my hasty actions.

"It's okay," he says in a low, soothing tone. "It's an observation. We all have moments in life when we leap before looking. It's something we especially do when we're young."

"You jumped without looking?"

"I took a job within the syndicate." He rubs a hand through his hair, smiling.

"Do you regret it?"

His expression becomes unreadable. I squirm, uncomfortable in the silence and in his change. He ruffs up his hair with one hand, scratching as if he's got the worst itch, and then he morphs back into the easygoing guy. "No regrets," he says with an odd smile. "It's best to look ahead and prepare."

"And that's what you do?"

His lower lip protrudes and his shoulder lifts in gentle, modest agreement.

"I'll try that. If I'm looking forward and preparing, I need to do so with eyes wide open. I hate feeling like I've been naive or…foolish." I bite out the distasteful word.

He brushes his thumb over my cheek thoughtfully.

"You know," his hand snakes beneath the covers, landing on my hip, and he tugs, shifting me closer, "it occurs to me we're doing a lot of things backward."

"What do you mean?" Since I'm closer, I let my hand flatten against his chest. His heartbeat pulses beneath my palm.

"Getting to know each other after we've...entered an arrangement. After we've..."

"Made love," I supply.

His eyes narrow. "Had sex. Willow, this is still temporary. It will end. One day."

I blink in acknowledgment. "But we don't know when. It can't be too soon or—"

"It won't be too soon. I promise you; I won't leave until it's been long enough that your independence is assured."

"I appreciate that."

"Is that why you approached me, Willow? Did you think if you didn't give me this, that I would..." He doesn't complete the sentence, and his distressed expression tells me everything.

"I wanted this," I assure him. "I always thought you were handsome. Is it so wrong if a woman wants sex?"

"No." He pulls back the comforter, exposing me to below my hips. His fingers trace along my clavicle, down my chest, to the valley between my breasts. He cups one breast gently, as if weighing it.

He is my husband, but I sense it's best not to remind him of that. What I can do is play to his requirements. "As long as it's only with you?"

His gaze lifts from my breast. His eyes lock on mine, and my heart pitter-patters out of synch. "As long as we're in this arrangement, only with me."

He lowers his head and takes a nipple into his mouth. Wet heat and suction elicit a moan, and I swear I feel his mouth deep inside me. My back curls forward. He releases the nipple and seeks the other one. My fingers toy with his hair, and his hand slides between my legs. I spread my thighs, opening for him.

His finger dips inside and a deep growl vibrates from his mouth, still latched onto my nipple. He pushes up and hovers over me.

"Flat on your back, princess." I roll onto my back, compliant. "Since we're in agreement," a smile plays across his lips, "let's do this the right way this time."

His warm body covers mine, and I hold him, caressing his back as he lowers his mouth and claims my lips. This time when we kiss, it's slow and languid. Playful and exploratory. My inner thighs brush against his outer thighs, over his coarse hair, as my fingers roam his spine and shoulders, kneading the flexed muscles.

"You have the most beautiful eyes. I'm not the first to tell you that, am I?"

His lips fall to my neck, and I stretch, giving him all the access he desires. He nibbles and sucks until he arrives at my breasts.

"I'm going to show you things I know that college boy didn't."

He continues pressing kisses down my stomach until he hovers over me, down there. He spreads my legs wide, and I close my eyes, fingers teasing his thick hair, lost to his touch and his skill.

He studies my body with a devotion I've never felt before. He's an astute student, studying my every reaction, learning my loves. Or perhaps worship is a better word choice than learn. My last thought as I fall asleep nestled against him is a reprimand.

Don't be naive. This isn't forever.

CHAPTER 18

SAM, AKA LEO, AKA SAINT

The ring slicing the air in the dead of night awakens me with the force of an electrical charge. The warm body at my side rolls into me, tugging a pillow over her head. She'd only do that if she felt secure, and yeah, she's right to feel secure, because she is.

Another shrill ring has me exhaling annoyance.

There's only one person who would call me on the mobile by my bed, and it won't be good news. I do my best to pull away without disturbing her and snatch the phone.

"Nick," I answer, striding to the hallway. I lift the robe hanging on the back of my door with one backward glance at the slumbering woman. *I'm going to hell.*

"Why do you sound awake?"

"You called. Do I need to fix coffee? What's up?"

Darkness blankets the city, and I scan the horizon to get my bearings. What time is it? The answer resides on the corner of my phone screen.

"I have a problem." He's calling at nearly four a.m. Obviously, something's gone to shit. A light flicks on beneath the bedroom doorway, and I step into the office and close the door. "It's personal."

"What's up?"

"It's Lina." Ah, his sister. "I'm in Doha. I can't get there."

"Where is she?"

"London. I got a call…something's wrong." He swears under his breath. I can't make out the exact word choice, but I get the gist. "I think she's using again, and I don't want it getting out."

"Do you have an address?" An unidentifiable sound filters into the room. I open the office door and am met with a sleepy-eyed Willow leaning against the wall. She's in one of my white button-down Oxfords, and I force my gaze away from her long, lean legs.

Focus. I need to get dressed and out the door quickly.

"Her security is with her, right?"

Surely, he didn't let his sister out without security.

"She blew them off."

God dammit, Lina.

"How do you know where she is?" I head down the hall to my bedroom.

"I have a tracker on her. Security found her, but she's unconscious. He thinks someone roofied her."

"But you don't?" I set the mobile to speaker and set about getting dressed as quickly as possible. At least security is with her. Nick has too many potential enemies who might jump at the chance to gain leverage.

"I'd like to, but I don't know. The club she's at…she's not acting like someone bent on staying straight."

"And she threw security," I add as I pull back a drawer, review my handgun options, select the SIG, check the chamber, set it on the counter beside the mobile, and search for my holster that can be covered by the right jacket.

"Dante. I'm gonna fire the fuck. I swear she's paying him off to let her go party."

"Your sister is what? Twenty-eight? He's not her babysitter."

"He's whatever the fuck I say he is."

"Did you send me the address?"

"Yeah. She's at Fabric."

Ah, shit. I'll need sissy shoes.

"The bouncer will expect you. She's in a private room. Do you think you can get her out of there without being snapped?"

Lina loves to make the tabloids, but even she won't want to be photographed being carried unconscious out of a club.

"I'll handle it." I pull on my cowboy boots. That's probably what the bouncer will look for when expecting Leo.

"I'm flying back. Do you think you can keep her at your place until I'm there?"

"She'll probably want to head home." Keeping Lina against her will isn't a gig I want. She's a spoiled hellcat, and that's one hundred percent Nick's fault.

"I'll send a doctor ahead of me. If the tests are positive, I need you to keep her. Do whatever you need to do."

"I'll call you when I have her back here."

I sling open the closet door. Willow's wide blue eyes track me with a trace of fear. Fuck. She doesn't need to be scared.

"Leo?" Nick asks through the speaker.

I hold a finger to my lips, giving Willow the universal quiet sign.

"Yeah?"

"Thank you."

"No problem." And I mean it. He's a friend. That's the thing about going undercover that no one really talks about. If you're any good at what you do, you genuinely like the people you're spying on, and for someone like me, five years in, you develop real friendships.

I pull on a jacket and slip the mobile into a pocket.

"Sorry to wake you," I say to Willow.

"You're armed. Are you…" She sucks in her lower lip and those blue eyes lose focus. "Are you going to work?"

The mafia princess apparently learned a unique set of terminology growing up.

"Nothing like that. A friend's sister partied too hard. I'm going to get her. I'll bring her back here." In the hallway, my gaze falls on the opened door to the guest bedroom. Nick knows that what Willow and I have is an arrangement, but I don't trust Lina to keep her mouth shut. "Can you ready the guest room for her? We'll put her in there. Maybe, ah, clear out your stuff? Don't give her any reason to talk?"

I check the time, and my pulse kicks up a notch. Dante's probably the only security Lina has, which means he's a target until I get there.

Willow hesitates and her thumbnail slips between her sweet lips.

"You okay?"

She nods and drops her hand from her mouth. "I'll get everything ready. Call me if you need anything."

Her bottom lip glistens, as if she just licked it, and an urge to kiss her swells from nowhere. And for a brief second I consider she probably doesn't have anything under that shirt, and that's the thought that has me spinning on my boot's heel and charging out of there without a backward glance. Last night was fantastic, but…fuck, I don't know what the hell I'm doing.

At this time of the morning, there's no traffic on London streets, and I berate myself the entire drive. Five years I've been doing this, five years I've been good, and then she comes along. Of course, she came along in my shower. Still, I know better. I am better. And then, it's my mom's voice that whispers, "You're always too hard on yourself." But am I? My dad's voice pipes in with, "Your mom's too soft on you. On all of you." One thing I do know, if I'm hearing my parents' voices, I'm in over my head and acting out of line.

In no time at all, I screech to a halt in front of the club. The valet steps up.

"A hundred pounds if you drive this to the back entrance. I'll be out in under five."

"Yes, sir."

I scan the sidewalk but don't see any lurking paps. Doesn't mean they aren't here.

The club door opens, and a tall Black man with a head full of braids dressed like a K-pop band member waves me in. "This way."

"How bad is she?"

"Bad enough. You need to get her outta here." He leads me up a narrow staircase and around a winding hall. "You gotta tell her we can't have this. We'll block her ass. Overdose shit's bad for business."

Bass pumps through the floor. The ceiling height up here requires both of us to crouch. He opens a black wooden door into a small room that reminds me of the servants' quarters in *Downton Abbey*, a show my youngest sister loved and forced me to watch. There's a narrow bed and a wooden chair with an exhausted Dante bent over his legs, phone in his hand, texting someone.

Lina's sprawled across the mattress in a skin-tight black leather dress that has risen over her ass. She chose to avoid panty lines tonight, and she waxes, something I never needed to know. Her skin is pale, but her lips and cheeks are flushed. If her lips had been blue, it'd be a different scenario. I lift her wrists, check her arms. No needle marks. She's wearing skimpy shoes that show her toes.

"What's her drug of choice?" I ask Dante.

"Magic flying dust. Passed out isn't Lina's jam. At least, not in the last couple of years. I'm telling you; someone drugged her drink."

"We have bartenders and security who watch that shit," the bouncer says from the door.

"Well, check your tapes. Because I'm doing a blood test, and if she was drugged here, you'll be hearing from us." I shift Lina, trying to decide the best way of hauling her ass. She's too fucking tall.

"I'll help you," Dante says.

"What? You take her feet and I take her head?" It would be like moving a sofa through that narrow staircase. "Here. Help me get that dress down." I glance at Dante, wondering why the hell he left her dress like that. Nick definitely needs to can his ass.

"Doesn't go down much more than that," Dante grumbles.

Her knees are bright red, like she went down hard on them.

"Did she pass out suddenly?"

"She was loopy. Fell multiple times trying to dance. I'm telling you, man. She was roofied."

"Help me get her on my shoulder. Fireman's hold."

He helps, and it's a challenge, but I've hauled a lot heavier over much longer distances than what faces me.

"You stay behind. Get his name. Watch the tapes." Dante nods while twirling a ring on his finger. Black ink covers most of his neck, and I'd bet if his suit jacket didn't cover his chest and arms, he'd be one giant sleeve. He's intimidating, which is why Nick hired him, and it'll earn his keep tonight. "Get as much information as you can." I wait until the fuck lifts his gaze. "We need to know who and why."

"That's pretty fucking obvious," he argues. "Someone wanted to fuck her."

Maybe. "If you want to live to see the weekend, you'll get the name. Hear me?"

The bouncer widens his eyes at that, but I don't give a fuck. Nick doesn't exactly aim for the squeaky-clean image.

Dante shoves a handbag in my hand and grunts. He's either telling me it's Lina's or he's telling me to sod off. I did my part by warning the wanker. If he wants the ability to wank again, he'll listen.

The valet's eyes widen when the back door opens, but the guy's sharp, and he jumps out and lowers the front passenger seat so I can lay Lina down. I buckle her in so the lap belt will keep her in place, pay the valet, and head out.

When I turn out of the alley, a car moves out of the line of parked cars. Headlights prevent me from seeing inside or identifying the compact car's make and model.

I flick on the signal, turning right. The car follows. There aren't many vehicles out at this early hour. When I turn left and the car does too, I'm more annoyed than anything. Who the fuck would mess with Nick?

I can't see inside the trailing car, and with Lina with me, I won't take unnecessary risks.

At the next intersection, I approach slowly, ready to stop at the yellow. The light turns red, I look both ways, and blast through the intersection. Trouble is, there's not a lot of traffic, and the tail blasts through it too.

It's a chase. On the off chance someone is tracking her phone or something in her handbag, I roll down the window and sling her handbag out. I lose the tail in a New York minute, but to be safe, I drive out of the city for a good forty-five minutes before winding my way back in a circular direction to home.

The sun skims the Thames by the time I pull into my underground parking garage. Lina's out cold, but she's twitched here and there.

When I park the car and come around to her side, she rubs her face and opens one eye.

"Where am I?"

"You're safe."

"Leo?"

"You think you can walk if I help you?"

"Whyyy hmm your car?" She pushes up off the seat with a dazed expression.

"Come on. Let's get you up to the guest room so you can sleep this off."

She rubs her face and smacks her lips. I wait, one hand on the door, as she wakes and gets her bearings.

"I only had three drinks."

Nick called at almost four. Three doesn't sound too realistic for hours in a club, but if Dante values his life, he's pieced together what really happened.

She wobbles on her heels, but with one arm draped over my shoulder, we make it into my apartment without incident.

At the top of the stairs, Willow meets us, her blonde waves flowing around her shoulders in an angelic veil and questioning blue eyes taking us in. Lina's head is against my shoulder, one arm wrapped around my waist, and those blue eyes travel down.

Shit. Lina's barely dressed. This can't look good.

CHAPTER 19

WILLOW

"Do you need help?" My words are gravel against my throat, but he's safe, which is the most important thing. Horrible fears terrorized my brain for hours, thanks to stories from Scarlet and Orlando. Flashes of funerals and tear-soaked faces plagued me.

The woman Leo holds against him wears a skimpy dress that reveals every inch of her waif, model-like form; the fabric so tight there's no room for imagination to play. She's gorgeous, but she's a hot mess. Mascara coats the skin below her eyes. Red lipstick stains the skin outside her lip line, although there's little trace of it on her pale lips, and the whites of her eyes are bloodshot. She's been through hell.

"The coffee's hot. I put the kettle on when the elevator dinged. It should be ready in a minute if you'd prefer tea. I have biscuits, fresh bread. That should ease her stomach, absorb some alcohol."

The woman draped against Leo lifts her head and her eyelashes flutter.

"Hello. I'm Willow. What can I get you? Are you thirsty? Hungry?" The stale smell of cigarette smoke, beer, and sweat wafts off the two of them.

"Is this the wifey?" the woman asks. "You really got married? And she's what?" She pushes off his chest and wobbles on her stilettos. I hold out an arm, lest she come crashing forward, and Leo grips her elbow. "Are you even eighteen? Did you go and break the law, Leo?"

Her words are slow and slightly off. I haven't spent a lot of time around partiers, but I've been to parties and seen those who imbibe. She seems like she's still drunk or high. My experience is too limited to know which.

"I found your first aid kit. And the pain pills." I glance back at the table where I have a mini-medical clinic prepared. "Do you want some water?"

She stumbles forward and pushes her index finger into my chest. "How old are you?"

"Twenty-two."

"Ohhhh," she drawls. "So legal." She sways, and Leo swoops her up. Her head dangles over his arm.

"Is the bedroom ready?"

"Yes." I push forward, speeding ahead of him to pull back the comforter.

He slows in the doorway, careful to enter so he doesn't bang her head.

"Will you get Lina undressed?"

"Kinky," she says with a grin.

"Her shoes, at least." He pushes past me. "Lina, you need to go to sleep."

"Should we be worried…" Leo pauses in the doorway to listen to me. He looks both exhausted and annoyed. "About vomit?"

"She hasn't so far. She'll be fine."

He leaves us, and I fiddle with the strap on her heels, removing them. The edges of her toes are tinged with a black, oily stain, as are the tips of her shoes. The smell on my fingers after removing her shoes is nasty.

Her eyelids close and she curls onto her side. I tuck the comforter around her. The drapes are drawn already, as I don't like the proximity to the windows in this room. I flip the light switch on the way out and pull the door closed.

Leo sits at a bar stool, a coffee mug in front of him. The kettle whistles, and I rush to remove it from the flame lest the shrill cry disturb Lina.

"I'll bring her a glass of water. She'll want it when she wakes." I pause, scanning him for injury. "You're not hurt?"

"No." He shrugs out of his jacket, and my gaze falls to the gun holstered at his waist. I focus on pouring the glass of water. This shouldn't surprise me. My father is a businessman. He's not an enforcer. But I've heard the stories. And Leo is a part of the syndicate. He may call them an alliance, but they must be fierce if they have mafia and cartels under their domain.

In the bedroom, I find Lina passed out cold. I set the glass on the bedside table and softly retrace my steps to the kitchen.

"Can I fix you breakfast?"

Leo shakes his head and pushes the coffee away. He raps the counter with his knuckles. "Thanks for doing all this."

"No problem. I didn't know what to expect. I called Scarlet

and asked. If you came back with severe injuries, she has a contact in London I could've called, but I figured you'd have your own doctor."

"That's what the bandages, scissors, and towels are for?"

"I followed Scarlet's instructions. I didn't know…you were gone for so long, and you took your gun."

"You said you're twenty-two. Did I miss your birthday?"

"It was over a week ago." I move to the sink to wash my hands of the stench from Lina's shoes.

"I was gone." He's speaking to himself, but I hear him.

"It's fine. No worries." This is an arrangement, after all.

"I stayed away to avoid temptation." He snorts. "Lot of good that did me."

I dry my hands and inhale deeply. That deep tone, he sounds like he's full of regret, even though he said he has none. Does he regret helping me? Me being here? Sex?

"Come on," he says, extending a hand. "Let's get some shuteye."

I take his offered hand, and we walk side by side through the living area. The sun peers above the skyscrapers and Big Ben, and there's a haze of blue between the buildings.

He stops by the banister that overlooks the stairs and the foyer below. He releases my hand and pushes a button. There's a low grinding of gears, a whirring mechanical sound, and the stairs fold, then the entire structure flattens against the wall, leaving us with an opening two stories below to the polished concrete floor.

"Can't trust she won't try to leave," he mutters.

"She could still jump," I say, peering over the railing in spite of the ensuing dizziness.

"She could," he muses. "Would probably break an ankle. She

won't. Now I can sleep without worrying she's escaped." Pressure and warmth on my lower back snaps me out of the foggy haze and disbelief that the two flights of stairs folded into nothing, and I follow Leo back down the hall to his bedroom. "Did you move your things in here?"

"Even my toothbrush. She shouldn't suspect anything."

"Good." He enters his closet and places his gun back in the drawer. "Get in bed. You've got to be wiped, too. You could've gone back to sleep, you know."

"I didn't know…I…You…I" I clench my hand into a fist to stop the stuttering.

"Willow, it's okay. I went to rescue a friend's wasted sister. It's not warfare."

I follow his instructions and get into bed, still wearing the leggings and oversized, long-sleeve t-shirt. We've been intimate, but I don't want to get undressed, and he wants to sleep, anyway.

The mattress dips with his weight. He adjusts the comforter then tugs me across the bed until I'm nestled against his body.

"Growing up, did people come home injured often?" he asks.

"Not in my home. My father never…but I heard stories. When I got older." All it took was asking questions and listening, and the people around me shared plenty.

There's pressure against my crown, as if he just kissed me.

"I'm not like that. Enforcing rules isn't what I do. I'm a broker, but I have to be armed. And we have to be smart. That's why we have security."

"And Lina?"

"My friend's sister." He strokes my arm. "I wondered if you'd ask me about her. She has no idea what this world is. No idea that you're related to the Italian mafia or what her brother is a part of. Thanks to him, she's never worked a day in her life. She's a clubber. Does shit on social media. Nick says she's an influencer. I don't grasp how that works, but Nick feeds her bad habits."

"You don't sound like you approve."

"Nick gets frustrated with her, but it's his own damn fault."

I shift, and my leg drapes over his.

"She and I…we've never." His fingers comb through my hair. "In case you were wondering."

"I wasn't." His eyes narrow inquisitively. "She's not what I envision as your type."

"Hmm." The shades are drawn, blocking the light. The sheets are cool, but his body is toasty. My eyelids grow heavier as the earlier adrenaline fades. "You would be correct. She's not my type at all. Out of curiosity, what do you see as my type?"

I lick my lips and grin. My face is tucked flat against his chest, so he can't see. "Me. I think I'm your type."

"It seems you are correct."

"A good thing for the arrangement, right?" I keep my tone purposefully light and playful. The last thing I want is to scare him away, or to earn a reprimanding reminder of our temporary status.

"You know, Willow, we don't have to… Sex isn't… I'd protect you no matter what. You know that, right? With or without sex."

"I know. You're a good man."

He snorts. "You say that, and yet you thought I went out to kill."

"You're a good man to me."

His chest rumbles and I expect him to argue, but whatever he's thinking, he keeps it bottled inside.

My fingers trace his breastbone, settling over the rhythmic beating of his heart.

"If I'd known about your birthday, I would've ordered you a cake."

"Twenty-two isn't a big deal. Maybe to Taylor Swift, but not to most people."

He chuckles. Then, with a low, pained groan, adds, "Jesus. Fucking twenty-two."

CHAPTER 20

SAM, AKA LEO, AKA SAINT

"She's still sleeping," I say to Nick, mobile pressed to my ear, gaze latched on Willow's perfect ass as she goes about pouring us coffee.

After a few hours' sleep, I woke with a raging hard-on, all because of the nimble beauty prancing around the kitchen. Thankfully, she was more than receptive to my advances.

"I'll be there in a couple of hours."

"Did you hear from Dante? Did he learn anything from the videos?"

"He's not answering my calls."

"Hmmm." I threatened him… "That doesn't sit right. Have you traced him?"

Willow's wide blue eyes meet mine. Her hair is darker, soaked wet from our morning shower. The color sets off those eyes like gemstones.

"Figured he was sleeping something off."

"When I saw him last, he was stone-cold sober. And I threatened his life if he didn't get the tapes from the club. He swears someone drugged her."

"He's fucking her," Nick practically growls. "Defending her coked-up arse, and I'm supposed to believe a horny random did this? Much more likely, she got her hands on a bad batch of the drug du jour."

I get why he's suspecting the worst in Lina. She's been through rehab twice—that I know of. But he's off on Dante.

"Someone followed me from the club last night."

"Probably paps. They've been bloodthirsty pricks ever since they figured out I'd bury any shit on Lina."

Guaranteed payday. One call to Nick with a photo, and they get a lump sum payment. I couldn't see shit behind those headlights. Maybe Nick's on to something.

"I'm going to ask Ash to locate Dante's car and phone."

"Whatever gets your rocks off. I'll be there in less than three hours to relieve you of Lina. The doc will beat me there. Let him in and force Lina to let him test her. Drug her if you have to."

A dial tone sounds loudly in my ear, and I end the call. I shoot off a text, then push out a stool and pat it for Willow to sit next to me.

"What you hear, in this flat, you can't share. Not with anyone. You got me?"

She nods, and I squeeze her thigh. Those lips are so tempting.

"Quiche will be ready in about twenty minutes," she says.

"Scarlet. The one you called last night. What did you tell her?"

"No details." Those sapphire eyes flash innocence. "She was married to a guy who did a lot of fighting. I told her you'd gone out with a gun, and I asked for her suggestions on how to prepare."

"She's your bestie?" I remember the redhead from our wedding. She didn't seem too enamored with me.

"She's my cousin. Before and after her marriage, she lived with us. Yes, to answer your question. She's my best friend." She smiles over the lip of the mug and then sips what looks like tea.

"Well, I've got a few more rules for you. If you call her, use a burner phone. Destroy it after you talk to her. You never know who's listening or who might try to get a trace. I have a box of burners in my office. That's all you use from here on out to call her, and if you're going to be talking to her for more than a couple of minutes, call her from the studio. Just in case someone is tracing from her end. You hear me?"

She nods slowly, absorbing my words. I don't know what the fuck is going on, but my instincts tell me something is not fucking right.

"And if someone is coming up in that elevator, and you don't know it's me, or if you're ever scared, you push that button that collapses the stairs. Got it?"

Another slow nod.

"After breakfast—well, no, after Lina's out of the flat—I'll show you the panic room."

"You don't trust Lina?"

I don't trust anyone. "I travel frequently for work. If I'm not home, you need a game plan. After Lina's gone, we'll map it out."

"Is there a war going on?"

Her word choice is telling. Her father may not have taken an active role in the criminal underworld, but as a part of the broader family, she's at ease with the vernacular.

Always is the answer. But what I say is, "Some things that happened last night don't add up. It's just a precaution. Best to be safe. What about other friends?" She's a likeable person. Two weeks in London, and she had an oaf following her around. "University? Anyone you talk to regularly?"

She blanches. "Acquaintances, mostly."

There's a story there. "What's that face for?"

"I didn't have a lot of friends at university."

"I call bullshit on that. A sweet girl like you?"

"A student got wind that I was a member of the Lupi Grigi. Rumors have always swirled around my father, even though he's a business leader. The security guy lurking in the background everywhere I went didn't help."

"Were students mean to you?"

"No, not mean. But…distant. No one wants to invite the mafia into their lives. And if they want to, you have to question why." She shrugs. "It was for the best. I grew close to some people… Jules, for example. His friends. The rumors. The tension. It highlighted how selfish I was being. Putting Jules at risk. Possibly his friends." Accusation crosses her narrowed eyes. "You know what interrogations can be like. It was better no one knew me well."

I understand what she's saying. At far too young an age she had to worry about the safety of anyone coming around her. In that way, she's like my sisters. Forced to confront mortality and grow up too young. I want to caress her cheek, to tell her none of that was fair, that she deserves so much more, but I hold on to my coffee mug. "What about within your..." I stumble on the word *family,* because I need a more expansive word. "Network?"

"I don't... I never clicked with those women. Maybe if I'd gotten married...but..." She shrugs dismissively and pushes off the stool. "Scarlet and Orlando are my two closest friends. You can trust me. I won't share your secrets with anyone. Not even them."

My phone buzzes with an alert that the garage code has been entered. It's Nick. He's the only one in possession of my code. The building gives each tenant a unique code. I confirm it's Nick by checking the security cam.

When I step out of my office, I do a double-take at Lina and Willow sitting around the kitchen table. Willow lent Lina clothes. With their hair up in ponytails, nostalgia stabs me. My sisters would often sit just like that, a mug of something, most likely hot chocolate, clasped between their hands while they jabbered about girl stuff.

The doctor came and went, saying he'd send the lab results directly to Nick. I can't imagine Nick's heard anything yet.

I stand over the banister, awaiting Nick's arrival. A moody fog hangs over the city. Traffic alerts reported serious delays on South End Road due to police activity. Up here in the clouds, peace and quiet reign.

"He's here, isn't he?" Lina asks.

"He has arrived," I answer.

"I suppose I should change," she says, pushing out from the table.

"Oh, no. You can take those clothes. It's fine. And I have some shoes for you, too." Both women sport thick wool socks.

"Is he in a rush? Or will he stay for a while?" Lina asks, standing over the sink with a mug.

"Your guess is as good as mine." He'll be tired after a long day of travel, and given he'll drive the nearly two hours to his estate, he'll likely want to get on the road. But he may wish to debrief in the security of my flat before moving on.

Lina tilts her head thoughtfully, then pours more tea from the kettle.

The elevator door slides open, and Nick steps out in a perfect crisp suit and shiny, pointed leather dress shoes. The extensive growth along his jaw means he's either growing a beard or he hasn't shaved in days.

"Did you attend church services?"

He snorts derisively. "This is what I was wearing last night."

As he climbs the stairs, I discern the wrinkles in his shirt and darker circles beneath his eyes. His attention shifts from me to his sister as he climbs the stairs. She holds up her mug in salute, and he shakes his head.

"What?" Lina calls out defensively. "I did nothing wrong."

He ignores her and steps past me with a curt, "Your office."

I follow him but glance back at the women. Willow watches over the rim of her mug, and I swear her concern washes over me like a brisk stream. Refreshing and disconcerting.

Nick sinks onto the sofa, and I close the door. Nick keeps Lina in the dark on his business practices, and I sure as fuck don't want Willow learning anything that could endanger her.

"Did your meetings go okay?" I ask.

"We found Dante. Dead."

Whoa. Not the expected response. "How?"

"Knife wounds. Scotland Yard has the case."

"Where?"

"A back alley near the club."

"I asked him to get the security footage from that night. Has to be related."

Shit. I threatened him with his life if he didn't get answers.

Nick's head hits the back of the sofa. "I've got a man who will give us everything they learn."

The syndicate owns quite a few, so I trust he's right.

"Doctor said Lina was drugged. Alcohol level nonexistent and no cocaine."

"Someone targeted her. It's the only answer, given I was followed."

"Or someone targeted you." He rubs a hand over his face as if he's attempting to wake himself up.

"You think they drugged Lina, expecting me to show up?"

"It's possible. Think about it. I'm out of town. You're my best mate. Who else am I going to call?"

"You employ a security squad. That'd be something else to assume I'd be the one you would call." It's hard to imagine anyone knowing Nick that well.

"Leandro Massimo is currently MIA."

"He doesn't have the intel or the intelligence to concoct that kind of plan."

Nick moves his jaw around, stretching it, then stretches each of his hands. I can't tell if he agrees with me. Hell, what do I know about Leandro's skills?

"How's she doing?" Nick gestures with his head in the general direction of the living area.

"She's been fine. Didn't fight me on staying until you

arrived." I mentally prepared for a brawl, but she's been a polite guest and cool with Willow.

"Not Lina. I just shared her medical report with you. The wife. How's she?"

"Good."

I don't appreciate his knowing smirk. But before I can derive a response, he pushes up off the sofa and exits the office.

"Let's go, little sister. I'm tired."

"You can stay at my flat for the night if you like," she offers.

"We're not staying there."

"Don't tell me you want to go back to Cumbria."

"Up." He snaps his fingers. "Let's go."

"But I promised I'd take Willow to lunch tomorrow. And we're going shopping. There's a sale at Harrod's."

Lina is not a friend I would choose for Willow. Or anyone I cared about. But that's something I'll deal with later.

"Dante was found stabbed to death outside the club," Nick announces.

"Who would do that?" Lina's expression is suitably horrified.

"No idea, but we're not staying in London."

Lina stiffens, lowers her gaze, and stands. She bends over Willow where she's seated and wraps her in a hug. She says something to her I can't hear, then straightens and joins Nick.

"I like your wife. Good job on that one," Lina says to me.

"Lina-approved. Cleared to spawn," Nick says.

Lina and I simultaneously flick Nick the middle finger, and he chuckles.

Willow exits the hallway and offers a pair of wellies to Lina. "These should fit, I think."

After Lina takes the boots, I pull Willow into my side, earning an annoying-as-fuck smirk from Nick.

We remain by the banister, watching as Lina and Nick descend the stairs. "Your security waiting in the car?"

"You going to escort us if they're not?"

"Yes."

"Don't be daft. Yes, security is with the car. And you beef up yourself, toodles. For you and the missus."

CHAPTER 21

WILLOW

Lina blows kisses goodbye, and I return them with a smile. The second the doors close, Leo backs away, letting me go. There's no one to perform for now.

I rub my chilled arms and stride to the kitchen. "Would you like a cup of tea? Do you have work to do?"

The kettle is light, so I set about making a fresh pot. His shoes scuff the floor, a dull sound that alerts me to his whereabouts, yet even with that awareness, a bolt of surprise fires through me when I turn and he's there, leaning over the counter, intent.

"It's Saturday. We've still got some daylight hours left. What're your plans?"

"No plans, really," I answer.

"No plans to meet up with Geoff?" His eyes light with amusement. Cocky amusement.

"After your reception yesterday, I doubt I'll hear from him again."

If I didn't know better, I'd say, based on his smug expression, he's quite pleased.

"His loss. If you've no plans, I'm keen for a tour of your studio."

"Really?" I set the kettle on the stove but flick the gas off. "You don't strike me as the art type."

"Is my flat not decorated to your liking? I've got sculptures."

He's got two Greco-Roman black onyx bust reproductions and monochromatic artwork in modern black frames. "I doubt you picked those yourself."

He grins. "Guilty as charged. But that doesn't mean I wouldn't like to see your art."

"Well, I received a notification that the shipment from Italy arrived. You can help me unpack it. On one condition."

He raises an eyebrow. "Go on."

"These are the pieces I'm planning to show to the agent. You've got to be honest with me. If you think it'll flop in London, you've got to tell me. If it's total shite, don't spare my feelings." That's something Orlando and Scarlet would do. "It'll be much worse if the agent arrives and turns right back around because he thinks—"

"Let's go. Get your shoes on."

Nerves light my stomach. My hands cool and the desire to change plans comes out of nowhere as if a dragon arose and instead of shooting flames, the monster shot doubt straight into my veins.

This is one dragon I must slay. I step back into his bedroom and into the closet where I placed my stuff.

Not everyone will like what I create. But someone out there will.

Foremost, I create for myself.

Haters teach. Either constructively, so I improve my art, or by strengthening my skin.

Leo is not a hater. I'll read the truth in his eyes. That might hurt more than anything he says, but I don't paint for everyone. My style might not be what he seeks. And that's okay.

"What's going on in that head of yours?"

I jump, palm pressed against my sternum. "You scared me."

"Wanted to see what was taking so long. Do you have enough room in here?" He examines the walk-in closet. It's a slightly smaller mirror image of his closet.

I didn't pack most of what I own. There's a ton of unused hanging space and drawers I haven't used. "It's good. I'll spend some time organizing and make it neater in here."

His closet is color coded, with the hanging clothes separated in sections by color, whereas mine has yet to be sorted. I ran out of hangers, so there's one trunk that's open against the wall that's a haphazard mess.

He disappears, and I slip on a pair of trainers and bump into his chest as I exit.

"Forgot to give you this."

The black credit card in his hand reads Willow Gagliano.

"My assistant said it was better to give you a card with the name on your identification. Since there's no reason for you to legally change your name…" He holds it out, waiting for me to take it. There's no need to legally change my name because this is temporary. "Use this for anything you need."

"You know, I have some money. You don't need to pay for everything."

"My wife should have a credit card I supply. Take the card."

I take it from him and absentmindedly slide it in a back pocket. "Ready?"

Silence descends. It's not an uncomfortable silence, per se, but I can't stop myself from wondering why a weight has settled on my chest. Is it the discomfort with financial matters? The reminder that this is an arrangement with an as-yet-undetermined end date?

He's wearing jeans and a loose long sleeve t-shirt with the outline of bullhorns on the back, UT on the pocket, and frayed edges along the sleeves. Instead of his odd-looking cowboy boots, he's also in trainers, and while I know he's quite a bit older, this look shaves years.

In our Saturday outfits, we could be mistaken as friends from university, rather than an influential arms dealer and the young art student he's mysteriously befriended.

"The workstations aren't far away at all, are they?" he asks as I open the door to the brick building that might be mistaken as a refitted warehouse.

"Nope. How long have you lived here?" I ask.

"In this flat? Four years."

"Where'd you live before?"

"A different flat." He extends his arm, holding the door for me. The worn brick floor bears a sheen from age and polish, and my shoes squeak, a shrill sound in the mostly vacant space. "Is it quiet like this because it's a Saturday?"

"Yes." I unlock the door to my studio. It's a one-room space with three spacious windows with iron grids on one wall. My paints are in boxes on the floor, and the dry brushes are put away in leather wraps. Cleaned, damp brushes gather in glass jars, handles down, tops airing.

"I've ordered some pieces for storage," I tell him. "I thought about shopping in the area but figured it would be easiest to find what I want online."

"So, this is where the magic happens?" he asks, traversing the space, slowing when he arrives at my easel and the work in progress. It's a flurry of reds and oranges. Another piece, one filled with blues and grays, leans against a wall. "Angry?" he asks, pointing at the reds. "Sad?" He lifts an eyebrow and gestures to the blue painting.

"Something like that." I like how he immediately interprets the pieces with emotion. To me, modern art is all about communicating the human condition. "Not everything I paint is a reflection of me."

"Have you ever read *The Picture of Dorian Gray*?"

"No…haven't heard of it."

"Oscar Wilde. I read it in college. But there's a line in there… Something about every portrait is a portrait of the artist, not of the sitter."

"Huh."

"Do you agree?"

"I suppose there's some truth to it."

"And if it's true in a portrait–"

"It's true in an abstract piece…or landscape," I finish for him.

"You said there's a shipment to pick up?"

"Yes. I think the front desk has it." Although I'm not as sure I want him to see my art now.

"Where's that?"

"In another building."

"Well, let's go."

When we return with the pallets on a wheeled trolley, he's

shaking his head. "I can't believe you thought you'd get this on your own."

I hadn't, actually. There are normally lots of people milling around.

"You planned on asking Geoff, didn't you?"

"I met Geoff twenty-four hours ago. If you keep mentioning him, you're going to make me believe you're jealous."

He narrows his eyes, and I'm torn between backing up or stepping forward and showing him he has no reason to be concerned. I'm attracted to him, and for now, he's the only one I want.

"We need tools to open this. I'll be back." The door closes and the lock clicks. He locked me in here.

He might believe such behavior is normal, but I don't. We lived in a small Italian town, and the family maintained order. Crime was rare. At least, I never heard of crimes. Papa never locked me in a room.

Maybe it's London that breeds fear? Or perhaps the syndicate isn't as good at maintaining harmony? The dead man Leo spoke of supports that theory. The news shook Lina.

If I'd brought a mobile, I would call Scarlet to get her take.

When the lock clicks again, he's carrying a bag that he drops on the floor with a heavy thud.

"It's not jealousy. It's self-preservation. We're playing a role, and it's important that our acting convinces everyone around us."

"Got it," I say, feeling sufficiently chastised.

He waltzed back in and picked right up where we left off. What does that say? He's offended at the notion he could be jealous?

He takes the back of a hammer and pops open the top of a

crate. One by one, he helps me pull out the canvases, the products of my university years.

He backs up, hands on his waist, studying them propped up on the floor, resting against the walls.

"You're talented."

Joy floods my cells, drowning all the negatives.

"Truly, you are. This is what you should do with your life."

"That's what Orlando says, but it feels pretty fantastic to hear it from someone else."

"If I had a sister, I would do everything I could to support her dreams." He side-eyes me. "Orlando's young. If he were older, you would've had a more potent ally."

He's thinking of my situation, where I had few options and needed to beg a stranger.

"What's your family like?" I want to learn more about him. This might be an arrangement, but we live together. We're lovers. I'll never forget him; of that, I'm quite certain. I owe him so much.

"They're good people." He crosses his arms over his chest and moves to a landscape painting I did of the sun setting over the ocean. It's not the modern style I gravitate to, but it was required for my portfolio class. "I need to return to Texas, and they'd love to meet you. Think you can get away?"

"Tell me when."

CHAPTER 22

SAM, AKA LEO, AKA SAINT

With the office door closed, I flip the lid on the box of burners, pull one out, and dial.

"Jack here."

"It's Leo."

"Hold."

I drop down on the leather sofa, kicking my bare feet up on the pouf, perfectly situated so I can see if a shadow crosses below the door.

"I'm back. Calling on a Saturday?" Jack asks.

"Need I remind you I work twenty-four-seven and have been doing so for more than five years?"

A grunt crosses the line. He can get annoyed all he wants. I really don't give a fuck. A click sounds, and I assume it's a door closing.

"What's up?"

"I need to coordinate a visit with my Texas cousins."

"Is this your bride's idea?"

"No. Nick's."

"Why?" He's right to be suspicious. And concerned. Jack doesn't want these people anywhere near his family, even his extended family, if things go south.

"He's looking for updates on some of your most recent product offerings. And he wants me to get a sense of what's happening on the American sales front."

"And he's using the new bride as an excuse?"

"Something like that. I keep telling him it's an arrangement, but he's convinced it's more."

"Is that right?"

"Showed up for the ceremony to perform as my best man."

"Nomad left that piece out of the intelligence briefing."

"If I bring her, you'll need to get a team on it. When I exit, they might come after her to ask all about who she saw on her Texas trip."

"When you exit, we're doing it so no one comes looking. Period."

"Does that mean you've cooked a plan?"

"We've got a dozen. But it's not time yet."

"Right." I've been hearing that for at least four years.

"What's the update from Qatar?"

"Don't have one yet. There may not be one. Nick had to leave early for personal reasons."

"Sources are telling us Russia had their hands all over that meeting."

"Could be true. Things happened. I couldn't press for details without raising suspicion."

"Anything happen we need to know about?"

"Nick's personal bullshit."

"Speaking of personal, how's life married to the mob?"

"The arrangement removed her from the mafia world."

"It's my understanding that's a world you don't leave."

"She did."

"Be careful. That wasn't part of the op."

I divert my attention to the overcast day and a plane flying high above the skyscrapers. He can take his criticisms and shove them where the sun doesn't shine.

"What's done is done. Sources say Russia's purchased some serious firepower to replenish its arsenal. Have you heard anything about that?"

"No. I wasn't called in to negotiate for them." Nick doesn't do any work for Russia. Putin assassinated his parents. He works around the Russians, not with them. "If you're trying to track it down, I'd focus on Titan Shipping. Alessio Gagliano is leveraging some ships for the shadow fleet to get sanctioned goods out of Russia and to buyers. Would make sense if he'd traffic sanctioned goods into Russia too."

"Is the syndicate orchestrating that?"

"Not Nick. There might be some players brokering the bigger ticket transactions. There's money in sanctioned goods. But Nick sent me down to that meeting to learn more about Titan's role in the shadow fleet, which says to me the syndicate is not orchestrating that piece of it. He wouldn't need the intel if one of his partners was a part of the deal."

"And Gagliano is your father-in-law, right?"

"That he is."

"You've created a new definition for deep cover."

"It's a talent."

"On another note, tensions with China are rising."

"When are they not?"

"True. But we're thinking the move on Taiwan is imminent."

"Syndicate won't touch that."

"But the kingpins will shift positions in preparation. They'll do everything they can to minimize losses and maximize gains from conflicts."

"And?" What, exactly, does the CIA want from me?

"Keep your ears open."

"Won't satellite imaging and monitoring market fluctuations tell you all you need to know?"

"You're done, aren't you?"

I lift my gaze to the ceiling. He's right. I'm exhausted with this game. But I'm not a quitter. "It's all feeling senseless. The syndicate is wealthier and more powerful now than before I started."

"You've been a saint to last this long."

Is that his idea of a joke? "My next update will be through Nomad. Figure out my trip for my bride to meet my family. Nick's going to ask me about it."

"We'll look into it. And hang in there. You've got to trust me. What you're sharing with us? The intel is invaluable."

A shadow crosses below the threshold of the door, and it pushes open. Cornflower blue irises warm me like a bolt of sun through a cloud-soaked day.

"Let me know if there's anything else we can do to help Lina." I end the call, knowing Jack will understand my nonsensical sentence means we got interrupted. And not a moment too soon. There was a time when I ranked Jack Sullivan as hero, but five years into this, and I'm about done with the guy.

"How's Lina?"

"Nick's taking care of her. She'll be fine."

"You know, she's convinced it was just a random guy from the bar."

"Men can be monsters." I push off the sofa and stalk toward her.

"You're like my father. You're not going to tell me what's going on, are you?"

I pin her against the wall with one hand on each side of her face, my gaze falling from those gorgeous eyes, down the slope of her nose, to those full, rosy lips, and farther down her creamy, smooth skin to her décolletage.

"My business is boring. But you know what's not boring?" My hand cups her breast over her shirt, and she responds with a gasp. "You."

Her fingers tenderly trace the outline of my erection through my jeans. "Apparently so."

I grin and bend until my nose presses to her shoulder and I breathe in her flower garden scent and kiss and suck my way up the length of her neck. She tilts her head, giving me room, but it's the tips of her fingers, lightly teasing my tip, that's going to push me right over the edge.

"If you unzip my jeans, you'll have better access."

A flicker of a smile crosses her lips before I claim them. Kissing her is fast becoming my favorite activity. She moans into my mouth, and I press her into the wall, trapping her hand between us. Her leg lifts, effectively cradling me against her, and I groan.

There's pressure on my chest, pushing me back, and I break the kiss, concerned. Does she not want this?

Her lips are glistening and swollen, and she's panting. All good signs.

Those luscious lips curve into a smile and the tip of her

tongue covers the center of her upper lip. My breaths are coming out at a quick pace, but they skid when her knees bend and she lowers herself to the ground.

Kneeling before me, she unzips my jeans, releasing my hard-as-stone cock. She grips the base and licks her lips. Thank god for the wall because without my hand planted against it, I might crash.

The tip of her thumb rubs over my crown, smearing the leaking pre-cum. I suck in air, fascinated with her every move. Hot, wet heat wraps around me, and I brush her thick hair out of the way, for her, and for me, because I don't want to miss a second.

The rest of the world falls away. My fucked-up role. China. Russia. The shadow fleet. It's just me and her. Her mouth. Warm and hot. Sucking. Licking. Taking me deep to the back of her throat. My balls tighten, and a desperation to be inside her surges.

I pull her up, lifting her, reaching my desk in seconds. My laptop, files, and pens fly, clattering to the ground.

Her chest heaves, and she lifts her top as I grasp her waistband, tugging down her loose pants in one swoop. Pale pink panties are all that's left and I shift them out of the way and ram into her.

Jesus.

"So fucking tight," I grunt.

Her fingers clutch my shirt, her thighs rub my hips, and her pussy constricts. I'm in heaven.

"You." Thrust. "Are." Thrust. "Exactly." Thrust. The desk shifts. "What." Thrust. "I." Thrust. "Need."

She pants her pleasure, words incoherent. Her nails dig into my back. Her heel kicks against my ass. I pound against her, feeling her tighten, knowing she's close.

"Fuck. You feel so good." It's a shame I found her so late into this stint, because she's perfection. I'll never get enough.

Her eyes lock on to mine, and I round over her, grinding over her with each thrust.

I watch her as I move deep inside. The intensity between us is surreal.

"Fuck."

"Harder." Her nails dig into my shoulder.

With a cry, her pussy constricts my dick so hard I lose control. *Jesus*. I come so fucking hard the world goes black.

CHAPTER 23

WILLOW

The agent Leo recommended provided a list of muted colors he believes will sell well, or in his words, will mesh with the London elite's decor. Inspiration from these hues is elusive, compounded by my mind circling back to last night with Leo.

From a starry-eyed, romantic perspective, he's gorgeous. Sexy. When I approached him in the shower that first night, I expected we could enjoy each other, and intimacy would increase the value of our nontraditional arrangement.

What I didn't expect is the closeness intimacy would breed. I absolutely love what he can do to my body, and he's far more skilled than Jules. Or at least, sex is better with Leo. But as much as I love the physical, it's our time after, in the dark, where we talk and touch that I treasure. His walls fall. Well, not really. He doesn't talk about business, and I get the sense he's holding himself back, but he asks lots of questions. After sex, he doesn't roll over and sleep. He wants to talk. That means something, no?

I can't wait to meet his family—not just to meet them, but to learn more about him. And does that desire mean I'm falling for him? If I care, is that such a horrible thing? We'll likely be together for years. Maybe over time he'll fall for me too.

My mobile vibrates, and the name Ludovica Gagliano flashes on the screen. I welcome the break from plotting my next piece, since I'm making no progress, anyway.

"Mamma," I say, letting genuine happiness color my greeting.

"*Mia bellisima figlia,* how are you, dear? Do you have a minute?"

"Of course." I sink down into a puff chair I purchased for the studio. "I'm at a good place for a break." She knows when I'm in the middle of something, if I don't want to lose my pace, I won't answer.

"Things are good?"

"They are. My agent found two galleries interested in showing my work."

"I'm so proud of you." There's a hint of sadness to her words. She rarely calls during the workday, as she's typically busy in our community. She volunteers at the local library, and she helps with the elderly.

"Is everything okay, Mamma?"

"It's fine. I'm calling to check on my daughter, a married woman. Can I do that?"

"Of course."

"In this time of, I believe the word is vicissitudes, this time of change, what I need to know is, are you happy? Does your husband make you happy?"

"He does." My mother understands it's an arrangement, but truthfully, almost all marriages in our world are arranged. In her time, arrangements were the only marriages. There were no exceptions.

"Is he a good man?"

"He is," I answer with conviction.

"You do not regret your choice?"

In her eyes, I had a choice. That's laughable.

"I'm happier than I could have hoped." I'm telling her the truth, and it's an unexpected realization.

"That's good, then. That makes it all worthwhile."

Odd.

"Ludovica, who are you talking to?" The man's voice is familiar.

"My daughter."

"Mamma, who is that?"

"Security detail." There's frustration in her tone. "You have your security with you, yes?"

"I do. Leo insists." Of course, I won't allow John to be in the room with me while I work. I need to be alone when I paint. Leo rented the room next to mine for John. There are small cameras installed in the corners, and I'm fairly certain John sits behind his computer in his office, watching me from right next door. It's something I try not to think about.

"That's good. How many does he employ?"

"I spend my days in an art studio. There's one bodyguard with me at all times, and that is more than sufficient."

She sighs.

"That's all Papa ever hired for me." I don't know why I'm defensive. John has probably never been more bored in all his life. Pretty much all I do is walk between my studio and the flat.

"He asked me to use a burner phone when I call Scarlet, in case someone would track it."

"That's wise."

"Is something going on? Is everything okay back home?"

"We're fine, *bella*. Do what your husband says. Be a good wife. He'll keep you safe. Remember, it's important to listen. The men deal with things we don't always understand, and we need to trust in them."

"Mamma, what's going on?"

"I love you, *bella*. Stay safe."

The call ends, and I stare at the blank screen. I'd call Orlando to check that all is okay at home, but he's in school.

Vicissitude. Variations in circumstances or fortune.

I pick up the burner phone I carried down in my bag and dial Scarlet. She lives in the same house as my parents, and she listens. She rarely speaks to my parents, but she always listens.

"*Ciao*!" Her excited greeting has me smiling. The rain outside is heavier now, and droplets stream down the glass in rivulets.

"*Ciao, bella*," I reply.

"To what do I owe this pleasure?" She reverts to English as readily as Orlando and I.

"I got a call from Mamma. Is everything okay there?"

"What did she say?"

Scarlet's question roils my sixth sense. "What's going on?"

"Rumors. There are always rumors. What did Aunt Ludovica say to you?"

"She sounded sad. Wanted to know if I'm happy. She mentioned vicissitudes." I struggle to remember. "We didn't talk for long, but she sounded off. Wanted me to obey my husband.

Her security interrupted us, but she wanted to make sure I had security. Are we at war again?"

When I was much younger, we were at war with the Cosa Nostra family. Hushed conversations not meant for children's ears would begin, and we'd be sent outside or to the playroom.

"The rumor is that Massimo isn't happy with your father for giving you to Leo."

"Because of Leandro?"

"That's the rumor. He doesn't feel respected or some such bullshit. But Leandro hasn't been around. Some say he left on business. But…"

"Scarlet, just say it."

"Others say he went to find you. Aunt Ludovica must've heard that rumor. And maybe there's more to it than what I've heard if her security detail was near." She's right. Mamma doesn't like them nearby.

"You think he'd go after Mamma? Where's Papa?"

"He's away on business."

"Well, that's normal." But as I say it, unease takes residence in the pit of my stomach.

"No one's questioning your father's absence. But, given everything, just be careful, okay?"

"Why did you say that? Do you think Massimo hurt him?"

"Don't let your imagination run wild. The rumors are about Leandro's absence."

"What would Leandro even do if he found me? I'm married."

"That man is a psychopath. It's a good thing you're in another country." Movement in the doorway catches my attention. It's John, peering in.

"Do you need anything? I'm going to the lavatory," he says.

"No, I'm good," I tell him.

"Don't leave until I return." He pulls the door closed and the lock clicks.

"Was that your security?"

"Yes," I answer, frowning at the locked door.

"How is married life?"

I rest back against the chair, scanning the ceiling. My cheeks warm as I remember last night.

"It's good."

"You're one of the lucky ones. An arranged marriage that delivered love?"

"I don't think they're as rare as you believe."

"Oh, trust me, they're rare."

She's jaded, but after her experience, I can't blame her for her views.

I could tell her I'm falling for him, but it's unlikely he will reciprocate, and without reciprocation, it feels hollow or foolish. I don't want to be foolish.

He's concerned about my age and reminds me daily that this is temporary. Not that I would ever share these details with Scarlet. I love her, but she'd leap into protective big sister mode. And there's no need to say the falling bit out loud.

Our conversation reverts to Italian, and we talk a while longer, with her filling me in on mundane details. It's a gorgeous day in Italy with blue skies. She's been swamped at work due to some tax deadlines. She works within Titan Shipping's accounting department, and it often sounds like she carries the department. Dad recruited her years ago, not long after Vincent's death. She'd been listless, and my mother feared she suffered from depression.

When our call ends, I resume painting.

I've never understood Scarlet wanting to work for my father as a bookkeeper, because to me, working with spreadsheets all day would be torture. She'd been training as a nurse, but that required she come into close contact with the Lupi Grigi men, and, as she once told me, the men she comes into contact with in the office are preferable, and in the office, she doesn't have to touch them.

By the close of the day, I have a vision for a set of three pieces in muted colors that reflect life's daily subtle variations and time's more momentous shifts, and I steal my mother's word. I title the series Vicissitude.

I wrap up, exit the studio, lock it, and, as I approach John's office, he exits.

"Do you have an umbrella?" he asks.

"I'll be fine. Rain won't hurt me."

Without a word, John returns to his office.

Geoff comes out of his studio down the hall, and I wave. He steps toward me, but when John appears with an extra umbrella in hand, Geoff changes direction. My stomach sinks. Does Geoff believe I'm with organized crime? That's what happened on campus. Once students figured out I had security trailing me, they connected dots. Why else would a young woman have a bodyguard?

Those first two weeks, John didn't come with me to the studio, and I lived the life of a normal person. But since Leo's return, he has insisted John follow me everywhere. It doesn't quite seem fair, but then my mother's call and Scarlet's rumors have me wondering if there's more going on, and Leo doesn't trust me to handle it. Meanwhile, I'm the one who handles issues. If I didn't address my challenges head on, I'd be married to Leandro. And if I didn't take the first step, Leo would've never touched me.

John escorts me wordlessly back to my apartment. I sense his shadow, even though the clouds mask it, and I catch glimpses of him in rain-streaked glass reflections.

"Goodnight," I tell him when we arrive in the lobby, but he doesn't make a move to leave. "Are you going home now?"

"Aye, I am. After I see you to the forty-first floor."

He joins me in the lift, and, wordlessly, we ascend. When the doors open, he peers in.

"It doesn't appear Mr. Sullivan is back," he says.

"Was he out today?"

"Business meetings. If you don't mind, I'm going to look around before I leave."

"Go right ahead," I tell him, as I have no choice in the matter. He heads up the stairs as I remove my wellies. I give him a few moments, then climb the stairs. He passes me on the stairwell.

"All's clear. See you in the morning. Don't leave or let anyone up until Mr. Sullivan gets home."

"Aye, aye, sir." I salute him with my finger, and he might smile. He might not. For someone who spends an awful lot of his time near me, he hasn't warmed to me much. But I suppose he's not family, whereas so many of the men around my father's home were.

Wistfulness for my family home sweeps in out of nowhere. The paths along the beach where I spent so much time, the faint scent of my mother's gardenias on the breeze, and the sun's warmth on my skin, I miss them all with a yearning I haven't felt since those first university days. I had been naive to believe I might be allowed to live in Florence forever. That the *famiglia's* rules didn't apply to me because of my father's status.

The rain outside soundlessly patters the thick-walled glass, and the dense clouds blur the skyscrapers into nonexistence. Inside, I fix tea and biscuits and await Leo's return.

CHAPTER 24

SAM, AKA LEO, AKA SAINT

A dull pain pulses behind my temples. Meeting with bankers ranks as my least favorite activity, and today has been nothing but contract reviews and signing documents confirming fund availability from specified accounts, product value, and delivery method. We're trading in weapons and arms, but at these prices, all parties want to minimize risk and ensure the transactions look as pure and legal as a Catholic Church property transaction.

My windshield wipers slow as the parking garage door rolls up. The multi-level underground car park provides spaces for all occupants within the building. Four spots are allocated for my unit. A black Audi four-door sedan is parked in one of the four spots that's farthest from the elevator bank entrance.

The black Audi is John's. Why's he still here?

I double-check the time on my wrist. He should've left

thirty minutes ago. He texted me on his way out. Did Willow change her mind and decide to work late? Is she still at the studio?

When I exit the car, an engine idling rumbles through the concrete cave. I still and listen. The car isn't on this row, and it's not moving.

I pop the glove box and remove my Glock. I slide the chamber, checking to ensure it's loaded.

I tuck it in the back of my trousers, scanning the other automobiles for anyone who might see me with a weapon. Across the way, I survey John's car. His passenger side window is smudged with a dark substance.

Instinctively, I know. All of my senses heighten. The scent of exhaust is stronger, the garage lighter and warmer, the engine's rumble louder. I wrap my fingers loosely around the grip of the Glock. My skin awakens, the dull headache miraculously eliminated as adrenaline surges.

There's a body in the driver's seat, the window down, head slouched to the right. Blood and brain matter splatter the passenger window and the seat. John lowered the window to talk to someone.

Why talk? To whom?

My stomach freefalls as my gaze whips to the elevator bank. I slide out the mobile. No service.

Gun poised; I rush to the elevator. God damn forty-first floor.

The glass digital reading shows the number forty. A down arrow appears.

Were they on my floor? Or is it chance?

I could rush up, but then, if they have her, I'll miss them. Is that why they talked to John? The code.

He wouldn't give it, though, would he?

I take cover behind my car, positioned to see the glass door that leads to the garage level elevator well.

What do I know about John? He's not American. Nick hired him. Transferred him into my employ. British SAS? No. He'd been a cop. Or had he even been that?

He came to work for me four fucking years ago. I don't remember shit from his resume.

Did you give them the code, John?

I fumble with the phone, flicking through to the video feed of my place. The video shows the foyer, the living area, the kitchen. She could be in our bedroom or the bathroom. Or my study. Or the guest room. Empty room after empty room.

I run my finger over the time range, sliding it backward. My eyes sting and my throat clenches. Three men.

The elevator dings, and I set the phone on the tire.

Blink. Prepare.

Three men. Plus the idling car.

One tango steps out, gun lowered at his side, scanning the area. He holds the glass door. Leandro pushes Willow out of the elevator.

Fucker.

The second tango exits behind him.

Wait.

Take clean shots.

Willow exits. One bruised eye, a bloody lip, tears.

"*Chiama* Marco," Leandro growls.

Call Marco.

"You are sick," Willow cries.

He's got her hands tied behind her, but she's fighting. Struggling against him.

Good girl. I should've given her fucking self-defense lessons like I gave my sisters.

"There's no signal. I'll go get him."

"He should've taken one of these spots. Where the fuck is he?"

"Probably didn't want to risk getting booted. Visitor spots are next level."

Crouching, I come around the front of the automobile, behind the three amigos.

Pop.

One falls forward.

Pop.

Second down.

Leandro spins, one hand behind Willow. The other hand flails, attempting to locate his gun.

"Uh-uh," I scold, rising from my crouching position, gun aimed between his eyes.

His head is too close to Willow's.

"She's mine," he grunts.

"Wrong," I say. "Get your hands off my wife."

"She's mine," he repeats. "She was promised to me."

"She's. My. Wife," I repeat. "I would tell you that if you come near her again, you'll die, but today is your death day."

He scowls.

"Let my wife go."

He underestimated me. Believed the men he hired could protect him.

He locates his gun, but it's snapped in.

Tears spill from Willow's glassy blue eyes. I meet those tearful eyes head on and mouth the word *down*.

She drops, throwing a fumbling Leandro, and the bullet rips through his brain.

She trembles, mouth opening as she takes in the carnage.

There's still one tango in a car.

"Was it just the three of them?"

She nods. Her pupils are blown out. Shock is taking over.

I brush a finger over her cheek, listening for any engine fluctuation.

"You're okay, baby. You hear me? Is anything hurting?"

They clearly hurt her, but I need to know if they broke anything. She walked out. I circle her, scanning her. She's not handcuffed. The fucker used zip ties. Blood oozes where it's cutting into her skin.

I set the gun on the roof of the automobile, snag my pocketknife, and slice through hard plastic.

She pulls her hands around, clutching her wounds.

"Get upstairs. Go straight to our floor. Do you hear me? Remember where the button is for the stairs?"

She nods. "I was in the bedroom when they came in. I thought it was you. I didn't know."

"It's okay, baby. Get up to our place. I'll be up in a minute."

"What are you going to do?"

"Take care of this." I press my lips to her forehead.

I love you.

The thought blindsides me. I breathe it away.

"Go. I'll be up as soon as I can."

I watch, hand on my gun, not taking my eyes off my wife until she's secure in the elevator. I wait until the digital reading shows the number 41.

My skin tingles. This isn't over.

I pop John's trunk and place all three bodies inside. The

concrete's a bloody mess. This place needs a cleaner. But I need to get out of here. I need to get a call in to Nick. Get bobbies we own on the scene.

That means I don't have time to surprise the tango. He's probably figured out he doesn't have signal down here, so he's waiting for one of his buddies to come up for him. Watching for them to walk up the incline. Or he'll loop the garage.

I get in the elevator and monitor the signal bar from the moment the doors close. The second I have signal, I dial. The lift stops at the lobby level, and a woman in a business suit and trench coat enters.

"Leo. I heard from Goldman. Funds cleared," Nick says.

"We have a problem." The woman side-eyes me, but the lift stops two floors higher, and she exits. The doors close, and the lift begins its rapid ascension.

"What now?"

"Leandro De Luca attempted to kidnap Willow."

"Fuck."

"He's dead, and so are two of his men. One is hanging out in the garage in the getaway car."

"Bloody hell."

"Leandro had to be the one behind Lina. He wanted to find me, so he went after her when you were out of town. Everyone knew you were at that conference."

"I'm going to kill him."

"Beat you to it."

"Any idea if Massimo knew what he was doing?"

"Didn't get to interrogate him. He had a gun to Willow's head." The elevator doors open, and I slam a fist against a tile panel. The tile lifts, and I press the button for the stairs to expand.

"God damn. The last thing I want is a war with the Lupi Grigi."

Willow appears over the banister, clutching her arms to her chest.

"Did Leandro say anything to you? Did Massimo know?"

"Who is that?" Nick asks in my ear.

"Willow."

"He said my father should have never agreed to give me to the syndicate. That the syndicate sold out the Lupi Grigi. And they would get revenge, starting with reclaiming me."

"You hear that?"

"Fuck." He'd been playing with fire when he tried to weaken them by taking out the capo last year.

"How'd they find out?"

The stairs slide to a halt, and I climb them two at a time. I don't have an answer for Nick, so I don't give him one.

"Never mind," he says. "Get Willow and come here."

"What about the bodies?"

"Where are they?"

"In John's car. Two in the trunk, one in the back. No witnesses. But there's blood at the scene. We need to pull the security footage before someone checks it."

"And John?"

"They killed him. Driver's seat."

"Fucking certifiable." He spits out garbled curses, saying a lot of what I'm feeling. "You're safest here while we sort this. Pack up Willow and come to the estate. I'll send cleaners."

Leo is stiff and silent, eyes roving, both hands on the wheel, a loaded gun resting between us.

We didn't pack. I don't have clothes, but I haven't mentioned it because I assume we'll acquire what we need. I haven't spoken because I don't want to break his concentration. Back at the condo, he tenderly washed my cuts, bandaged my wrists, kissed my forehead, gave me aspirin, and we left.

He scans his surroundings constantly, as if he expects a car might sideswipe us or bullets rain from the sky.

Did I do this? I didn't allow anyone in. Leandro and his men didn't call up. I don't know how they found me. I've done exactly as Leo told me and haven't shared my address with anyone other than my parents. Scarlet pushed for it, wanting to update my contact information, and I told her I couldn't share it. But I had my art shipped to the studio. Is that how they found me?

I steal a sideways glance at Leo. For the first time, he reminds me of his namesake, a lion. He's scanning the concrete jungle, a killer poised to attack.

We turn onto an expressway. The outline of London skyscrapers comes into view in the reflection of the side view mirror. Traffic is slow moving, heavy with homeward bound commuters.

Leo rests his elbow on the divider between us and rotates his wrist, holding his hand out, palm up. An intricate mesh of deep lines crosses his palm. If only I'd paid more attention to the palm reader in Florence.

"You okay?"

I nod in answer, but his attention is trained on our surroundings. His fingers wiggle.

"I am," I say.

"Then give me your hand."

With everything going on, my insides still thrill at his request. I place my palm over his. He weaves his fingers through mine. I slide in the seat, shifting closer to him, mindful of the gun.

He lifts our joined hands and rubs the back of my hand against his rough, unshaven jaw, then presses his lips against the skin.

"If I had shown up any later, he would've taken you."

"I tried to fight him."

His gaze cuts to me and his jaw flexes. "I can see that. I should've taught you self-defense techniques. Did your father not teach you?"

I always have security, but saying so feels like blaming Leo, and I don't want to cast blame. None of this is his fault.

"I can't believe he came for me. He's *pazzo*!"

"Did he say anything to you? Like what he was planning?"

"He said I belonged to him." He'd reached out and cupped my breast and squeezed like a demented creep. To a man like him, women are possessions. "He believed my father agreed to give me to him. He's *consigliere*. Our capo's brother. Is my father, my family—will Massimo go after them?"

"Did your father promise you to Leandro?"

"Not to my knowledge. It was undoubtedly discussed. But now that I think about it, maybe. The way my father rushed our wedding was highly unusual."

"Like he wanted to avoid confrontation. Or avoid giving Massimo the opportunity to deny it."

"Massimo agreed. My father wouldn't marry off his daughter without the capo's approval." But as I say the words, I doubt them. Did Father move forward with a plan to beg forgiveness after the marriage? Did he go away on business, hoping Massimo would calm down over time?

As the distance between us and London increases, the road clears incrementally, and we drive faster into the night.

"If I'd gotten home five minutes later..." This idea clearly bothers him, and I squeeze his hand to reassure him I'm fine.

My fears differ from his.

"I thought you'd come home and wonder what had happened. That you'd think I left willingly. You showed me the stairs and the safe room, but I... I was in our bedroom, in the closet, when he appeared out of nowhere. I was trying to decide what to change into. I didn't hear him." My voice cracks. He hasn't said or done anything to blame me, but I need to explain.

I need him to know I wasn't going willingly. "I would never go willingly."

He lifts my hand once more to his lips. It's not so much a kiss as a pressure against my hand, as if he needs to hold me the only way he can while we're driving.

"I love you." My words are whisper soft, too soft to be audible.

He lowers our hands and says, "Recline your seat. Close your eyes. Your adrenaline is going to crash, and you're going to become tired. Sleep it off. I'll wake you when we arrive at Nick's."

"We're going to Nick's?"

"He has an estate. It's secure. We'll be safe there."

"Leandro is dead. Why wouldn't we be safe?"

His gaze flits between the rear and side view mirrors. "Would the capo avenge his brother's death?"

"My father said he's a fair man. He said he would be a good leader."

My father shared so little with me. I know far more about the shipping business than I do about the inner workings of the Lupi Grigi.

"In all likelihood, he'll want to avenge his brother's death," Leo declares. "He'll need to make it known his family can't be touched. The question is, how will he go about doing it? Will they come after only me, or will they come after you, too?"

The weight of his question wraps around me, squeezing with the force of a vise. "Most of what I know about Massimo and the Lupi Grigi amounts to rumors." The tales aren't good, but surely they're exaggerated.

"Which is why we're staying at Nick's estate." It occurs to me that if he's right, if Massimo will choose revenge, he's in danger. "Massimo's coming after you?"

"You don't need to worry about me."

"How can you say that? If something happened to you because you agreed to this arrangement, all to help me—"

"Hush." He releases my hand and reaches across the seat to touch my thigh. "We'll get this settled. I'm not afraid of the mafia. They're a support service for the syndicate. They may not see it that way, but if Massimo doesn't back down, he'll get a masterclass in world order shoved up his ass." He turns off the expressway and his muscular hand squeezes me with a firm, resolute grip. "Recline your seat. Close your eyes. I'll wake you when we're there."

I do as he asks, reclining my seat to ensure I don't block his view. I shiver, and he cranks the heat. How did it come to this?

The car door opens, and I blink, taking in a dark shadow bending over me. A scream rips through my mouth.

"Shhh." It's Leo. "It's just me," he says in the deep timbre I hear in my dreams.

I press a palm over my hammering heart.

"We're here. Come on, baby. I was going to carry you in."

My eyesight adjusts to the dim light, and his familiar smile comes into focus. It's a slight smile, one that says he has indeed relaxed during the drive, allowing the Leo I love to return.

He helps me out of the car, and our feet grind the gravel leading to marble steps in front of an impressive English estate. An expansive lawn surrounds the house, and trees line the border of the lawn in the distance.

An oak door with aged hardware opens, and Nick stands in the threshold.

"Do you have bags?" Nick asks. He's dressed in flannel pajama bottoms and a silk robe.

"No. We came straight here," Leo answers.

"Take her up to your suite. I'll be in my office."

Leo takes my hand and leads me up a grand staircase to the second floor. Most of the lights are off, but enough light exists to cast a series of oil paintings, all equestrian hunting scenes, in a soft glow. A logical choice for art, I suppose, given this house is undoubtedly a country estate.

We arrive at the end of the hall, turn right down another similar hall, and then arrive at a door that he opens without knocking.

"This is where I always stay when I visit."

"Those two weeks you were away when we first married. Is this where you were?"

"For a few nights, when I wasn't in Abu Dhabi."

The canopy bed looks like it came from the set of the *Catherine the Great* movie. He flicks a light switch and one bedside lamp lights, casting a golden hue over half the room. Gold swirls adorn the wallpaper. A thick golden-brown carpet covers the floor, and the antique furniture is ornate with gold accents.

My fingers brush over the silky-smooth gold comforter. "Nick has a thing for gold, doesn't he?"

"I'm not sure who decorated his estate, but I've always imagined he hired someone and never walked through the estate to see what they did."

"So, his room isn't like this?"

"I haven't seen his bedroom. No plans to either." He pulls back the comforter and steps aside. "There are spare toothbrushes, toothpaste, soap, shampoo, anything you could need in the bathroom."

"Bring many people to stay here?"

He taps the tip of my nose and smirks. "Jealous?"

A little. "No."

He presses his lips to mine, tucks some hair behind my ear, caresses my cheek, and breathes in deeply. "You're the first woman I've invited into this room." He steps back, and I see it, the warmth in his eyes. He hasn't told me he loves me, and he may not, but there's no doubt he cares. "Treat this room like it's your own."

"Are there any spare clothes?" There very well could be. An ornate armoire dominates the opposite wall, and there are doors in the hallway that lead toward the bathroom.

"You're welcome to anything of mine in the closet. Are you feeling okay?"

My face is sore, my eye throbs, but given John died… "I'm fine."

"I'll be back as soon as I can. And tomorrow we'll take care of getting you everything you need."

"Leo?" I call to his retreating back.

He turns, giving me his undivided attention. "I'm glad you haven't brought anyone else here."

His expression is hard to read, but solemn feels like the best description, and my heart sinks. "We can't forget our situation."

"But I'm yours." Can't he see that? For me, it's no longer an arrangement. I only want to be with him.

"You're not my possession, Willow."

"But I am." Can't he see it? Doesn't he feel it?

"I can't keep you." His lips contort into a sad smile, and he leaves the room.

CHAPTER 26

SAM, AKA LEO, AKA SAINT

Five years, I've pulled this off. Five years of celibacy, five years of refusing to risk a person getting close, and I go and help a young woman and fall. I fell the moment she came to me in the shower. Maybe sooner. Those bright-blue eyes—strong, intelligent, and kind, but also in need of protection. She pulled strings I'd tamped down. Reminded me what it is to be close to someone, to be real with someone. The attempted abduction eviscerated any doubt.

She said she loves me. I pretended not to hear–a shit solution. She's fallen too. Which means when I leave, and the day will come when I leave because I have a family to return to, she'll hurt. She'll mourn me, and I'll watch from afar. Only, whereas I knew one day I'd come home to my sisters, I'll never come back for her.

I ache, knowing what's coming. Knowing what she's going

to go through. This operation is so fucked up and has been since takeoff. The plan had been for me to be missing in action for a couple of months, long enough that if I were caught, no one would connect me to my real identity. No one would take vengeance on my family, a real risk considering the organizations and governments I'd be deceiving.

But the months turned into years. I left my sisters so many clues that this was happening, hoping they'd piece it together. I'd thought I'd get one more time with them so I could lay it out for them. They didn't have clearance, but I was going to break policy, to shield them from the pain. Trust in their acting skills. And then it all happened so fast.

Light spills out of Nick's office. He's in his office chair, a bottle of scotch on his desk, and two highball glasses holding healthy pours.

"You're going to want a drink," he says, gesturing to the liquor.

"After the day I've had, I want the bottle," I say, sinking into one of the leather chairs. There's a fire going, and the room has the smell of a campfire from my youth.

"Sir, do you require anything?" The woman at the door speaks like you'd expect her to be in uniform, but she's in a casual dress with slippers.

"No, we're good, Freya." He lifts his glass and pauses, "Unless… Do you need food?"

"No," I say, shaking my head. I'm too numb and exhausted to want food. "This scotch should knock me out."

"You can retire, Freya. Thank you."

The tall, middle-aged woman nods, her gaze set on Nick. I glance between the two of them. Nick doesn't keep a full staff, but here this woman is, presumably living on the premises.

Freya steps into the hall, and Nick calls, "Please close the door."

"Who all is here?" I ask after the door clicks closed.

"Lina."

"Oh?"

"Tell Willow under no circumstances is she to cave to any of Lina's ideas."

"What's Lina up to?"

"She's itching to leave the estate."

"You won't let her?"

"There's no temptation on the estate," he says as he picks up an iPad and flicks it to life.

"You can't exactly withhold all temptation." While he fusses with the device, I add, "We gain the strength of the temptation we resist."

"Is that biblical?"

"Ralph Waldo Emerson."

"Where did you say you went to school?"

"Not Oxford," I say, shooting him an amused grin.

Nick has the most prestigious academic record of anyone I've worked with. He's a mostly good man who skirts the law and is intelligent enough to never get caught.

"Massimo De Luca called me earlier."

"Apologizing or declaring war?"

"Eh, middle ground. He feigned ignorance of Leandro's plans but said it was our fault."

"Because I married someone he wanted?"

"Apparently, Willow's father promised Willow to Leandro."

"I don't believe that's true." Alessio likely would've caved with pressure, but I don't believe he had already done it when he blessed our union.

"Truth doesn't matter. What I'm telling you is what Massimo believes." Nick pointedly looks at me, and I get what he's not saying. It's a point he's made repeatedly. Truth is immaterial. The only thing that matters is what one believes.

Truth was a twentieth-century inconvenience, and it's a twenty-first-century myth.

"He suspects the syndicate is behind the heroin bust that landed his capo in prison but doesn't have proof."

I'd been aware of Nick's scheme. Kept Interpol abreast. But they observed and didn't get involved. "Who knew?"

"I'm working through that. Massimo may have been probing. Trying to figure out if Leandro was playing him to justify coming after Willow. It might've been conjecture on Leandro's part. Guy wasn't stable. Had a history of being delusional."

"Perhaps some of the law enforcement groups that normally would've been paid off to re-direct a bust suspected something? Shared their suspicions with Leandro?"

"Perhaps."

"Where'd you leave it with him?"

"I agreed to send his brother's body back to him so he can have a proper funeral."

"And in exchange?"

"Officially, we let bygones be bygones. Willow stays with you."

"Her father?"

He waves a hand. "I don't think he was ever going to do anything to Alessio. He's too wealthy. Wields too much power. And some portion of that pea-brain recognizes that his brother was demented and a woman forty years younger wasn't a suitable bride."

"So, it's over?"

Nick's brow furrows, and he pushes the iPad across the table. "Not at all. The Grigi are slow learners. They need another kneecapping."

On the screen, there's a list of weapons.

I flip to the next page. Another list.

To the next page. Another list.

"What's this?"

"Cargo on three Titan ships. Two other ships are carrying sanctioned oil. We're going to bust one of these ships."

"Are the weapons going in or out of Russia?"

"Saudis and Chinese are fortifying Russia. I'm thinking if we do this right, we'll piss the Russians off, and if we can lay blame at Massimo's feet, make him look incompetent, they'll take him out."

"Won't that just make Gagliano look incompetent?"

"Massimo orchestrated the sale. Putin will blame the man who took his money."

"You don't want to go the legal route?"

"Would get too suspicious. Plus, the paper trail at this stage is too complicated for the international courts."

"So, your goal is to have the Russians eliminate Massimo in the hopes he's replaced by a more capable leader?"

"Tensions are high. Putin's patience is thin. If the Russian cartel steps in to eliminate Massimo, the world will assume Putin taught a lesson. Any of those ships represents a tidy sum. But you're the arms expert. Which one is going to piss Putin off the most when it doesn't come to Papa?"

I flick between the pages. "Any of these ships could blow away a small country." I glance up. "Chemical warfare? Is this real?"

The door opens, and Lina steps in wearing a silky floor length nightgown. "Is it true?"

"Lina, when the door's closed, knock."

"Oh, my god. Like I care if the two of you get blitzed. Freya said we have guests. Plural. Is Willow here?"

"She's sleeping," I answer.

Lina claps her hands. "Finally. Guests. I've been bored out of my mind." She drops into the seat across from me.

Nick pushes up and grabs his sister by the arm. "Out you go."

"Piss off."

"Lina, you are trying my patience."

"I am always trying your bloody patience."

"Precisely my point." He hovers over her.

"Did you know we lost Internet. Again?"

"We didn't lose Internet, Lina."

"Yes, we did. I was in the middle of streaming a movie, and tits up."

"Fuck, Lina," he grumbles. "I'm going to go fix her goddamn television. Look over that list, and let's discuss when I'm back."

"What list?" Lina asks as Nick shoves her out of the room.

"Contrary to what you believe, Leo and I work. It's a new concept. One you should contemplate."

The door clicks closed. I listen to the steps moving farther away and scan the room. Nick's office is a camera-free zone, unless he's lied to me over the years. No time like the present to discover the truth.

I whip out my mobile. It's not a burner, but I'll switch out the card. I snap photos of each list.

Nick wants to take out one of these ships. But we need to take them all out.

CHAPTER 27

WILLOW

The morning light peeks around the sides of the drapes, lighting an otherwise dark, damp room. I shift, moving the comforter over my shoulder, and let a leg wander closer to Leo.

He's asleep on his stomach, with one arm cast in my direction. He woke me a couple of times, tossing and turning.

Last night he came to bed late, and I can only presume it has to do with what happened with Leandro. I asked him if all was okay, and he said yes and for me to go to sleep. I snuggled into him, but he didn't try anything. Last night marked the first time we slept together and didn't have sex.

I'm not sure what I've brought him into. I thought the marriage would end all risks, but—yet again—it appears I've been naive. Ultimately, my father gave my hand to Leo. What Leandro did, arriving at our flat intending to take me, was psychotic. Going after Lina so he could assess where Leo and I were living, absolutely obsessive. But now, where does it end?

Is the syndicate now at war with the Lupi Grigi? He said we're safest here, at Nick's estate. Does he worry his flat in London, forty-one floors in the sky, isn't safe enough when we're being hunted? Is Massimo after us? Or just me? I could turn myself in. Leandro is dead. If I turn myself in, would Massimo be appeased? Would he leave Leo alone? Is he taking his anger out on my family?

The dim light smooths over the lines around Leo's eyes, shaving years. His strands are in disarray, with some portions flattened straight, others sticking out in awkward directions. The peaceful slumber contrasts with the uneasy night. His long lashes flutter and his lips curl into a smile.

"Morning, beautiful."

My fingers smooth over his shoulder, and I wiggle closer.

"Were you watching me sleep?"

"I didn't want to wake you." The answer is evasive, but it's not a lie.

He softly touches the skin below my eye, the one that took an elbow when I fought Leandro's men. It's a little sore to the touch, and I imagine the bruise darkened overnight. Thin scabs formed over the torn areas of my wrists.

He pushes onto his side, releases a groan, and rubs a hand briskly over his face.

"Something's wrong. What's going on? What's happening?" Last night, he said everything was okay, but he was protecting me, the same way Father would.

"Everything's fine." He rubs sleep from his eyes then caresses my cheek. "How'd you sleep?"

"Fine." I look straight at him, needing to see the truth. "Did we start a war?"

He blinks and then squeezes the bridge of his nose. He slings his legs over the side, away from me. A chilly draft sweeps beneath the comforter.

"Massimo won't send anyone here."

"What is he saying? How did he react to the news?"

"Of his brother being a lunatic? The way one would expect." I swallow down his non-answer. "I've got to go away for several days. You're going to stay here. You'll probably spend quite a bit of time with Lina. But I need you to remember something for me… She doesn't know shit. You can't fill her in, you got me?"

"Why doesn't she know?" In the Lupi Grigi, we're taught at an early age the importance of family. From what I understand, that's essential in organizations like ours. Many were surprised I didn't learn about the family business until I was sixteen. Why wouldn't Lina know what her brother does? For that matter, how is it she's not married? Is the syndicate run differently?

"Don't have an answer for you, love. It's not my business. But it's what Nick wants, so that's what he'll get." With a sad expression, he traces my bottom lip with his finger. "I've got to shower. Pack."

"We didn't pack any clothes."

"I have spares in the closet. Lina has some clothes you can wear during your stay. Or you can shop online. There's an address Lina uses in town, and one of the guards will pick up packages."

"And Lina doesn't get suspicious?"

"Her head's in the clouds."

She doesn't want to know the truth. He walks naked into the

bathroom, and the globes of his well-formed buttocks gleam as his muscles flex with each step.

His phone lights up as the sound of a shower filters into the room. I get out of bed and open the drape, revealing a cloudy morning with no direct view of the sun. The phone vibrates again.

He's going away again. For days. Is Lina the only one who doesn't want to know the truth? Is he going to attack Massimo? Or is the Lupi Grigi nothing to worry about, and he's simply leaving me here to go visit another woman he has on the side? Scarlet says all the men do that.

I pick up his mobile. It's not like the burners he routinely tosses in the rubbish. When I brush my thumb over it, it asks for a code.

With the mobile in hand, I stick my head into the bathroom. Steam envelops the ceiling, and moisture coats the painted wall. Either the bathroom doesn't have a fan, or he didn't turn it on.

"Leo, someone's trying to reach you. Two texts have come through."

The shower is in a clawfoot tub, and there's a plastic hanging curtain. His head peeks from behind the curtain. White suds cover his head, and there's a razor in one hand. I step up closer and spot a mirror hanging on tile near the front of the tub.

"I'd get you in here if there was more room."

"Be careful shaving. If you slip, you'll cut yourself."

"No shit." I hold the mobile up to him and the device unlocks with facial recognition. He frowns as he reads. "It's nothing. I'll be out in a few."

"I'm going to turn the fan on," I say when I spot the switch.

"There's a fan?"

I roll my eyes as I exit the bathroom, leaving the door ajar to allow some steam to escape.

And then I glance at the mobile in my hand.

The texts are from a number with no name applied.

Package en route.

Crystal

I flick to read more, but there are no messages. The history has been deleted. It's probably a precaution. My brother called Leo the arms dealer. While that sounds more legitimate than drugs, it's my understanding the trade isn't always legal.

His email is also empty. Who doesn't have any email history? How is that even possible? Nothing filed.

I switch over to the camera. I've never seen him snap a photo, but wouldn't it be lovely if he secretly loves landscapes or architecture?

No such luck. He has all of a dozen photographs in his collection. I must have seventy-five thousand uploaded. Yes, the two of us have differences. I zoom closer to see what ranked as important enough for Leo to snap a photo. Documents. How bizarre. I zoom in. It's a weapons list. Contracts. Bills of lading. Manifests for five of my father's ships. I recognize the ships' names. What's he doing with these? And where did he get them? From my father?

The shower stops, and I close out of photos and set the mobile on the bedside table. While my discovery is better than finding plans to meet a mistress, a pit forms in my stomach. I never knew what Leo got out of our arrangement, but this discovery leads me to suspect he did, in fact, get something out of marrying into the Titan Shipping business. But why not tell me? What is he doing?

CHAPTER 28

SAM, AKA LEO, AKA SAINT

Mixing in with the parishioners, trench coat pulled tight, head bowed, nose appendage and glued mustache itching, I enter the church. Unlike the others, once inside, I veer right and head down the familiar hall through quiet passageways.

Interpol rents out the conference portion of St. Martin's on meeting days, but my gut roils. Something's not right. I pause outside the conference room door, listening. Organ music drifts, the faint chords chiding those who do not attend the service. There are no footsteps, no voices.

When I open the door, Nomad sits at the table on the far side facing the door, forearms resting on the table, hands where they can be seen, a glass of water before him, and a cell phone. The standard fare has been laid out on the side table. Water, wine, bread, biscuits.

"Good morning," he says.

I clear the space behind the door out of habit and shut it, clicking the lock.

"No one else is here," he says, relaxed as ever.

I exhale, hoping to slough off the foreboding sense gnawing at me.

"You got the documents?" I remove my trench coat and lay it over the back of a nearby chair, then pull out a seat, sit, and remove my hat.

"Work is underway to stop the ships."

"All of them?"

"We can't let those ships reach their destinations." He taps one finger on the table. "You agree, right?"

"That's why I sent it over. Destroyed the mobile card."

"You're concerned?"

"Short list of people with access to Falcon's iPad."

Falcon is the name Nomad and I apply to Nick in conversation. It's a precaution to minimize the chance someone stumbling on a recording could piece together our discussion.

"Might be just me and Falcon." If he shared documents, the list of suspects would be wider. But I was in his office. The rim of his device is shown in the photos.

"We translated the data. Nothing will trace to you."

"Good," I say, but it's bullshit. The bust will trace to me simply because I am one of the few with access. I rap my knuckles against the table as a topic transition. I have a flight out of Heathrow and little time. "Tensions between the syndicate and Lupi Grigi are a live wire. Ironically, it mostly has to do with my arrangement."

"Your illegal nuptials?"

"It's a clusterfuck. Falcon plans on taking out the *Irina*. So leave that one alone."

"If Falcon takes them out, I doubt the paper trail will lead to a prison sentence."

"Correct." The former capo who pissed off Nick will never get out of prison alive. "But that's not the goal this time around."

Nomad raises one smooth eyebrow, asking for an explanation.

"He's hoping the Russians get pissed at their incompetence. Wants to weaken the wolves. Replace the head of the pack. He doesn't take kindly to them drugging his sister. He's cutting them where it hurts the most. Speaking their language."

"Might they pull out?" He's asking if the Lupi Grigi, the gray wolves, will break ties with the syndicate.

"And be at odds with every other family? Put themselves in unhindered competition against every single South American cartel?" He blinks comprehension. "But it'll likely get nasty. If you get wind they're looking to buy from another source, I'd appreciate the heads up."

"Are you being targeted?"

"Possibly." A memory of Willow being held at gunpoint hits with the force of an adrenaline injection, and my fingers curl into a fist.

"You think it's time to eject? Might look mafia-related. It's been, what...three years?"

"Five." I grit the answer out, annoyed my half-cocked so-called handler can't keep up.

My gaze roams the flat white ceiling. This addition to St. Martin-in-the-Fields has little character. We could be sitting in a conference room with a glass window overlooking an interior courtyard in any building in America.

"You're going to bust all five ships. Well, four, minus the

Irina?" My request for confirmation is born partially out of a need to know the plan, but also because I've been on too many ops where they sat on the intel.

"*Algeciras* was pulled by the Japanese last night. Hasn't hit the news yet."

"That's fast."

"Exited international waters first."

Normally, matters like this are handled more delicately. We've tracked shipments via satellite and let land forces take over. We've even let shipments change hands successfully and busted storage locations a month after delivery. And sometimes, if the exchange met G8 purposes, we let them be.

"What's going on?"

"China's on the move."

"Edging toward a world war." It's a statement. It's the fear that led me to sacrifice everything five years ago. The CIA determined the syndicate pulled strings across eight sectors and every developed nation. And I had the opportunity to join them. I consider recent meetings and communications. "Work hasn't ticked up. There's nothing to indicate—"

"You didn't negotiate these." He points to his phone and the packing list I sent him.

He's right. That product is being moved by Lupi Grigi ships, and yet the syndicate had no purchasing role. At least, I didn't.

"You've had a proper good time. If you want to teach the masterclass, you've got to know when to call it."

"Know when to fold 'em?" I ask, correcting the Swiss Brit.

"Keen on poker?" he asks, clearly not getting me.

"Kenny Rogers." I scratch my head, digging into the areas where the hat band holds firmly. "Kenny Rogers is as American as apple pie."

"Is that right? I'm not sure I'd recognize the chap."

"Well, he's not The Beatles." I stretch out my arm, checking the time. Is it time to call it? If I jump ship now, what will happen to Willow?

Chances are Massimo and Nick will sort their shit. But it's risky. If Massimo's knocked out, it could get bloody fast. And if I split now, Massimo might demand Willow back. Especially if my extraction leaves any doubts. If they harbor any suspicions I'm a narc, Willow would be tortured to death by whichever fucker got her first.

"I can get plans rolling," Nomad says.

"I thought you always have plans in place." I narrow my eyes.

Jack once said they have a dozen plans, but of course, that statement rings of CIA bullshit, unless one counts self-reliant techniques like swimming across the Atlantic.

"All plans were actionable for the first year. Like fine wine, they've aged. Won't hurt to dust them off, right?"

"Dust away." I consider those ships. It doesn't feel like this is just Russia's war of aggression. And there's Willow. "I'll stay in place. Let's review the plans next time."

"When do you think that'll be?"

"A month, maybe? I'm in the desert for the next week." I'll need a new flat now that Massimo possesses my London address. "Might stay with the Falcon for a bit." It's harder to get away when I'm staying with Nick.

"I'll plan accordingly." He lifts a folder from a black leather attaché case. I open it.

The first photograph is of Sloane, my younger sister, and for much of my childhood, my best friend. She's holding a vanilla ice cream cone and smiling, genuinely happy. The guy walking beside her is a fellow SEAL, Max Hawkins. He's her husband

and, I suspect, the reason Arrow has been able to capture happy moments. For years, I'd get photos of her entering or exiting buildings with a muted expression.

Sloane and Sage both found good men, and if the photos tell the truth, they have good marriages. I missed their weddings. I've missed everything. Like always, the thought has me shoving down anything clogging my thought processes. Missing family events is part of the job.

The second photograph is of Sage and Knox in a parking lot. There's nothing little about my littlest sister anymore. Knox's hand falls protectively to her back, and her stomach is swollen with pregnancy.

"When is she due?" I flip the photo for him to see.

"Mid-November. Can't recall the exact date."

The next photo is of Sage in a carpool line at school, waving at a student, then one of Sloane and Sage at what appears to be the sidelines of a marathon, probably cheering on their husbands. I flip through a half-dozen photos, checking for smiles, and close the folder, breathing deeply. Sentimentality is not my friend.

Six Days Later

It's nearly midnight when the gate lifts and the gravel crunches over the winding road that leads to Nick's mansion, or as he likes to call it, his country house. I stop the car in front, before the massive fountain. There's a separate parking garage in the rear, but this late, I'll leave my car out front and deal with it in the morning.

It's been a long few days of product testing, negotiating prices, and wining and dining. The meetings in Saudi Arabia had been scheduled six months earlier, and after the Leandro incident, it was tempting to bail, but with tensions high between the syndicate and part of the Italian mafia, and a sense that an unknown player is in the mix, rescheduling didn't feel like an option. It helped that Willow was at Nick's estate. No one would dare to come after her here. If they tried, they wouldn't succeed.

Over the last week, I couldn't shake her from my thoughts. During the day, I'd watch a bazooka explode in the sand, and I'd wonder what she would think if she saw it. Someone would introduce their wife, and I'd compare the wife to Willow. After dinner, escorts mingled, and I wished for Willow. She's the only woman I want. I'm not an idiot. I know she's gotten under my skin. But there's no winning here. The day will come when I leave, and I'll leave her in this world.

One night I dreamed we were in Asheville. I think we might've been in the front yard of Knox and Sage's home, a place I've only seen in photographs, but I have a good idea of what's around it, because I visited Sage in the original house, before it burnt down. The dream was disjointed, and people appeared and disappeared.

When I woke, I had to go for a run to shake the sensations rattling through me. She could never come to Asheville as Willow Gagliano. To do so would open my sisters, my family, to revenge attacks. And I've put them through too much with my staged death to turn around and put them at risk now. On the flip side, if Willow assumed a new identity, she'd leave her family behind, never to see them again. And I've lived that scenario, and it's one I could never put her through.

The front door clicks, and my pulse picks up a notch. Nick steps out, and there's no denying the disappointment. I hoped for Willow. Ridiculous of me. Soon enough, I'll be dead to her.

I haul the suitcase out of the trunk and slam it down. But where is Willow? Why didn't she greet me?

"Miss me, did you?" I call, making light of Nick greeting me at midnight, as he'd expect no less.

"How else would you enter? Blast your way through the door?" There's a gravity to his tone that I recognize. He's pissed. But why?

I step past him, into the foyer. One lamp lights a corner, and the house is silent.

"Lonely without me?" I ask, maintaining the light facade.

"It's been something." His dress shoe clicks against the floor. "Leave your bag. Follow me to the office."

I do as he says, following like a lapdog, but listening intently for sounds.

"Where's Willow?"

"Gone a week, and you didn't text your wife?"

It's true, I didn't. Electronic devices are a necessary evil. I only use them when there's no other option.

"Told you. It's an arrangement."

He stops at his office door and stands in front of a glass panel. The door unlocks.

"That's new," I say.

"Overdue," he says.

"How are things with the Lupi Grigi?"

"According to sources, the funeral for Leandro De Luca is this weekend."

"Massimo hasn't been in touch?"

"Not a peep."

When I step into the office, he closes the door, and the click that follows sounds an awful lot like a deadbolt.

"Where's Willow?"

He sinks into his desk chair, and his eyes narrow. "She's sleeping off the afternoon's festivities."

My stomach muscles clench. When he gestures to the chair across from his desk, I can only look at it. "What do you mean?"

It takes every bit of control to remain calm as my blood pressure skyrockets.

"Chill. Your arrangement is fine."

His emphasis on the word arrangement has me wanting to shove my fist into his face.

"Lina and Willow got high this afternoon." Holy fuck. My hand's on the doorknob when he calls, "They're fine."

An intense desire to strangle the fucktard lights from within, and he chuckles.

"Pot. Ganja. I told you. I'm not keen on Lina doing the other shit."

"You recognize Lina has a drug problem." It's like I'm talking to a toddler. "No one recommends an addict do drugs. Of any sort."

"It's a compromise."

"Dumb as fuck compromise."

He snorts. "That's what I like about you, Leo." He points at me. "You've always been willing to play it straight with me. I took it as a sign of your character. But now I'm not so sure."

"What're you talking about?"

"Sit." He points at the leather chair across from his desk. I never twisted the knob when I reached the door, but I'm fairly certain my only option is to do what he says. The question is… what does he know?

"The Marina Militare boarded the *Mina*."

"That was your plan, right?"

"Three ships within Gagliano's shadow fleet have been detained."

"You didn't do it?"

"No, Leo Sullivan, I did not." He steeples his hands and glares.

It's a pointed, angry expression, albeit controlled. Nick is a master at controlling his temper.

"What're you implying?" I'm careful with my reaction, keeping my hands still and my eyes trained on Nick.

"We have a mole."

"I've been in Saudi Arabia all week."

"That is true."

Nick checked up on me. What the hell did Nomad do with that list? Has Nick figured me out? Did he do something to Willow?

Nick's gaze drops to the desk and his tap-tap-tapping index finger. I've seen him do this before. But intimidation tactics won't work on me. Neither will torture.

"Saint."

For a brief second, that one word stops my heart. Survival skills kick in, and my muscles tense, ready to react. If needed, I'll kill him. At this angle, both his hands are in view. If that changes, I attack.

"Have you heard that name?" he asks after minutes elapse. He's baiting.

"No."

His aristocratic brow furrows.

"Not as relates to an individual outside a religious institution," I clarify.

"Are you religious?"

"No," I answer but regret it instantly as he may have picked me out on London surveillance entering St. Martin's, even though I always disguise my features in order to trick facial recognition on CCTV.

"Yet your vices are few." That finger continues tapping. "No drugs. Little to no alcohol. Might as well say no alcohol. No sex. At least, until an arrangement blessed by God occurred. I have it on good authority sex is now a part of the deal."

"What did Willow say?" So help me, if he hurt her…

"Oh, five stars. Highly recommend."

"What?" I'm halfway out of my seat. If he fucking—

"She recommends you." His gaze flicks up to mine. "In the sack, you score well." Humor crinkles the skin around his eyes.

I relax back into the seat. "Lina."

"Girls talk." He shifts and steeples his hands, elbows on the desk. "And you've no idea about a Saint? Because it's my understanding code names are derived from behavior."

"Wouldn't know about that."

"Right. Because you've never been in the military?"

"Nope."

"It's my understanding a code name can come from one night, one moment in time, or an overarching behavior the group picks up on." He raises an eyebrow with expectation.

"Sounds about right to me." Our gazes lock. "I wouldn't know."

"Neither would I."

I've never questioned Nick's background. He's an Oxford boy. Well-educated.

"Have I ever told you MI6 recruited me?" he asks.

"No." If I've been monitoring a British asset for the last five years, I'll strangle Jack Sullivan. I breathe that flash of anger away and ask, "You turned them down?"

"Something like that."

"Ever regret it?" I have no idea if I've landed in safe waters or if he's still baiting.

"No." He pushes up and stares out the window into pitch black. Although, perhaps from where he's standing, he can see the stars. "I'm more effective at maintaining world order in my current position."

"World order?" Narcissistic much?

"Financial stability," he explains. "There was a time in our human evolution where sex made the world go round. Hence the reason marriages served as currency. Those times have changed. Sex is readily available. In modern times, gold churns the earth."

Given I'm in an arrangement with someone who was bartered by her father, I'm not sure I completely agree with him. But the essence of his philosophy rings true.

"How did you end up at the syndicate?"

"Luck." He slowly turns. "I'm a lucky man."

He may harbor suspicions, but he has no evidence.

His references to Willow don't sit well with me. I need to know she's safe. I push up from my chair and flatten my hand across my midsection, smoothing my shirt.

"Was there anything else?"

"No."

"Then I'm going to go check on my wife. Take stock of the damage from an afternoon spent with Lina."

He gives the slightest of nods, but it's enough to take as

permission. My fingers touch the cool metal knob, as he says, "Saint."

I twist the knob and cock my head to better hear him. "What was that?"

"Keep an ear out for that name."

"Will do. You have my word."

CHAPTER 29

WILLOW

The door creaks, and I peer into the darkness.

"Leo?"

"Hey," he breathes. The door clicks closed. "Heard you had quite the day." The mattress sinks with his weight. He caresses my cheek. "Still stoned?"

"Oh, my god, it was not like that."

"No?" He grins. "How was it?"

"Lina smoked a joint. She passed it to me like twice."

"Like?"

"I did not get stoned."

His fingers systematically unbutton his shirt. It's dark in the room, making his eyes the color of midnight.

"Was Nick pissed?" he asks.

"At Lina?" He shrugs out of his shirt and rises, headed into the bathroom. "No. Maybe. Lina couldn't stop laughing. Nick didn't say much. They went off to the kitchen together, and I came back to our room."

"You didn't eat with them?"

"Nick gave me a mobile he said I could use to check in with my family. And Scarlet."

He pauses, both hands resting on the bathroom counter. "How are they?"

The sink water flows, and he splashes water on his face.

"Good. My mother says they're good."

"Did you speak to your father?"

"He's away on business."

"Still?"

"Should I be concerned?"

He puts a toothbrush in his mouth. I push off the bed and come to stand in the doorway of the bathroom. He's barefoot. He must've shed his socks when he removed his shoes. His skin along his back is smooth, although the bathroom light reflects on a thin white scar along his side, and a raised, jagged scar on his shoulder.

I come up behind him and press my lips to his shoulder and wrap my arms around his waist. He finishes brushing his teeth, and I ask, "How was your trip?"

He turns in my arms. "Hell."

I push back, wondering what could've happened. Is there more bad news?

"You weren't there."

When I look into the depths of those warm brown eyes, all I see is sincerity, and I melt.

"I couldn't stop thinking about you. I ached for you."

His fingers brush my hair away from my face.

"But you never called." I missed him too. His not calling left a shitty feeling.

His shoulders rise and fall. "Had a job to do. But I've never been so… It's like…" His eyes close and his lips press together in a firm line. "You're always right there. I close my eyes, and I see you. I'm with you always, even when I'm away. Don't ever doubt it."

His lips fall to mine. The kiss is slow. Tender. Loving.

Might I hope this kiss promises a future?

He walks me backward until the backs of my thighs hit the mattress. He left the bathroom light on, and a golden glow crosses the mattress.

He moves slowly and with intention. Each touch lights within, inciting a burning need.

He lifts my nightgown and lets it fall to the floor. A buzz goes through my body, a low hum that has my lower belly clenching. He sets me back on the bed, over the comforter, and I feel his gaze, covetous and hot, as he undoes his belt and his clothes fall to the floor.

When he climbs over me, his lips and fingers explore, worshipping every inch of my skin, his tongue yielding teases and pleasure. A brief, suckling kiss on my exposed nipples makes my entire body twitch. His movements are slow, as if we have forever, as if dawn won't break, and we have this night for eternity.

The hard heavy weight of his cock against my hip, and my thigh, assures me he needs me, he desires me, and as his tongue and fingers slay me, he has every intention of bringing us together. An incendiary need rachets up within me and I tremble, coming undone.

Those dark eyes watch, taking me in with an intensity that reaches my marrow.

"You're so beautiful." His soft words are full of adulation.

He rises over me and I reach for him. My fingers tangle in his short silky strands. His arm muscles flex and veins protrude from the strain of holding himself high. I tug him down, wanting his mouth on mine. My thighs spread, welcoming him, needing him. I'm a heartbeat away from pleading.

When he sinks into me, my hold on his back tightens. His movements are slow and reverent. The pressure on my core as he stretches me, fills me, and rocks against me, re-awakens my sensitized self, and all too soon, I once again come apart. He cups my cheek, holding me in place, dark eyes boring into me as he too falls. As he pulses deep within me, I strain to hold him as tightly as possible. His head falls to the crook of my neck and I press my lips repeatedly along the side of his face and over his crown. There's no other word for it, no other description, than making love. We've had each other in so many ways, against the shower wall, on a floor, an exploration of sinful positions, but missionary has never felt more perfect or right.

CHAPTER 30

LEO, AKA SAINT, AKA SAM

The sun has yet to rise, but my skin crawls as if it's the morning of a mission. Willow sleeps naked, cuddled into my side. I should enjoy the moment, but I can't. Energy courses through my veins with the fury of springtime rapids.

Saint. He didn't stumble upon my code name. He heard it. But from whom? Where?

I slip out of bed, careful not to wake my slumbering bride.

Exercise. I need a good run to clear my thoughts and work through my fears.

Dressed, I pause to take in her sleeping form. She'll need a new home. One that's not so high in the sky but is secure. Is there time to train her? Fuck. I should've been working with her since day one. But how would she have received that? Yes, you married me, and now I'm going to teach you self-defense and leave you.

I'm so lost in self-flagellation on my way through the house I almost miss the creak.

In the shadow, I slow.

Listen.

"Anyone there?"

Nick's staff might get an early start.

"You've a good ear."

"Nick." Where is he?

"Appears neither of us could sleep."

My vision adjusts, and I make out Nick in the foyer, deep in the shadows. The only light source is the fading moon. Like me, he's dressed for a run.

"Time change." A logical lie.

"It's a bugger."

He stretches an arm out, gesturing to the door. "Shall we?"

"Going to join me?"

"Is that a problem?"

"Not at all. If you can keep up."

He doesn't smile. No, he glowers. Something's up.

We step out the door. Dampness blankets the chilly air. Somewhere, past the tree line, the sun teases with glimpses of gold. I don't need to see the light to know she's there with her promise of a new day.

"You lead," Nick says.

I take off to the path that winds through the woods.

If he's planning to shoot me, he wouldn't ask me to run.

Nick's a good shot, but it takes training to run and shoot.

Whatever this is…it's mind games. That's what it is. He suspects me. No doubt.

Dew coats my running shoes, dampening my socks and my legs up to my calves.

I push forward. He wants mind games, we'll play.

Adrenaline pumps. My body awakens. Senses heighten.

The cool air stings my eyes.

My fingers burn.

Sweat drips from my brow.

Willow. A vision of her in bed flashes.

Secure. Safe.

Her arms around me, her giving body.

Eyelids fluttering closed.

There's nothing like watching her orgasm.

God, she's gorgeous.

The narrow trail in the grass breaks open before the woods.

I'm a fool to be out here.

I should be in bed with Willow.

The trail head opens near an old pine.

A weight crashes into me, slamming me into rough bark.

I push back.

Nick's arm presses me into the tree.

My left hook misses, grazing his ribs.

A sliver of light reflects.

A sharp pain sears my neck.

I still.

"What the fuck?" I growl.

Be tough. Don't act guilty.

"Who are you working for?"

He knows. Come clean or deny?

"Did you bring me out here to kill me?"

The blade presses harder against my throat. But he's not pressing the edge into me. He's fishing.

"Didn't have a plan. But here we are."

"What the fuck is going on?" One last grasp for innocence.

"Drop the act."

I force my muscles to relax. Bark digs into my spine.

A haze of blue lightens the horizon.

The scent of damp earth fills my nostrils. Damp earth and sweat.

"I trusted you." It's an accusation.

"I haven't done anything–" The knife's edge cuts into my skin.

"No lies."

I meet Nick's gaze head on and speak the truth. "I am your friend."

"Is it about money?"

That's what he would expect. I pointedly glare. "No."

"How'd they get to you?"

"I want the same thing you do."

"Yeah?" The blade flattens against my neck once again. "What's that?"

"Stability."

"Who are you working for?"

"You." The sharp blade deepens the slice. Warmth trickles down my neck.

If I don't take control, he'll kill me. And what will he do to Willow?

I grab his wrist, shove, and trip him with my leg.

The move catches him off guard.

He stumbles.

Free of his hold, I circle him, arms wide, on my toes, on the ready.

He wants a fight. Let's fight.

He grins. It's an evil grin. My blood mars his knife.

"What are you?" he asks, watching me while he cleans the

blade on the bark.

The action does a piss poor job of clearing my blood.

"Come on. It's out in the open now. You work for me. Who else?"

Fuck. This is it.

"Others who also want stability."

"You sure about that?"

"Nick, I am your friend. I'd die protecting you." Speak the truth when possible.

He leans against the tree. "Funny thing. I believe you."

I've no idea if that's sarcasm or honesty.

"Who?" he asks.

"Can't say."

"Out here you can." He gestures to the forest. "Only me and the gods to hear you."

"What about Willow?"

He narrows his eyes. Twirls the knife like a baton. "That's what you're worried about, eh? Your arrangement?"

Depending on his answer, I might need to kill him. If that's the case, I'll need to do it out here. Away from his security. We'll need to leave before anyone misses him.

"Tell you what. Friend." He snarls that last word. This won't go well. "How about I promise your lady love's safety?"

How could I trust you? It's on the tip of my tongue, but if I pursue that angle, we're at a stalemate.

"You trusted me with Lina. I'll trust you with Willow." An eye for an eye. It's a language he comprehends.

He chuckles. "An arrangement, my ass."

My fingers stretch. On the ready.

He raises the knife.

I hold my hands up in a defensive posture. "I don't want to fight you. Work with us. The goals are the same. In essence."

"Go on."

"It's an unofficial group." It's the truth. "Doesn't appear on paper."

"One of those CIA jobs, eh? Designed to fly outside of Intelligence Committee awareness?"

No need to confirm or deny.

"Bloody Americans." He spits and kicks at the spot on the ground. "Goal?"

"Intel." That's obvious. "But, Nick, the sands are shifting. There're cracks in the alliance. Activities aren't adding up. Those ships. That's strengthening Russia. That's not what you want either."

Putin killed his parents. Nick skirts international law, but we share enemies.

"There's no leaving the alliance. You know that."

"Wouldn't want you to leave. Work with us."

"What would I get?"

"A partner." He scowls. "When you want them," I add.

That's what every asset is– an opportune partner. Information is shared when it's mutually beneficial.

He scratches his ear. "I'm thinking that's a no," he says, pointing the end of his blade in my direction. "You can't expect I'll keep a traitor around."

Fuck. I don't want to kill Nick.

"How'd you find out?" Who else knows?

"Let's say it's best you go dark."

Light breaks through the mist across the field.

My knees bend slightly, preparing.

"Get out of here."

I straighten, breath held. What did he say?

"Go. I'm gonna finish my run. When I'm back, be on your way. Understood?"

"Nick?"

He sheaths his knife. And waits. Solemn and astute.

"Thanks for being my best man. You were the best I could've asked for in this world."

He answers with a jerk of his head and silently mouths the phrase *in this world*.

"I'm going to leave a number. You ever need anything. If things spiral with the alliance…it's the number for you to call. You change your mind…the goals are the same. Stability."

He opens his mouth, thoughtful. His jaw shifts back and forth. "Get out of here. Stay low."

I hold a fist out. It's a weak goodbye gesture.

"Watch your back." I mean it. And he senses it. At least, that's my hope.

CHAPTER 31

WILLOW

When I wake up, the sheets on his side of the bed are cold. A bag lies on the floor beside the armoire that holds my clothes.

Is he leaving again?

I'm in the bathroom with a toothbrush in my mouth when he stomps into the room.

"We need to go. Pack anything you need to take with you. You can shower at home."

Panic strikes, but he's gone.

I quickly get it together. Whatever's going on, at least he's not leaving me this time.

The bedroom door swings open as I zip the duffel closed.

"Is Lina up?" I should say goodbye to her, if we have time.

"No. We have a lead on a flat."

"We're moving?"

"Can't stay where we are." He reaches for the bag. "Ready?"

"Shouldn't we say goodbye?"

"Already did."

I follow him through a quiet house. I'm sure Lina's still sleeping, but I keep an eye out for Nick.

Leo's Range Rover is outside on the gravel, and he throws the bag into the back seat.

"Is everything all right?"

He doesn't look at me. No, he's scanning the horizon. His demeanor is the same as when we fled the garage after the incident with Leandro.

There's a thin red line across his throat. "What happened?"

He side-eyes me as he lightly touches the injury. "Ran into a branch running this morning."

"Did you put something on it?"

"It's fine." His focus returns to the road.

The stilted silence in the car has me scrolling songs on Spotify, searching for something to lighten the mood. The dense cloud cover and increasingly heavy traffic only exacerbate the negative vibes reverberating off Leo.

I select a channel that touts itself as The Beatles channel. It's not all Beatles' music, but it's selected by fans of the band.

"Can you listen on headphones? I need quiet."

I don't possess headphones, but I don't wish to argue, so I press the screen and silence returns. He side-eyes me and huffs.

There are so many things he could be angry about. A news alert came across yesterday about a Titan ship being detained, and I can't help but wonder if it's related to the shipping manifests I saw in his pictures file. I didn't ask Nick about the ship, as years in my father's home taught me that women don't inquire about business matters. Plus, Leo said Lina isn't aware of what they do, and I shouldn't say anything to her, and she was almost always around.

Leo could also simply be angry about me getting stoned with Lina. But then again, last night he hadn't seemed mad. Still, of the options on the table, that's the easiest to tackle.

"Are you mad about yesterday?" His gaze remains fixed on the road ahead. "Leo? Seriously?"

"What?" He blinks and rubs a hand over his eyes.

"Do you want me to drive?"

"No."

He's not this worked up over pot. My father, who has a zero-tolerance rule on drugs, would have gone ballistic. But Leo's not conservative like my father. He's progressive and open. Or at least, that's what I thought. This silent, brooding shit—something is bothering him, and he won't open up. The pot is the only reason I can think he'd be angry at me. And that doesn't make sense. Which means it's more, and he's treating me like my father would treat my mother.

He reaches for my hand, and with his touch, my incensed thoughts fizzle. We drive like that for the next hour and a half, silent, fingers linked. Occasionally, he lifts our linked hands and presses his lips to my knuckles or to the back of my hand.

I've no idea why he's out of sorts, but the more I give it consideration, we left without him saying goodbye to Nick, at least that I saw. Perhaps they argued. If it weren't for the middle divider between us, I would slide next to him. Something is wrong, and I want to make it better for him, but I don't know how. I do the only things I know to do. I remain silent, don't turn on the music, and hold his hand.

When we return to the garage, Leo parks and tells me to stay. He exits the car, and prickles climb my spine as he rounds the vehicle, searching for god knows what. More people coming for us? Is this not over? Is that what's the matter? Did he get word Massimo is coming after us?

Leo opens the door and holds it for me.

"Everything okay?" That phrase must be the one I say to him more than any other.

"All good. Let's go."

My gaze tracks to the spot where John's car had been and then the spot where Leandro and his two employees died.

"Come on," Leo says, his tone softer now.

"Are they coming for us?"

His lips purse and his head shakes. "I don't believe so. But you need to stay close until I make some additional arrangements."

It's not until we're in the elevator that I ask, "You mean replace John?"

"Yes."

When we return to the flat, he promptly enters his office and shuts the door. Years of growing up in my father's home have taught me that if you want to listen, you can't stand in front of the door where your shadow can be seen. You either have to locate a connecting vent or stand at the side of the door.

There are no vents in Leo's office that I've noticed, so I loudly step away, letting my shoes clatter on the floor, all the way to the kitchen. Then I remove my shoes and slide my feet back into the hallway, flattening myself against the wall as I inch to the door.

As expected, he's talking to someone. His tone is firm with a chord of urgency. I can't decipher the words, and I inch closer to the door, eyeing my shadow. I move to the light switch and press it, removing the light source. Then I return to the door and press my ear to the wood, feet still planted to the side of the threshold.

"I need you to do something else for me," Leo says to someone I have to believe he's speaking to on a mobile, as no one else is here. "When I'm gone, you've got to look out for my arrangement. I'll leave resources."

His arrangement? Is he talking about me?

"At least initially, when I'm gone, watch out for her. It's important. Do whatever you have to do."

When I'm gone. The phrase ricochets through my mind, unlodging facts. Shipping manifests on his phone. The detained Titan ship. He's an arms dealer who never parties. Orlando assumed he was gay, but…he's a plant. When the law seized the heroin shipment last year, everyone had been talking about it. The rumor had been that there were undercover officers within the ranks. That's what Leo is. That's why he's always said what we have is temporary. He's leaving.

"Forty-eight hours," Leo says. "You've been a good friend. Thank you." There's a pause. "I'll see you on the other side. And yes, I'll need those updates."

A drawer opens, the sound a mix of rattle and squeak. There are no voices. I twist the knob and push the door open.

Surprise flashes. Either he forgot I'm here or he can't believe I had the audacity to open his office door.

On the top of his desk is a smashed SIM card.

"Are you working undercover?"

CHAPTER 32

SAM, AKA LEO, AKA SAINT

What the hell do I say to her? The less she knows, the safer she is.

She steps up to the desk, swipes the remnants of the SIM card into her palm and balls her hand into a fist. She gestures with her head to the doorway, urging me to follow her.

Curious, I do as she asks, silently following her through our bedroom and into the bathroom. She lifts the lid on the toilet, empties her hand, and flushes.

She's protecting me. How does she even know what that smashed remnant on the desk was? Did she see Alessio smash SIM cards?

The shower turns on—both shower heads. The noise is loud, but she also flicks on the fan.

I doubt anyone would place a listening device in a bathroom, but she's got the bases covered if they did. Alessio

Gagliano may have protected his daughter from their world, but once she started paying attention, she learned.

I cross my arms and lean against the bathroom cabinet. I'm both incredibly turned on by this cunning woman and scared that I'm going to fuck this up and endanger her.

It's taken five years, but I've grown lax. I invited a woman to live with me at a time the CIA and our counterparts have become increasingly aggressive.

Big, trusting blue eyes take me in. A cornflower blue I'll never forget. The first woman, other than my sisters, I'd risk everything for. She edged her way under my skin, and I've no idea how, but one thing I'm certain of is I've fallen. I love her with all my soul. I'll never forget her, but I will leave her, because I love her too much to force her to leave her life behind.

"I can't tell you anything," I begin the second she places those expectant and unforgettable eyes on me. "I wish I could. But you can't know anything."

"You're afraid they'll torture me to gain information." Her matter-of-fact statement is delivered with calm and an edge of anger.

"You're very calm," I say.

"Not on the inside." She maintains distance from me and her arms cross protectively in front of her. "Who's coming after you? Where are you going?"

"What did you hear?" Shit.

"I'm trying to piece—" She closes her eyelids and her lips purse. "I don't care who is coming after you. Take me with you. Don't leave me."

My heart implodes. I wasn't supposed to have to say goodbye to her. I have nothing prepared for this moment, and I sure as hell am unprepared for how difficult it is to breathe or for the excruciating pain slicing through me.

She places herself in my arms, and her youthful, sweet scent surrounds me. I close my eyes, blocking out the world, and it's only the two of us. *Wishful thinking.*

"Wherever you're going, take me." Her plea brings me back, a reminder of what I must do. If it was just me, running away with her with a plan to kill anyone who tracked us down could work. But it's not just me. It's my sisters. My friends. The life I left behind and all those I love.

"I can't."

"You're going for good?" Her voice quivers, and it's like shrapnel in the aftermath of an explosion, painful and lethal.

The plan is in motion, but it might not happen for days. Weeks. How the hell am I going to survive days of goodbyes?

"I love you. I know it was supposed to be an arrangement. I know it wasn't supposed to be real, but it is. To me, it is."

I close my eyes, resting the side of my face against the top of her head, clinging to her. It's real for me too. God, I love her. I don't know when I fell for her, but I don't remember ever loving someone like this, ever hurting like this for another person.

"If you don't love me, that's fine. I can go wherever you need to go. I'll do whatever you need me to."

With her clasped tight against me to avoid her tear-filled eyes, I admit, "Fuck, Willow. I love you too. So much. Too much to take you with me."

She claws away, struggling against my hold. Her tear-streaked face kills me. Dead on sight.

"I can't," I insist.

I want to, god knows I want to, but wanting is not justification.

"Are you having Nick arrested? It wouldn't be the Lupi Grigi coming after you. It would be the syndicate. Are all the syndicate partners going to be hunting you? Was that what Leandro—"

Damn, she's smart. But she's grasping. Desperate to piece it together.

"Leandro wanted you. There was nothing else. You'll always need to be wary of Massimo. I don't trust the Lupi Grigi. Your father's place in the family helps, but they're vengeful."

Her bottom lip trembles, and fuck if the room doesn't blur. "Don't leave me."

"You can't leave your family. I can't take you from them."

"You're my family."

"To leave them for good is a pain you will never know."

"Because you left family behind…" Her bottom lip trembles as she pieces it together.

I pull her back against me because I can't bear her tear-filled eyes. It hurts too much. I have to be strong. For her, for my sisters. Jesus. This isn't goodbye, but now that she's figured it out, it needs to be. *Fuck*.

I choke back emotion. Gather my strength. "We have some flats to check out. Ones that aren't in skyscrapers. You'll like them better. You'll be happier."

"Don't say that."

Steam fogs the glass and mirrors. I stroke a thumb over her lower lip. In a perfect world, I'd tell her I'll never leave. I'd strip her of clothes and take her in the shower, the very shower where we began.

But it's not a perfect world. And the countdown has begun.

The pain slicing through me aches more than anything I've ever experienced, and given my background, that's saying a lot. I've swum miles in frigid water, carried weight until my muscles fatigued, and watched from afar as my sisters cried at my memorial. But I am without choices. And I don't give up. I never give up. I soldier forward, and I complete my missions.

CHAPTER 33

WILLOW

It's a soft blur, a nightmarish out-of-body experience where I watch as he gathers three burner phones from the box, places them in an outer coat pocket, lifts a handgun from his desk, and loads the chamber with a steely, unreadable expression. He's quiet and avoids looking at me, as if by evading me, all issues resolve.

The man who moments earlier tearfully declared his love for me has morphed into a cold, determined stranger.

It was always an arrangement. He's never lied to me. Yet he's working for someone in an undercover role. That much is clear. What does it mean? Will he disappear, only to reappear in court to testify against syndicate members? Will he testify against Nick? Or other groups who purchased weapons illegally through him? Did our arrangement aid his efforts to entrap the syndicate? Will my father face charges for shipping illegal cargo, or will those charges be placed against the corporate entity? It's not like my father loaded the cargo himself.

In a haze, I lean against the balcony, watching Leo descend the stairs to the elevator. When he reaches the floor, he calls, "Collapse the stairs."

Why? Who does he believe is coming after me? I press the button beneath the railing, and the elevator doors close. The floor vibrates from the shifting of the stairs. Like an earthquake, the vibrations seize on cracks and fracture my chest. It hurts to breathe.

He's leaving. Maybe not today, but soon he'll be gone. And once the truth comes out, he'll be my family's enemy.

I stumble back to our bedroom, lift my mobile, enter the bathroom, move to run the shower, but stop because background noise won't make this call safe. It doesn't matter if I must watch my words. I need to hear Scarlet's voice.

She picks up on the first ring. We speak about nothing. I can't open up to her or the dam will break and I'll tell her everything, and I can't do that. Not if someone might be listening on her end or monitoring my call. Both scenarios are realistic if the *famiglia* or the syndicate suspects Leo is the mole. And based on our premature departure and my observations today, he believes someone suspects him.

He saved me. I'll die before I do anything to risk his life.

When I'm on the phone with Scarlet, my brother passes her, and she hands me off to him. He sounds happy enough, but we discuss nothing of importance. Our father is away on business, and our mother is somewhere in the house, and somehow that little update transports me to our family home, and I smell the sweet gardenias and feel the salt breeze across my brow.

After the call ends, I curl into a ball in the middle of Leo's bed. Hours pass, and I eventually move into the den. Perched on an armchair, vibrations filter through the fabric and the stairs slowly expand.

It has to be Leo. He can control the stairs with his phone. But it might not be him. The eerie calmness blanketing me is cognitively unsettling. As the vibrations rumble, I slowly awaken and self-preservation kicks in.

If it's not him, I'll run for the panic room. The lift door slides open.

Leo steps out into the foyer. His stern, blank expression tells me which Leo has returned. He climbs the stairs and wordlessly traverses the flat to his office. I follow, and he must sense my presence, because, without a backward glance, he says, "Look at these. Two potential flats. Let me know which you prefer."

He's behind his desk, fussing with the keyboard and mouse, and he rotates his monitor.

"That's where you were? House hunting?"

"Needed to be done. You can't stay here."

"Why?"

"It's not safe."

"What about my studio?"

"We'll find you another one."

"I have an agent. Anyone who wants to find me can find me through my agent."

He closes his eyes, and his jaw flexes. When his eyelids flicker open, he astutely avoids looking at me. "Your new security detail starts tomorrow. Check out these properties. You don't like this flat."

"Who says?"

"Willow." Exhaustion pierces my name. "You close the blinds

in the bedrooms and always stay away from the edge. You don't like heights."

True. I dutifully bend to view the photographs on the monitor, although it's difficult to take in what I'm seeing. If I have to say goodbye to him, I'd prefer to stay in a place that holds memories.

"I can come with you," I say as I press an arrow for the next photograph. I don't know why I say it. The words feel pointless, as I inherently understand he will not change his mind.

"No. You can't." He steps away from the desk and fiddles with something on a shelf on one wall. Three shelves shift forward, contents firmly planted as if glued to the protruding shelves, to reveal a storage space. He removes a black duffel and drops it on the sofa.

He leaves his office, and I stand there, frozen, inspecting the gap in the wall. Guns hang on the side. Three handguns and two assault rifles.

Leo re-enters with an empty black duffel that is a replica of the stuffed one on the sofa. He unzips the full one and lifts a zipped leather bag.

"This is cash." He unzips the empty duffel. "I want you to keep this on hand. Cash is the only untraceable entity. In this bag, there are pounds, euros, and US dollars." He removes the outer coat he's wearing and slips his hand inside. "Here's an EU passport with an alternate identity. Two more passports will arrive later in the week — one United States, and one from the UK. You need to store them in this bag. Do you understand?"

He tilts his head, listening with his back to me.

"I'm heartbroken, not deaf."

"You—" He stretches an arm out as if pushing back on an invisible force.

"Please don't." I'm not above begging.

"I don't have a choice."

"You do have a choice. Choose me."

"I am choosing you. I'll always choose you."

My eyes fill with unshed tears and hope.

"What's best for you." The brief bubble of hope bursts with his determined countenance. There's nothing I can do or say. Unless… Can I convince him his beliefs are wrong? What's best for me is for us to be together.

He steps past me, gaze locked on the ground, and opens the box of burner phones. "Keep some of these in the duffel. If you suspect someone is following you or you are in danger, use these."

He pauses, and I half expect him to ask me if I understand, but he twists his head, and his neck cracks. His jaw flexes, his eyes a stone wall of resolution.

"This is an alternate plate for the automobile. If you ever find yourself on the run, switch the plates out. But do so after you get away from your flat, so no one can be certain which automobile is yours. CCTV canvases London. The chances someone will connect the plate change to your vehicle are too great if you do it in your garage or anywhere near a traffic cam."

I am listening, but I swear, once again, the surreal sensation threatens to drown me.

A loud beep sounds. He gently sets me aside and touches the mouse. The photographs of a flat in Notting Hill go away, and in its place, there's a view of the downstairs garage. That view switches, replaced by a side street view.

"Fuck," he snarls.

"What?"

"Ex-Mossad."

He presses a button, and the shelves move back into place.

"Where?"

"Black-haired man in the gray sedan."

"You know him?"

"Recognize him."

"Is he here for you?"

"Possibly." He pulls one of his burner phones from the box. "He takes odd jobs."

I move aside as he messages someone. On the opposite side of our building, on Olympic Park, there's another occupied car. The occupant dangles a cigarette out the car window.

"Can you zoom in?"

He clicks a few keys, and my view zooms closer, although the car I'm looking at doesn't stay centered and now it's nearly off the screen. But I see enough.

"That guy is Italian. He's Lupi Grigi." I can't remember his name, but I remember his face. His unofficial title, or what everyone calls men like him, is a foot soldier.

"Fuck." Leo puts his jacket on and scans me, his eyes running over me for the first time since this morning. "Get a hat. A coat. Shoes you can run in. Let's go."

"Where are we going?"

"I'm taking you to a safe place."

"We're not safe here?"

"Obviously not," he grinds out. "Go. Move. Now."

When I return to the office, everything is put away. The duffel he'd been filling now bulges. Barely visible ear pieces peek from his ears.

"Let's go."

"How are we getting out of here? Someone is watching both

sides of the building. Why don't we wait them out? They can't get into the building."

"We don't sit and wait. We move." He's already at the stairs. "Come on."

We don't enter the lift. He opens the closet door, then opens another door within.

"What's this?"

"Stairs."

"Huh. I always wondered why there wasn't stair access."

"We built the wall out to accommodate the motor for the stairs. I took the opportunity to disguise the stairwell entrance."

"Wouldn't anyone with floor plans know it exists? Or anyone in the stairwell?"

"First," he says, as the heavy metal door closes firmly behind us, "few people casually roam the forty-first floor of a stairwell." He pulls a handgun from somewhere on his waist and motions for me to go before him. "I'm right behind you."

"Second?" I ask, fixating on the metal end of his gun and the device attached to the barrel that I'm fairly certain is a silencer.

"Second what?" he asks.

I let one hand glide along the stainless-steel railing for balance. He's right at my back, and I push myself to go faster. "You said first. What's the second?"

"You always need an unexpected escape plan. That's difficult to pull off in a skyscraper."

"There's the roof."

"And that's one plan. But I didn't think you'd be down with paragliding through London."

"Flying high above with nothing but a rickety contraption to keep me afloat sounds like hell."

"Exactly."

The shuffling of our feet on concrete steps becomes the only sound. I always assumed there was a stairwell, somewhere, at least for the lower floors, but I've never seen a door with a stair label.

On every floor, we pass a metal door with a sign and a number. When we pass the number twenty, it's the halfway mark, and perspiration coats my skin.

"What's your real name?"

"You don't—"

"No one is listening in this stairwell. I just want to know… I'll never tell anyone."

"I wish I could tell you. I do. But I can't. If one of these guys were to get you, they're trained to get information out of you."

"I'd never tell them."

"Everyone has a breaking point."

He's saying they would torture me, and I'd break. Maybe he's right. They could bring Orlando, or my parents, or Scarlet before me, and I don't know what I would choose. Would I hold his secret or let them hurt someone I love? Would they do that for a name? No, they'd do it because they thought I knew more, which means they will do it if they catch me, period.

We pass the tenth floor.

"What's the plan? Will I be on the run forever?"

He doesn't answer, or if he does, I don't hear him. Maybe he perceived my question as rhetorical, but… "Why don't you take me with you?"

"I won't do that to you."

That's my opening. When we get in the car, I'll discuss it with him. Break his steadfast resolve. When I'm not out of breath and he's set down his gun. Whatever he thinks he'd be doing to me, I can handle it. I want to handle it.

He slows when we pass the second floor and flattens his body against the wall, the hand with the gun held high. We pass the lobby floor slowly, then quickly descend two more floors to the garage.

"They're going to recognize your car," I say, remembering the false plate he stuffed in my duffel. Both duffels hang off his left shoulder.

"Which is why we're going to steal one. Ideally one with tinted windows. Ready to go car shopping?"

"You're in a shopping mood today, aren't you?"

He glances back at me and lifts a finger to his lips. He pushes open the door. It opens directly into the garage, bypassing the elevator well.

A distant engine rumble floats through the garage. The faint scent of exhaust permeates the space. He checks his mobile, and a grin flashes.

"This way."

He takes me straight to a black Land Rover with tinted windows. He tosses our duffels in the back seat.

"Get in," he says. "Back seat. Lie down on the floor."

When he comes around to the driver's side, I do a double-take. He's wearing a baseball cap and a two-inch red beard. His hair's not red, so anyone glancing at a car going by won't suspect it's him.

He drives the vehicle slowly through the garage. He slides sunglasses on as we exit the building and enter the drive. We slow, and I presume he's waiting for the gate to open. Seconds pass.

The car proceeds slowly.

Minutes later, he says, "Okay. You can sit up. Put on that hat. Shades too."

I push up, do as he says, and climb into the front seat.

"Now where to?" My real question is how much time I have to convince him to take me along. Because, somehow, I'm certain this means he's leaving for good.

He doesn't answer, which is annoying, but his grim countenance keeps me quiet. We turn, and he watches his rearview as much as the road.

Rain droplets splatter on the shield. The wipers clear them away.

He accelerates, weaving through cars.

"Fuck."

With a growl, he floors the vehicle, and the sharp squeal of tires screeching pierces the air.

I reach for the seatbelt as he curses, "God dammit."

The seatbelt clicks, and I bend, attempting to see behind us through the side view. Rain coats the glass.

"Sit back," he barks.

He's flying through the rain-soaked street. Cars honk. He swerves, and my body jerks. My hands grip the armrest. Pedestrians stare. Buildings whir by. My body jerks with each hard swerve. I close my eyes. I can't look.

"It wasn't supposed to happen like this," he mutters. "Dammit."

He needs to focus on his driving. I'll ask questions later. A siren's wail joins the sound of honks.

Getting pulled over by a police officer will be a good thing. No one will hurt us if we're in a police car, and then we'll leave the station.

I'm whipped into the car door from a sharp angle he takes. My head hits the back of the seat from the force of his acceleration. I crack one eyelid open and see we're somehow on a road with few cars in front of us.

Rain lashes down. The storm is intensifying, or perhaps it's our speed.

"You okay?" he asks.

I swallow and will my heart to slow down a little. Sure, I was raised in a mafia family, but I've never been in a car chase. My stomach lurches.

"Are they gone?"

"We lost them. But more will be coming. You okay?" he asks again.

Leo's knuckles are white on the steering wheel, his jaw clenched.

I force my eyes open, my heart pounding in my chest. The world outside blurs into a mix of gray buildings and flashing streetlights. My stomach keels with each turn, the lingering adrenaline making me feel simultaneously wired and exhausted.

"You good?" Leo asks, his eyes flicking between me and the rearview mirror. There is genuine concern in his voice, a softness that contrasts sharply with the hardness in his eyes.

I nod, not trusting my voice. The reality of our situation sinks in. We're running, truly running, and I don't know where we're going or when—if ever—we'll be able to stop.

"We need to switch vehicles soon. This one's too conspicuous."

I glance back, half-expecting to see a parade of black SUVs in pursuit. The road behind us is clear, but that does little to ease the knot in my stomach. "What are we going to do?"

He takes a sharp turn down a narrow alley. The Range

Rover's sides scrape against the brick walls, leaving a trail of paint behind us. I wince at the sound, but Leo seems unfazed.

"It's complicated," he finally says, his voice low and tight. "This isn't your family. At least, they aren't the only ones."

The alley opens into a deserted parking lot. Leo slows the vehicle, his eyes scanning our surroundings. "We need to ditch this car. Can you run?"

A blistering barrage of gunshots ring.

"Fuck!" Leo shouts. "Is your seatbelt buckled?"

It is. I tug on it to show him, eyelids clamped closed as the engine roars.

"Is it?" he shouts.

"Yes!" I cry, squinting one eye as my whole body shifts left as he jerks the vehicle.

"How the fuck did he find us?"

Up ahead is a bridge.

"Fuck!"

"What? Who is it?"

We're in a rundown area I've never seen before. If I were to guess, these are warehouses. Maybe we're nearing a shipping district.

"Get down."

I lean forward, doing exactly what he says.

A bullet splinters the side mirror. I scream.

"Stay down."

Leo holds a gun in his hand.

He's driving like a madman.

The tires screech. Shots pierce the air.

The back window shatters.

"What the fuck?" he shouts.

"God dammit!"

He's so loud, it's as if he's shouting at the gods.

"Hold on. Do you hear me? Willow, hold on."

I close my eyes. The sirens return. Louder than before. A screeching of tires infiltrates the car. We maintain forward motion. Boom. My body snaps forward.

A loud crashing sound overtakes every other noise. I'm jerked, and my neck whips. The seatbelt cuts into my collarbone. Something big and fast explodes into my face. It takes a second to register, but it's the airbags on my front and side. My ears ring. Dots mar my vision.

We dip forward, floating, sailing through the air. My stomach remains somewhere up on the road, high above.

The seat belt is so tight against me that when we crash, slamming into water, my head moves but not my body. Dazed, I'm still—frozen in time until water bubbles around the windows.

"We've got to get out of here!" I screech. The back window is out. We're going to sink like a stone.

Leo's hand covers mine. "Willow. I'm so sorry. It wasn't supposed to be like this."

Muddy brown water climbs over the windows.

He's not doing anything.

He's sitting there.

Still.

Glassy eyes.

He's giving up.

His mouth moves, muttering nonsense.

"No," I plead.

I unsnap my seatbelt, pushing against the airbags for space.

We can swim out the back.

We need to get out of here.

I can barely see out of the vehicle, but I can tell we're moving. The stream is moving us.

Fast.

Like a boat.

Rain splatters the water, sending water up to the sky only to fall back down again.

The front of the vehicle dips forward.

The brown line rises.

We're sinking.

Falling to the depths.

"Willow, look at me."

He's calm.

Resigned?

This can't be the end.

CHAPTER 34

TWO WEEKS LATER

NIKOLAI JOHN IVANOV; AKA NICK; AKA FALCON

A stacked stone fence marks the perimeter of the estate's cemetery. Some of these gravestones date back centuries, although the weathered dates are impossible to read on the diminutive marble slabs.

When I first acquired this estate, I invited a historian to visit. She found the markers fascinating. I enjoyed fucking her.

The grounds crew maintain the space, but I had them clear a special corner beneath a sprawling oak tree. Alessio Gagliano wanted to bring his daughter home, but I insisted she be buried with her husband on my estate with my family.

Alessio didn't fight me, probably because he's too heart-broken to fight. Timing was also on my side.

The Gaglianos' red-rimmed eyes and dazed expressions speak of parents living a nightmare. Unlike their parents, her younger brother appears incapable of curbing his tears. Aware crying doesn't convey strength, the teen remains on the outskirts of the gathering.

I allowed the Gaglianos to bring their family priest, a Catholic man who required a significant donation to travel and perform the ceremony. I considered having someone else perform Leo's service to spite the greedy priest, but this isn't the time to wage petty battles.

A photographer I hired camps out roadside with a long-range lens. I plan to submit some of her photographs to a local paper. I expect the Gaglianos will appreciate photographs as well.

Caskets encased in a watertight steel capsule rest in deep holes, and black folding chairs are lined up opposite. Lina and I stand in the back to give privacy to the Gaglianos. Plus, I have no desire to hear the priest.

Scarlet Gagliano casts furtive glances in our direction throughout the service. The ginger is debating my proposal. She's a widow, and from what I understand, she doesn't have much of a life back in Italy.

My source said she'll never remarry. She cut off her husband's dick, let him bleed out, and now men fear her. Rumors say when he was in and out of consciousness and unable to fight her off, she placed his dick in his mouth and clamped a hand over his lips, forcing him to die choking on his penis.

Centuries ago, she would have been accused of being a witch, possibly burned at the stake. His death was ruled self-defense, so she's free to roam the streets, but the court of popular opinion didn't rule in her favor. Many of the Lupi Grigi men teach their wives lessons, so my source explained that while it is generally agreed that he took his lessons too far, breaking her jaw and wrist and slicing her with a knife, some believe she deserved it as she was unruly.

Right or wrong, none of the thugs wants her near their crown jewels. Fools.

I hope she accepts my offer.

She's stunning in her uniqueness. That vibrant, thick, red hair and pale skin don't blend with any of her family. The shape of her green eyes is reminiscent of her mother's, but nothing else is. Her father died years ago. I'll have to dig up a photo because she looks so different to me than the rest of the Lupi Grigi, and her distinctiveness reeks of an illicit affair.

Scarlet's mother hadn't been forced to remarry after her father's untimely death. Sister-in-law status to a wealthy shipping magnate comes with perks.

The mafias and cartels create their own fucked-up world. Their seemingly archaic rules and expectations allow them to function in a society that would otherwise lock them up like the brute monsters and drug lords they are.

In my world, these vast, organized criminal organizations are a necessary evil—a military for ambitious business and banking leaders. Perhaps "enforcer" is the most apt designation.

A successful strategist deals in solid business fundamentals. But some mergers and deals need greasing. Moscow rules apply. Old-fashioned *kompromats* boast a high success rate, especially among politicians. Even so, all the world's problems can't be solved with talk. No, sometimes people need to die.

I check my wrist, wondering how much longer the priest will jabber.

CHAPTER 35

THIRTEEN DAYS EARLIER

SAM; AKA LEO; AKA SAINT

"What the hell do you mean, she's dead?"

It's a good thing Jack Sullivan is thousands of miles away, speaking on video, because if he was in the room with me, I might kill him with my bare hands.

"They called off the rescue. You're both presumed dead."

"Why the fuck would they call off the search?"

"You don't keep up with the weather, do you?"

It's nighttime, and we're in international waters. A trawler pulled us from the river and took us out into the ocean, where we transferred to a yacht.

Willow's washing the Thames off her in an onboard suite.

"What weather?" We're tossing about. Waves are high. It's raining.

"A cyclone's about to hit. It's one reason we moved up the timeline. They won't risk rescuers. They'll assume your bodies washed out to sea, and a search for the wreck—and, well, your bodies—will resume after the storm passes."

"Well, they're gonna find her alive. Let's come up with a story. Plant someone to say he found her and she's okay. Amnesia. Doesn't know what happened. You can find her in a day or two."

"I thought you were on board with this plan." Jack's warning me. I hear it, and he is my superior, but he's also the guy who got me into this mess.

"With my extraction? Yes. Willow wasn't supposed to be a part of it. She's supposed to be a widow."

"The extraction plans were for both of you."

Nomad is the walking dead.

"If that wasn't your plan, why was she with you?"

Dammit. Why was she with me? "Ashraf Cohen parked outside. He tailed us."

There's no way I'd leave Willow with an ex-Mossad assassin hunting her. Not to mention, the fucking Italian mafia, but we lost them. But Cohen…he found us. We'd lost him, and he found us.

I stretch my jaw, as it's tight from the pull of the regulator, and pinch my nose, reliving the shit storm from this half-baked, rushed-as-fuck plan.

"Saint. Do you read? Saint? Respond. Over."

Fuck the CIA.

Fuck this whole goddamn operation.

"Awaiting instructions. Over."

If this shit goes FUBAR, these bags will provide some air. Not much.

"Copy. Three minutes out. Stay with the vehicle," the operator said.

"Have you ever dived?"

She blinked, shocked and terror-stricken.

"Scuba?"

She unbuckled and glanced to the back where she wanted to exit. That level head of hers kept her calmer than I would have expected. A good thing. I needed her to stick with me.

"A few times," she finally answered. Thank god. That made the plan easier. Of all the extraction plans, we had to fucking go with this one. And thanks to the bullets, we don't have as much air as expected.

"Divers are going to approach us. I'll tell you when to breathe deep. A diver will offer you a regulator. Put the mouthpiece in first. Understand? Just like the airplane flight attendant says. Get the oxygen first. Then put your mask on. Oxygen on, then we swim. I'll be right at your side. You got me?"

"You won't leave me?" Her lower lip trembled.

"I won't leave this vehicle without you."

"That's not what I'm asking."

I shoved the airbag out of the way for a better view through the glass. The frigid water was up to our chins.

"Leo?"

"Let's get out of here alive. Then we'll talk."

I dipped below the water level, eyes open, scanning our surroundings.

A dark figure neared.

Details emerged on the diver wearing a full body wetsuit.

I pushed up until my nose was out of the water and my head hit the roof of the SUV.

"Leo?"

Fear rang in her voice. My fingers wrapped around her delicate wrist, and I squeezed.

"Willow." I waited for those blue eyes to lock on mine. "You're going to be okay." She needed to calm down, so I did what I had to do. "I love you. I've got you. Trust me. Let's suck in as much air as we can. When we're completely submerged, we'll hold our breath, then we're swimming out. I won't let go of you. Don't let go of me."

This plan could have backfired in so many ways. What a fucking shit show. If something had happened to Willow, I'd have a terminal list and wouldn't rest until I crossed every name.

"Sam?"

His use of my Christian name clears the cobwebs. I need to focus.

"You hired Cohen?"

"You're officially off this mission," Jack says. "You want updates?"

Yes, I fucking want updates. What the fuck? I grind my teeth, breathe, and answer like an angry midshipman speaking to a superior without regard for rank. "I want answers."

"The Lupi Grigi weren't there for Willow. They were there for you, at least that we know of, and Nick Ivanov."

"What?"

"We're hearing they suspect the syndicate had a hand in Gagliano's gray fleet being detained. The ships getting detained backs Leandro's claim that the syndicate was behind last year's heroin bust."

"Are they after Nick?"

"Possibly. Nick's aware."

"What's your source?"

"Intercepted conversations."

"How?"

"Lina. He's upped security."

Right. She had her watch and jewelry cleaned in London, and the CIA has been monitoring her conversations ever since.

I shake my head. Nick and the syndicate are no longer my priority. It's time to focus on transition.

"Who hired Cohen?"

Jack's smugness pisses me off until I realize he's looking at me like that because he thinks I should know the answer. It all clicks into place.

Motherfucker.

"No. She's got to go back. She will not lose her family because of me."

"Have you asked her what she wants? Because it's going to take some time for the judicial system to work its magic, but her family will crumble."

"Nick's going after them for revenge." It's a statement that I say more to myself. He won't forgive them for going after Lina.

"Nick's not the only one. The crumbling has begun. Infighting. Her father will be targeted. You sure you want her living through that?"

Once the other Italian mafia families smell blood in the water, it could become quite dangerous to be a Lupi Grigi living in southern Italy. Not to mention, if Nick's plan works, the Russian mob will go after them too.

"Talk to her," Jack says. "But I'm telling you, if we concoct a plan to send her back, no matter what we do, it'll raise suspicions. It's risky."

Jack's right. I know he's right. But fuck, this is not what I wanted for her. How did our plan get so fucked? Because Nomad, that's how. He fucked me over.

Thanks to him, the option she's being forced into is essentially witness protection for the rest of her life. She loves her family. She doesn't have any idea what it's like to walk away from her family, and it's a pain she shouldn't experience.

When I push open the door to the primary suite, a location doled out as if it's a reward, she's sitting on the bed, legs tucked beneath the comforter in a pale pink silk nightgown. She looks up, cheeks slightly flushed from her shower, her hair wet and dark. There's faint bruising below her eyes from where the airbag hit her. The bruise across her collarbone is darkening. The skin from the black eye Leandro gave her has yellowed. She's a patchwork of bruises, yet she's still beautiful. The sight of her slows my heart and squeezes my chest.

"How are you feeling?" What a stupid question. We crashed into the Thames.

"Sore. Is everything okay?"

She's worried. Can't blame her.

On the trawler, we said little. The men with us had been engaged for a specific piece of this op, and I wasn't aware of their clearance. Given the speed at which the operation unfolded, I doubt they had much more information than there were two people they needed to covertly rescue and transfer to a waiting yacht.

Once we boarded the yacht, I encouraged Willow to take a hot shower to quell her shivers, and I was escorted to an office onboard the yacht for Jack's debriefing. The plan is to sail across the ocean and dock in a harbor where there will be no record of our entrance into the US.

"Leo?" She lifts an arm, reaching for me, and grimaces.

"Did you take any Advil? Anything for the muscular pain?"

"I did." She inches forward until her fingers warm my forearm.

"You need a shower, too. Are you sore?"

I'm a little sore, but it's nothing compared to what it will feel like tomorrow. I'm old enough my body hates me for my choices. But that's not what Willow and I need to talk about.

I kick off my shoes and slide back on the bed, careful to remain above the comforter since my clothes reek of dead fish, thanks to the dip in the Thames and hours on a fishing trawler.

"Leo?"

God. Those bright blue eyes. How do I tell her?

"You're scaring me."

My gaze roams the ceiling. This is not how it was supposed to happen. "I'm so sorry, Willow."

"For what? Because I'm with you? Don't be."

She crawls next to me.

"Don't think you want to do that. I smell."

"You think I care about that?"

"You've showered. You're ready for bed." You're young and innocent, and unless I figure something out, your family is lost to you.

She palms my jaw, forcing me to look at her. Apparently,

that's not enough because she pushes aside the comforter, tugs on her nightgown, lifting it over her knees. I don't know what she's doing. Hell, I don't know what I'm doing. With the silk higher, she slings a leg over mine, so she's straddling my legs.

"What's wrong? You look like someone died."

"Someone did die. You. Willow Gagliano died today."

"And Leo Sullivan died too?"

"It wasn't supposed to go like this. This was not the plan."

"You don't want me with you? Is that what you're upset about?"

"Willow…your family—" She doesn't get it. How can she? I didn't either.

She pinches my chin, forcing me to meet her gaze. I don't want to look at her, though. Not when I failed.

"Listen to me. I love you. I'm where I want to be. If my choice is to live in a world without you or live in a world with you, I choose you. Every time. I choose you."

"You don't understand."

"*Perché*? Why do you say that? Because I'm young? Get that out of your head. I've got an old soul, and you rescued me from a cruel world. I fell in love with the man who cares when there's nothing in it for him. I fell in love with the man who might not always do right, but who always tries." She flattens her palm over my sternum. "I fell in love with the man who gave me wings."

"Hate to tell you, but I don't see any wings." In fact, I see a prison sentence she doesn't yet perceive but will one day.

"You believed in my painting. In my art. You believed I could make it on my own."

"And you would have if—"

"I still can. You strengthen me. And wherever we're going,

you'll still do that. The man I fell in love with didn't die. He's still right here, no?"

The room blurs, and I have to look away from her innocence. Jesus. My throat clenches and emotion wells up. I don't handle it well when things do not go according to plan.

"What's your name?" Her eyes narrow. "Can you tell me? Or will we be using aliases? The ones in the duffels?"

I lift her palm from my heart and press it against my cheek, then press my lips into her palm.

"You really want to stay with me? Even if it means never seeing your family again? Your friends? You might not be able to paint. We'll meet with relocation experts, but they may say painting is too identifiable." It probably is.

"Do you not listen? I want to be with you. With my husband." The curves of her lips curl into a teasing smile. "Yes, this began as an arrangement. But things change." In a softer, tentative voice, she adds, "It is real to me. We're real to me."

I press my forehead to hers. My eyes burn with love for this woman. Once again, something that was not my intention. Another plan gone sideways.

"We can make it legal when we're Stateside." *What am I saying? She has choices.* "If you want. You're young. If you want to date…we can do that too. You have options. There's no rush. You can build the life you want. It's all up to you."

What I don't repeat is that she shouldn't have to build a new life. She should have the life I planned for her. The safe one. In London. Pursuing her career with her family by her side.

She pulls back. "Why is our marriage not legal now?" Her eyes widen with realization. "Oh, your name. But then, will my name change?"

I shift, repositioning us slightly on the bed.

"Are you ready to hear it all? Once I tell you, there's no going back." Based on what Jack said, there's no going back anyway, but I'll find a way, if that's what she wants.

"The only way I go back is if you go back with me. I want this. I want us."

"Are you sure?"

Her blue eyes blur, but she's not the one with tears filling her eyes. It's me. And I do not cry.

"I won't leave you. Tell me everything."

"You're making a commitment here." I exhale, as much to clear my thoughts as to dry up the emotion blurring my vision. "From here on out, it's a commitment to be with me. If I piss you off one day, or I bore you, or you wonder how the hell you wound up with such an old guy...you'll be stuck with me."

"You're not that old. What are you? Forty-two?"

"Actually...I'm thirty-nine." She grins so wide it's like those three years made her day. "I lied about my age in my alias, partly just to command a little extra respect for the work I was doing, and then, well, years passed."

"I get to help you celebrate your fortieth birthday."

"I don't celebrate—"

"When is your birthday? Really?"

I let out a breath, and with it, I accept that she can't go back. If she changes her mind about us, she'll still need to build a new life.

"My name is Sam Watson. Samuel Lee Watson. Born on January twenty-seventh." I hold out my hand as if I'm offering to shake hers. "Nice to meet you."

"Sam." She says the name like she's tasting it. I like hearing her say my real name. I like my name wrapped with her European accent. "You go by Sam?"

"Yes."

"And do you have family?"

"Two younger sisters. One day, you'll get to meet them. They're both married. One is expecting her first child, so you'll be an aunt soon." As I say those words, it feels like my heart is going to burst out of my chest. I've missed my family so much. It's why I hate Willow has to miss hers, but talking about reuniting with mine brings home a wave of warmth.

"Do you have photos?"

"Not with me." I tap her nose. "But you'll see them soon. Once we determine it's safe." I wrap my arms around her, and she shifts until her chin rests on my shoulder. I know I smell, but I need this. To hold her like this while it sinks in that this is forever. The emotions have been real, but now we're forever. She's mine. I never have to let her go. I understand I'll need to earn her love, work for our love, and take care of her, but I'm capable. My parents showed me what it is to work for a loving relationship. My shoulders lighten, like a weight I hadn't known I was carrying has lifted.

"I want to meet them," she says, her voice light, as if she too is lighter.

"You will."

"How will you introduce me to them? I mean, what will my name be?"

"I suppose you can choose your alias, with Watson as your last name."

She digs a digit into my ribs, and I squirm, and she laughs into my ear. "Who says this American woman took her husband's last name?"

"I think we're going to have to say that you're from Europe. Maybe from Croatia."

"Why? My English is good. I dream in English."

"Your English is phenomenal. But you've got an accent."

"So do you, Mr. Cowboy Boots."

"That was part of my alias's persona. I have what's called a southern accent, but I played it up for the part of Leo."

"I noticed the strength of your accent fluctuated."

"It's typical for Southerners," I say, although I've noticed it's true for most accents. Alcohol, emotion, the situation—they can all diminish or strengthen an accent.

"The part of Leo, huh? So, what's Sam like? And that's who you truly are? No more aliases? Are you done with this?"

"I'm done."

"You have a boss?"

I nod slowly, as the answer isn't clean cut.

"I have to figure out my next steps. Our next steps."

"Maybe we can take some time together?"

"Oh, yes. I think after five years undercover, I'm due for some PTO."

"What's that?"

"Paid time off." I don't know if I'll stay with the CIA. It's something I'll have to think through. Technically, I'm still part of the Navy. Arrow took charge of the op so it would remain off radar. No one from the Intelligence Committee could have access to the op, as the syndicate has connections to the group.

Her chin rests on my shoulder. I could fall asleep like this, holding her.

"You can choose a name. Who do you want to be?"

"I've always liked Ella. Or Isla."

I dated a girl named Ella years ago, and that did not work out. That's a no-go. Isla isn't doing it for me. If Willow weren't such a unique name…"Willow means freedom." I looked it up one day when I was on a train returning to London. "Oddly enough, you freed me."

She buries her face into my throat and I just squeeze her harder. Now that I've got her, for better or worse, I'll be holding on to this one with everything I've got. A name comes to me out of nowhere.

"What about Lily?"

"Lily." She says it like she's trying it out on her lips. "I like it. Lily Watson."

"Sleep on it. We have some time, but not too much. We'll need to have all the requisite documents made for you."

"Sam and Lily Watson. It has a nice ring. You know what else I like?"

And then her lips press to mine as she shifts, grinding her heat and weight over me.

My hands clutch her hips, stopping her. Not that I want to stop her, but I can smell myself, and every single muscle throbs.

"Hold that thought." She skims past my cheek, and her teeth nibble at my ear. I slap a palm against her ass. "I need a shower. And painkillers."

She pushes back, eyes wide. "You didn't take anything? Get in the shower. There's a medicine cabinet in the galley. I'll get you some tea and see what I can find."

In the shower, a memory of our first encounter surfaces through the steam. This shower isn't tiny, like many boat showers are, but it's not designed for two. I lean my head back in the stream, and as the water pours over me, it feels as if the past is circling the drain, and we're sailing to the future. Leaving the past behind and navigating life to come.

When I exit the bathroom, a towel wrapped around my waist, Willow awaits, perched on the edge of the bed, holding white pills in her palm and a glass of water. I knock back the pills and chase them with a gulp of water.

"Thank you."

My gaze grazes over her, taking in her hopeful, bright eyes, her full, upturned lips, and the fall of the silk over her pert breasts. She tilts her head up, and I bend, taking her lips in a slow lazy kiss.

She grapples with the towel, and cool air envelops my bare ass.

I rub my nose over hers and grin. "Is there something you want, Mrs. Watson?"

Her cheeks flush. "If you're not too tired."

My body isn't too tired, and her hand strokes the evidence.

"The shower performed miracles," I say as I lift the hem of her nightgown, tugging it around her bottom, and over her head, only to drop it on the floor.

"You smell delicious."

"Do I? We'll need to find out what brand they stock so we can use it at home. I like the idea of smelling delicious to my wife."

Her grip tightens, and I breathe through the pleasure. The boat rolls, and I stumble. My shins bump against the bed.

"Is someone driving the yacht?" she asks, sounding only slightly concerned.

I reach around her, pulling back the comforter and sheet. "The yacht's fully staffed. They've got a night crew. We should reach calmer waters by morning."

I climb into the bed beside her, aligning our bodies and pulling a sheet over us. "You don't get seasick?"

"Never have. You?"

I bite back the answer and then chuckle. I can tell her everything. "Nah, I was in the Navy."

"The Navy? Battleships?"

I nip at her lips. "Something like that."

"How did you—"

I stop her question with my mouth, and her tongue complies. "I'll answer all your questions. But right now, I need my wife." *Oh, how I need her.*

With a smile, she lies back. Her fingers comb through my hair, and she guides me down to her.

I've made love to women before. I've loved women too. But I've never had what felt like forever before. As I cover her body in kisses, taste her, and bring her to the edge with my fingers and mouth, as she opens for me, giving me all of her with no barrier, only truth, I release into her with the force of a tidal wave. This is what forever feels like.

CHAPTER 36

FIVE DAYS LATER

WILLOW, AKA LILY

The crew members are polite but distant. They're all Jack Sullivan's employees, and Sam says we can trust them, but by the same token, they're trained to keep their distance.

Sam—it's still strange to call him Sam—correctly forecast the pain level from the crash over the bridge and into the river. We spent the first few days taking pain meds and sleeping quite a lot, either in the bedroom or on the deck in the shade. Or, at least, I've been sleeping. Sam's been in what he calls debriefs.

Today is my first day with no pain medication. My bruises are yellowing, and the rhythm of the sea has lulled my tight muscles into a serene state. With five crew members, we're never alone, but that's not the way it feels.

Named *The Honey Pot,* the yacht has a bright and airy interior with luxurious, neutral-colored accommodations, including five suites for guests, and quarters for the crew in three cabins.

Traveling day and night at a brisk pace, we've reached the Gulf Stream, a warm current that runs along the east coast of North America, and it's warmer where we are. We plan to travel south of Florida and dock in the Gulf of Mexico at a private port. Today, the tropical sun beats down on the boat with a welcome intensity.

"Here you are," Sam says, stepping right up to me and flattening a palm on my right butt cheek. "This is a tiny bikini." I'm wearing a swim coverup, but it's a stringy concoction that covers nothing.

"It's what they provided."

The approving hum next to my ear sends tingles down my neck and straight through me.

"Are you done with your meetings for the day?" I ask, hoping for some relaxing time with him.

"I believe so. Would you like to hang out on the deck?"

He's wearing swim trunks that hang low, close to his knees, a decidedly American style, but an American stocked the ship with the clothes. He's also wearing a short-sleeve button down, but it's unbuttoned. My fingers trace the fading bruises along his collarbone and across his chest.

"Should I get some sunscreen? You can take this off and save yourself from strange tan lines."

"Does this mean I get to apply sunscreen to you?" He fingers the lining of my swimsuit bottoms as he nibbles along my neck.

"Thomas already did that. But you can reapply in about an hour."

"Thomas?"

Choosing to ignore the gruffness in his tone, I push up on my toes and press my lips to his chin. "You've been gone," I chastise. "This would feel like a honeymoon if you hadn't been working so much."

He exhales what sounds like frustration. "Debriefings and... our funeral will be in a week."

"That's quick." It feels quick, at least. Time has simultaneously flown and slowed out here with nothing but the Atlantic as far as the eye can see.

"Your family is speeding it along. At least once they agreed we would be buried on Nick Ivanov's estate."

"Why there?"

"He's the closest Leo had to family in Europe. They debated flying our remains to the States, but the powers that be decided it would be risky to invite your family to my theoretical family home. It opened us up to unnecessary risks."

"What do you mean?"

"Family photographs without me in them. Running into a real family member in town who isn't aware Leo Sullivan exists. It's a high-risk scenario."

"How is there a burial without remains?"

"They have remains. After the storm, the search team found our bodies downstream from the vehicle. We were cremated."

"My family agreed?"

"Nick insisted you would want to be buried with your husband."

"Why?"

He raises an amused eyebrow. He's teasing me because he knows I plan to be by his side for eternity. While he's been absent during the day, our nights have been full of lovemaking, talking, and planning the future.

"No, I mean, why not have us buried in the Gagliano family plot?"

"Minimizing risk. We don't want someone digging up remains and running DNA tests."

"Who was cremated?"

"John Does."

"Who?"

"Unclaimed bodies in the morgue."

"But..."

"Anything can be had for the right price."

"These precautions...are you still—"

"I'm officially no longer a part of the operation."

"Is it over?"

"It'll never be over. At least, as long as countries distrust each other, intelligence gathering will occur."

"How is it not over if you're—"

"My tour is over." I open my mouth, full of questions, but he places a finger over my lips. "I'm no longer a part of the operation. That's all you need to know."

"You're still worried we might be in danger?"

"I'll probably always worry. At least for the next couple of decades." He presses his lips to my forehead and muses, "I've seen the worst in humanity. Power and greed lend justification to vile acts. Many criminals have no option other than prosecution. But with a certain level of wealth, options exist. And if faced with losing everything..."

"They do bad things."

"Yes."

"My father isn't a dangerous man." I've seen the men who

kill regularly, mostly the ones who keep businesses safe and members in line. My father isn't anything like them. Interestingly, the brutal men are the workhorses and rank lower in the organization.

"Few men are truly evil. Most men possess morals, but ethics vary. Your father is better than most. He grew up in a criminal organization, but he runs a mostly legitimate, global business."

"My father doesn't like… He didn't want us touching drugs. He once told me there's been a market for drugs for centuries and there always will be. That what our family does is bring discipline to the market and safety to our communities."

"Some criminal organizations are more successful than others at maintaining peace."

The skin on his outer arm has a lighter tone and is slightly raised in an uneven pattern, something that's more noticeable with his tanned skin. I run my fingers over the area. "Were you injured here?"

"I had a tattoo. Had it removed." He grins, glancing at the area fondly as if he can still see what he'd once had inked on his skin.

"Why?"

"It's not a good idea to have an easily identifiable marking. Especially one that screams U.S. Navy."

I bend and press my lips to the area, kissing both his skin and the starched hem of his shirt.

"What was it of?"

"A frog."

I crinkle my nose, and he laughs.

"Yeah, my sister didn't like it too much either."

"Were you drunk?"

"Pretty sure I would've failed a sobriety test." He caresses my cheek. His grin has settled into a relaxed, warm expression. With each day that has passed, our bodies have healed, and I'm sure that's partly responsible, but it's also like he's letting Leo the syndicate member go, and he's remembering who he was. Who he is.

The sun sparkles over the water, and it's a nearly perfect day with calm, rolling waves, but an exhaust smell circulates in the air where we're standing.

"Want to go sit?" We're on the lowest deck, but the higher one is free of the engine's smell.

"Sure." He links his fingers through mine, leading me to the narrow stairs. He steps aside and lets me pass.

On this deck, there's a curved white sofa that looks behind the boat. A circular table fits perfectly in front of the sofa, and there's a hidden panel which can pull out to turn the sofa into an oversized lounge chair. Sam bends to adjust it for us, and the door behind us slides open.

One of the crew, a woman named Marta, exits and takes over. Thomas follows, arms full of thick white towels, and they set up the area for us.

"Would you care for anything to drink?"

"Iced water with lime," I say. "Thank you."

"Same," Sam says.

I remove my swim cover-up and sprawl on the plush towel.

"Come here. Grab that sunblock." He does as he's told and sits beside me, giving me his back. "Do you burn easily?"

"No. And if I do burn, it's usually a tan the next day." He glances over his shoulder, and I feel his gaze roam my body. "What about you? How well do you tan?"

"I tan easily, but I also wear sunblock religiously. A young woman has to take care of her skin," I say, imitating my mother. It's hard to believe I won't see her again. I haven't debated with Sam as I don't want him to think I harbor regrets, but I have to believe that with enough time, I can see my family again. At least my mother, father, and brother. If they're too much of a danger thanks to their position in the Lupi Grigi, then I should be able to see Scarlet again. She will always prioritize me over the family she hates. She'd never rat us out.

"It wouldn't be a bad idea for you to change your hair color after we're stateside," Sam says, bending his head as I massage lotion into his shoulders, oblivious to the emotional wave that swept over me and my train of thought.

"Will I be in disguise?" I tug on him, forcing him to turn. "Are you in disguise now?"

He chuckles. "No. But it wouldn't be a bad idea for us to change a few things, so we're not instantly recognizable. I was thinking about growing a beard. I stayed mostly cleanshaven before, so I could easily attach facial hair as needed to alter my appearance. Growing a beard will be a welcome break from shaving. If my wife wouldn't mind it?"

I scratch my nails through the short growth darkening his jaw. "I think I'll like it. I love you in any form." I wiggle my eyebrows, and he grins. "You could grow your hair long," I say, moving my nails to his scalp and earning a low moan. His dark hair has a natural curl to it, and as it's grown longer, it's gotten wavier.

"Do you have a thing for men with long hair?" I still, thinking of my first boyfriend…my only boyfriend. He'd had straight, shoulder-length, sandy blonde hair that he either pushed behind his ears or held back in a man bun, out of the way when he painted.

"I don't mind long hair."

"Hate to break it to you, but if I grow this out, it's closer to a seventies Afro than sexy Italian."

I snort then press my lips to his shoulder. "You're sexy to me, no matter what." I tap him, letting him know I've finished his back. He takes over, applying lotion to his front.

"I would like to take care of my roots before I meet your family." I've been dyeing my hair blonde since my eighteenth birthday as an act of rebellion. Or maybe not rebellion, just a statement that I would not be like the other women in the Lupi Grigi. I'd been determined to make my path, to choose my hair color, my clothes, and my education. This turn of events is unexpected, but it's also a choice I pushed.

"Your roots are getting pretty long."

My hand flies to my part, not that I can exactly hide it. I am overdue. I like having some roots showing against the blonde, but… "Do you hate it?"

"No." He's smiling, genuinely smiling. "You're beautiful. With straight hair, wavy hair, any color…with those eyes, you'll always be stunning." He caresses my cheek, warm brown eyes thoughtful. "In any form, you'll always be beautiful to me."

The door slides open, and our drinks are delivered to us, and just as quickly, Thomas disappears back inside the boat.

"I imagine your natural dark shade contrasting with the blue in your eyes will be heart-stopping."

"Straight, dark hair," I say, fingering a section of the wind-blown salty strands. "I get the waves from braiding it at night."

"Come here. Lean back with me."

I do as he says, sprawling beside him. My sunglasses shield my eyes, but the sun's heat sizzles my skin and relaxes my muscles. This is the first day on our journey the air has been warm enough to lie like this.

Sam's fingers and the sun work in concert on my skin, scattering tingles across my limbs. I close my eyes, reveling in the ease of the moment.

My bikini strap slips from my shoulder and cool air circulates over my breast, and a hot, wet warmth encapsulates my nipple. Sam slips a hand beneath my bottoms and fingers my folds. My legs spread wider, giving him ample room.

The breeze, the sun, the salty air, and his fingers and tongue feel amazing, but we're outside.

"The crew," I gasp, attempting to push up to see inside the cabin.

"If they come out here, they'll leave."

"But…"

There's a tug on my top, and the stringy piece falls to the side. He sucks in my other nipple, circling his tongue as his fingers press against my mound, massaging in a way that feels incredible.

"Mrs. Watson?"

"Hmm?"

"What do you say we officially begin our honeymoon?"

CHAPTER 37

ONE WEEK AFTER THE FUNERAL

SAM

"According to a CIA source, Massimo De Luca's men have been inquiring about Leo Sullivan. Two men were hanging around his apartment building, showing his photo, and asking occupants if they knew him."

"I can't imagine they discovered anything useful. I didn't socialize," I say.

I'm in Jack Sullivan's home office. Liam Sullivan, Jack's brother, flew to San Diego for the meeting. The original plan had been for us to meet in Houston, but given my alter ego did business in Houston, and therefore the risk of being recognized was highest in that city, our yacht docked in a small marina on the Alabama coast. We drove to a landing strip where we flew a private plane to San Diego. There are no official records of our arrival in the United States.

"We're monitoring Massimo all the same."

"What do you think he's looking for?"

"Our source thinks he might be investigating his brother's death."

"I never denied killing him," I say, letting my tone convey my skepticism of that theory.

"No, but we think he's highly suspicious of the syndicate."

"Leandro was suspicious. Massimo concurring fits."

"Precisely. We're uncertain what he's hoping to find, but we're fairly certain his goal is to understand the extent of the syndicate's involvement in recent legal issues for the Lupi Grigi," Jack says.

Liam bounces a stress ball on the floor, listening with blatant apathy. From what I know of Liam, that checks. His passion lies in R&D. He doesn't have a military background and, to my knowledge, has never cared for law enforcement. He was perfect as my business contact on the Sullivan end because in all my undercover years working for the syndicate he never once mentioned anything not pertaining to the sale of arms. If anyone listened to our conversations, we never gave them a reason to doubt the legitimacy of my role in negotiating with various arms dealers.

"Do we have anyone monitoring Alessio?"

"We're watching him from afar. An inside source shared that the reason he wanted the funeral to occur as quickly as it did is that his son, Orlando, had a ceremony scheduled, and they didn't want to interfere with plans," Jack says.

"Ceremony?" A fifteen-year-old mafia teen… "He's a made man? He killed someone?"

"Sometime this weekend. I guess that means he killed recently, or he will soon."

Damn. Willow would hate knowing that. Her brother had an innocence about him, and killing will change him.

"I know you hate you took her away from her family, but you did her a favor. You took her out of a life in organized crime. She's better off here."

I understand what Jack's saying, and I appreciate why he's saying it. But she still loved her family. They're as much victims of the world they were born into as purveyors of it. Judgment Day awaits every person, and I am not the judge.

"What are your plans?" Jack asks.

"Well, I'm thinking once we leave here, we might drive up the coast. Let her see California. Maybe drive cross country, checking out places. See what kind of place she prefers, where she might want to settle. It's my understanding we can live pretty much anywhere?" I ask, looking to Jack for confirmation.

"We don't see any reason you can't. It's an off-the-books op. No accessible records exist tying you to it. The risk you need to resolve is your sisters. They need to keep your return quiet. They can't run an article in the local paper or do a small-town hero welcome for the soldier who's been suffering from amnesia in a hospital in Syria for five years."

"I'll be careful." The CIA provided a carefully sculpted explanation for my whereabouts, including a story for how I met my wife. They'd wanted to paint her as the nurse, but I vetoed that, given she has no medical training. The official story is I recovered in a hospital in Syria with amnesia, took a job fishing, and stayed in Croatia working the docks. It wasn't until after I met her in Croatia, where she was a sketch artist selling her work on the street, that I began to recover my memory, and found my way to the U.S. Embassy.

That's the story my sisters will be told. If need-to-know arises, Knox and Max, my sisters' husbands and Arrow team members, may be given clearance to learn the truth. Until then, they'll be fed the cover story. Will they believe it? I doubt it. But they'll understand the importance of playing along.

"Your sister's baby shower is soon," Jack says.

Liam continues bouncing the ball, creating a steady *whop, whop, whop* sound.

"Are they under surveillance?"

"No. Although the Swiss authorities inquired about Sloane testifying."

Sloane unwittingly uncovered a scam at her company, and she and Sage became targets by those attempting to keep it under wraps. That had been a challenging time for me to be deep undercover.

"Is she going to testify?"

"She agreed. If needed. But I'm not sure it will happen. The lead architect of the scheme was released on home arrest awaiting trial and recently committed suicide," Jack says.

That gets my attention. "Legit suicide? Not staged?" Staged would mean someone is still out there keeping things under wraps.

"A security camera in his home office captured the moment. A housekeeper found him within minutes."

There's not much to say. It wasn't my case, but I'm glad the bastards who came after my sister are no longer sharing our air.

"So, my sisters are in the clear, right? You aren't still monitoring them, are you?" All those surveillance photos Nomad showed me come to mind. "How'd you learn about the shower?

Knox?" That would make sense. Knox works with these guys, and it's his first child.

"I received an invitation," Jack says, shifting in his seat, as if taking offense to my question. "We're all close."

Close enough to cross the country for what will probably last about an hour? I can't imagine my youngest sister, Sage, doing anything extravagant. She'd probably have her friends over for cupcakes or whatever one eats at a baby shower.

"Knox made it clear he didn't expect us to attend," Jack says, as if sensing my incredulity. "Ava and I sent a present. But we're all close. We became closer after…"

Jack lets his voice trail. Yes, there's no need to dredge that up. I thank god daily it all worked out and my sisters are safe.

"There's a reason for me bringing this up." Women's voices pass through the closed doors, and there's a soft rap. "Come on in," Jack says.

Ava, Jack's wife, stands at the door, hand on the knob. Willow—I've got to start thinking of her as Lily—remains in the hallway. "Sophia and Fisher arrived." She pushes the door wider.

Jack comes around the desk and hugs his daughter. She's his daughter from his first marriage and must be in her late twenties or early thirties. She graduated from college and entered the FBI directly through a special program, but she's CIA now, as is her husband, Fisher. He and I shake hands.

Whereas I went deep undercover, these two specialize in quick undercover projects that carry substantial risk. They helped rescue my sister and even met with me once to assure me in person my sisters were a priority.

"Good to see you both," I say as I shake Sophia's hand.

"Lily and I are going to take a walk along the ocean. What

time do you think you'll be done? I was thinking we could make reservations at a restaurant downtown so she can get a feel for the city at night. She hasn't been to San Diego before," Ava says.

Jack checks his watch. "We'll be done in another hour or two, tops. I'm down with going out to eat. Are you?" It takes me a second to realize he's asking me.

"That works." I make eye contact with Lily to gauge her exhaustion level.

Ava set her up with a hairstylist this morning, and her hair has been blown out to perfection. I doubt the near black color of her locks is her natural color, but I was right that a dark color is a stunning combination with her magnetic blue eyes. And she is a magnet. She walks in a room, and I'm pulled to her. I don't want to look anywhere or be anywhere else.

"I'd love to," my wife says, understanding my unspoken question.

Ava smiles and pulls the door closed, taking my wife with her and leaving us to our meeting.

I'd hoped Ryan, Jack's Arrow Tactical Security partner, would make it down, but he got caught up on a different project. When we drive through Santa Barbara, he's invited us to stay over and has given us a choice of staying at his home or at one of the corporate apartments Arrow maintains near the office.

With so many of us in the office, we resettle at a round table that's off to the side. Jack's office overlooks a covered deck with direct views of the Pacific Ocean.

"Where were we?" Jack asks himself. He raps a knuckle against the table. "Oh, yes. The baby shower. Interpol will be in attendance. That's why I brought it up."

I crack my knuckles, waiting to hear the reason Interpol

needs to be at my sister's baby shower, and yes, I'm bracing for the worst.

"Nomad," Jack says in explanation. "Your sisters know him as Tristan Voignier."

My gut has trusted Nomad for years, although if he rushed my exit with Willow—er, Lily—in tow, I'll have some words for him. "How did he become friends with Sage?"

"Interpol got involved with the pharmaceutical scandal. Cross-border crime."

He's been showing me photos of my sisters for years, but they were taken by surveillance. I face Sophia and Fisher. "I thought the two of you—"

"They did," Jack interrupts. "But they all met at a legal proceeding, and your sister Sage seems to be good at maintaining friendships." I smile at that. Because yeah, she is. "Ryan was on vacation in Europe at the time of the big bust, and he got to know Tristan and his wife, and we all got together last year. And of course, part of Nomad's assignment was to stay abreast of your sisters so he would have updates for you."

He was good about it, too. At every meetup, he had an update. But he never shared he'd become friends with them. "I've missed a lot over these years, haven't I?"

"A great service to your country, but also a great sacrifice," Jack says.

Not one to dwell on commendation, I ask, "Do we know yet who rushed the extraction?" If it had gone as planned, I would've been alone. I would've had Willow set up with security in a new location.

"Nikolai Ivanov," Liam says.

Liam is the one who originally set up my going abroad under the guise of a Sullivan Arms salesperson.

"The immediate extraction was one of his conditions," Liam adds.

I let out a breath, confused. I left Nick a number but didn't know if he'd use it. "He's an asset now?"

"Our first meeting is in a week," Sophia says. "Fisher and I need your help. We'll be his contacts. Interpol is reallocating resources. We need to understand everything about his schedule. The players in his world. Anything that will help us so we can cultivate him."

"And keep him safe," I add, given that's the part she left out of her statement.

Fisher adds, "Absolutely."

That's good. I'm glad Nick's working with us. It's the best possible scenario.

"Why did Nick rush the extraction?"

Jack smiles. "Because you did what any good undercover operative does. You developed a genuine friendship with the man. And he said you needed your wife. That she was the best thing that happened to you."

"But...he didn't know the extraction details."

"No. But you convinced him to be an asset and gave him a number to call."

"And?"

"He called. Pieced things together. Nick can be a persuasive individual," Liam says.

"He's the one who hired Cohen? Nick sicced Mossad on us?"

"Ex-Mossad," Jack corrects. "We told Nick we needed more time. He told us he wanted to see us in action. Wanted to see us prove our worth."

"And you all jumped." Fucking CIA. "Prioritized an asset over an officer."

"You know what's at stake," Jack says in a tone that lets me know he's had enough insolence and he's on the verge of pulling rank. "Besides, our new asset made it clear you and your wife were his priority. He gave us no choice."

Dammit, Nick. He always has to believe he knows best.

"He also sends a message," Liam says.

"Yeah?" I ask, wondering what exactly he would have to tell me.

"He says that if you ever need him, to call."

My throat tightens a notch. Nick and I worked closely for years. We treated each other like family. But I thought once he found out I'd been his leak, he'd want me dead. I feared he'd kill my sisters if he ever got their real identity.

"You didn't share with him—"

"No," Jack says. "He knows you're alive but has no way of reaching you. Well, I suppose he could use his contacts—us—to get word. But, no, he doesn't know your real identity or what country you moved to." He places his elbows on the table and links his hands in a relaxed prayer posture. "Same goes for your wife."

"Which brings us to why we're here," Sophia says. "Ready to download? We've read the debriefs, but there's more we need."

CHAPTER 38

WILLOW, AKA LILY

In Phoenix, we stopped in a small gun store, and Sam purchased a black handgun he placed in the glove compartment, along with a box of ammunition. The purchase served as a reminder that while we might be theoretically untraceable, Sam doesn't gamble with safety.

We stood in awe at the Grand Canyon. Ate the most delicious beignets in New Orleans. Boarded a plane to New York City because when he asked where I'd like to visit, and I told him I'd always wanted to go there, we ditched the rental and presumably his handgun, and on Broadway we attended *Six*, a play about King Henry's six wives. From there, we rented a car and drove to Annapolis, Maryland. He pointed out restaurants he liked "back in the day."

Before we arrived in Washington, DC, he warned me he'd never move to the DC area unless I absolutely loved it. I enjoyed visiting the monuments I'd only seen photographs of, but I couldn't see us living there due to the crowds and the traffic.

From DC, we drove to Charlottesville, Virginia, a smaller, quaint college town where I learned he'd once dated a girl who went to school here. I'd asked what happened to them, and he shrugged, saying they weren't that serious. Because of my experience with Jules, I understood exactly what he was saying. I'd cared for Jules at that time in my life, but I was young, and I loved the freedom and rebellion he represented more than him. Knowing if we were ever discovered, my father would likely have him killed, made me end things earlier than I might have otherwise. But still, all things being the same, it's clear Sam also had relationships that were important but not meant to last.

From Virginia, we drove to Asheville along rolling highways lined by trees. We checked in to our Asheville hotel hours ago. And now, we're in the Land Rover he purchased outside of Charlottesville. We'd been in a rental, but when he saw the older SUV in a used car lot, he swerved to make a last-minute turn into the lot.

Sam assured me he'll buy me whatever I want, but I'm a nervous driver. I drove ten miles lower than the speed limit when we went to return the rental after he purchased his giant new automobile. I'm sure I'll eventually drive as it seems Americans love to drive, but I drove little in Italy. At home, my father's security accompanied me and therefore drove. In Florence, as a student, I biked whenever I found myself free of security. Here, the cars speeding along on the freeway feel enormous, and I'm still not used to the measurement system, which is disorienting on the dashboard.

We're parked on a neighborhood street with small bungalow

homes, broad-leaf trees, and mailboxes stationed at the end of each driveway. Sam's knee bounces up and down, and he's on his phone, checking texts. In the glove compartment is a small box of SIM cards, should he need to destroy the one in his mobile and replace it. He also picked up a new handgun when we arrived in North Carolina, as there's no waiting period to purchase one here.

Our windows are rolled down, and a soft breeze blows through the vehicle. The day was warm, but the temperatures are dropping quickly.

Over the last several weeks, Sam has spoken of his sisters with increasing frequency. Sloane is the one closest to him in age, and he said that when they were younger, they spent a lot of time together. His youngest sister, Sage, had been sick as a child, but he says she's healthy now, and she's the one who is expecting a child with his best friend from high school. He doesn't know the story of how they got together, but he said he couldn't imagine a better husband for his sister. And Sloane married a guy he doesn't know well, but he's been around him and believes he's a good guy. Sage's husband is named Knox and Sloane's husband's name is Max.

Knox and Max both have last names that start with the letter W, which meant they were assigned to the same homeroom. That's how they met, and they became fast friends.

"Do you think they'll be much longer?" I ask.

"Should be soon." Finished with his messages, he taps the phone against the steering wheel in the same rapid beat as his bouncing knee. I reach for his hand, remove the phone, set it in the drink holder, and link our fingers.

"It's going to be okay. They're going to be thrilled to see you." He's nervous, and he shouldn't be, but telling him not to be nervous won't do anything. "Tell me about them. Your sisters." He's told me about them, and the look he gives me says he's thinking the same thing. "Tell me a favorite story."

He exhales and lifts my hand to his mouth where he playfully nips at my skin.

"Come on, there has to be something. Is this the house you grew up in?"

"Here? No. I told you, I grew up in Rocky Mount."

"Is that near here?"

"Not at all. Sounds like it belongs in the mountains, doesn't it? No, it's farther east. About an hour east of Raleigh, where Sloane, the oldest of my two younger sisters, lives now."

"Which sister were you closer to?"

"Well, Sloane's close to me in age. She…she struggled in school. More in middle school. By high school, she didn't give a fuck. I mean, sorry. She didn't care about what others thought. But I was probably her closest friend."

"Why'd she struggle in school?"

He half-smiles. "Mom always said she sees the world differently. And she does."

"What does that mean? Is she–"

"If she was diagnosed with anything, Mom didn't share it. She was big on avoiding labels. For a while, there, I was one of the few who could calm Sloaney down when she'd work herself up." Pride rings through his words.

"It's odd your mom didn't share what was going on with you."

"She did. In her own way. And you gotta understand…my parents. We had tough years. Sage was really sick. It's hard on a family when a kid's in and out of the hospital. Mom had a group of friends who were all parents of sick kids, and they were tight. Guarantee you they backed Mom's approach. You asked for a memory… I can remember someone in a mall coming up and asking what was wrong with Sage. Said it like this, 'What's wrong with her?' I don't think Sloane heard, or if she did, it didn't register. But Mom, man, I thought she was going to lose it on the woman. It was just… We were all so protective of Sage, and Sage was dressed up to go out to the mall. It was a big deal, you know, and she thought she looked normal. And she did. She was just…really thin. Pale. Probably had a bandage or something. I don't even remember. But I remember Mom. It was like she doubled in size. Transformed into super momma bear. Had me and Sloane take Sage to get a cookie from the American Cookie Company. Told us we could get soda too." His slight grin tells me this is a fond memory, but tears threaten in my eyes. "I love my sisters," he says, sniffing back his emotion.

"I know you do."

"I hope they can forgive me."

"They will. They're going to be thrilled to have you home."

Between the houses, a view of the mountains peeps through, and a purple haze colors the dips and valleys beyond. A tiny, bright light twinkles and disappears.

"It's a firefly," I say, pointing to the gold pinprick. Back home, we used to have an abundance of fireflies in early summer. Beneath a tree, where the shadow is darkest, another light shines and quickly disappears.

Headlights beam down the street, approaching us. The car slows and turns into his sister's driveway.

"You ready?" I ask, reaching for the passenger door handle.

Sam squeezes my hand. "Not yet."

Another car turns onto the street and pulls up beside the other vehicle.

I watch Sam closely. His attention remains fixed on the driveway. The driver of the first car walks around the front and opens the passenger door.

A very pregnant woman with dark, wavy hair, presumably Sage, takes the hand of the man who came around to her door. She's smiling widely.

"Is that Knox and Sage?" I ask.

Sam's transfixed by the scene and gives an almost imperceptible nod.

The back of the vehicle pops open, and I assume Knox is holding a set of keys that allowed him to do that since he's at the front of the vehicle. The back is filled with boxes and bows.

A tall, thin woman with dark, straight hair, presumably Sloane, exits the other car. The driver of her car gets out after she's already walked away. He's a tall, broad-shouldered man with sandy blond hair.

"I'll empty the car. You guys—" The man stops speaking the second he notices us sitting in the vehicle. Sam parked in front of the neighbor's house, but we're not far away.

"I think he's spotted us," I whisper.

"Sage, why don't the two of you go on inside?" Knox says.

"I don't mind helping," Sloane says, oblivious to Knox's concerns, putting her arms around a brown cardboard box at the back of the vehicle.

The other man, presumably Sloane's husband, Max, approaches and says something in her ear. She immediately releases the box and rushes to her sister's side, taking her elbow and guiding her into the house.

"I'm fine," Sage says loudly enough for her voice to carry across the lawn.

The screen door creaks and closes behind the two women, and the two men stand side by side, squinting at our vehicle.

"Can we help you?" one of them asks.

"Stay here," Sam says to me.

He exits the car, and Knox stills. From inside the car, it's as if Knox's color blanches and his mouth opens slightly. Max's expression is unreadable.

Sam approaches, hands out to his side like the two men have guns pointed at him, but they don't. They're just staring.

"A lot of shit's gone down," Sam says. "But I'm back."

"Holy shit." Knox says with a trace of derision blended with incredulity. "Sage always said—how the fuck? I saw it. I saw the explosion."

"Magic," Sam answers. His back is to me, but he sounds cautious.

"Who are you working for?" Knox asks. Max remains silent, watching. "Not the Navy. CIA?"

"Man—"

"The explosion?" Knox asks.

"Staged."

Knox's mouth opens, incredulous. I can imagine it's a lot to absorb.

"You were never supposed to see it. You were supposed to stay in the bar," Sam says. None of this is what he's supposed to say.

Knox closes his mouth, and he cocks his head. "You hired—"

"They did. They hired her. A distraction. You weren't supposed to follow me." There's a plea to Sam's tone.

"And you let us..."

The screen door creaks open.

His pregnant sister steps out onto the front porch. "Sam?" She squeals, arms wide, running forward as fast as a woman with a distended pregnant belly can. "Sam!" she squeals. "I knew it."

Sam's smile is as wide as I've seen as she crashes into him. I can't hear what they're saying to each other, but the other two men look on with the same incredulous, dazed expression.

On the porch, Sloane watches, hands at her side, elbows out. I expect to witness the same unbridled happiness Sage exhibits, but Sloane's not smiling. Obviously, I don't know her and might be misinterpreting her expression, but her slight hands ball into fists and she steps back. Is she going to leave?

Her movement draws Sam's attention. He pulls away from Sage and holds out his arms to his other sister, but she isn't having it.

She stares in his direction. Her mouth opens and closes. Is she having a panic attack? No one makes a move to help her.

The streetlights flick on, emitting a slight buzzing sound.

My hand squeezes the door handle. He asked me to wait, but someone has to do something.

Max approaches his wife, but he keeps his distance. He doesn't touch her, but he's talking to her in a low voice I can't discern.

Headlights illuminate the street. The group on the lawn checks the approaching sedan and watches it pass, except for Sloane, who takes off, heading down a path around the side of the house.

"I'll talk with her," Max says, backtracking to the group. "She's just going to need some time." He places a hand on Sam's shoulder. "Good to have you back." He pats him once, and then he's off.

Sam and Knox shift, watching Max depart, and Sage looks past them to me. Our gazes lock, and my skin tingles with awareness.

"Sam…who is this?" Sage asks.

He turns, and the concern that had marred his expression lightens, and the corners of his lips lift.

"That's my wife. Your sister-in-law."

"You got married!" she exclaims, slapping his arm before charging toward me.

I step out of the SUV to greet her, sliding down to the curb, glancing past Sage to Sam.

Sage raises her arms and drops them. We both stand looking awkwardly at each other. Her smile is warm. I don't know what to do. Hug her? Introduce myself? In a flash, Sam is beside me, his palm warming my lower back.

"Lily Watson, I'd like for you to meet my sister, Sage."

He touches her shoulder, then brushes her hair behind her ear. "You look beautiful, sis. Pregnancy suits you."

She beams through a steady stream of tears, then holds both arms out to me. "A sister," she screeches. I bend to hug her, and, with her belly, it's a little awkward, but we're both smiling.

Her husband, Knox, steps up behind her. He's not smiling, but he's not glaring either. I think he might be shell-shocked. Sage wraps her arm behind his back, and he places his across her shoulder.

"Can you believe he got married?" Sage grins, taking me in with a warm, glowing gaze. "We're married, too," she says, gesturing to Knox.

"I am aware. I sent you an anonymous wedding gift."

"The yellow Kitchen Aid blender?"

"I remembered you loved Mom's."

"I had a feeling." She rubs her belly, looking up at him, eyes full of wonder. "You've been watching over us."

"As much as I could," he admits. Then, almost apologetically, he adds, "Officially, though, I was in a hospital in Syria with amnesia, but it's probably best we share that story as little as possible."

Sage nods slowly. "I don't need to know details. I'm so happy you're back." She swipes at her tears with a soft laugh before her attention falls back on me. "You are so beautiful. Where did he find you? Where are you from?"

Sam and Knox exchange a glance, and Knox says, "Why don't we go inside and they can share what they've been allowed to share? It sounds like there's specific information we need to learn."

Sage beams as if she didn't even hear Knox. "I told you he was still alive. I told everyone. They never found your body. I just knew. And this guy…he refused to listen to me."

Knox grimaces. "This is just what I needed. For her to be proven right. Again."

"Has she ever been wrong?" Sam asks with a sly grin.

Knox exchanges a loving glance with his wife. "Never."

"Spoken like a wise man," Sam says.

It might have been my imagination, but I think a flicker of a smile cropped up on Knox's face. But a shadow quickly falls.

This is what Sam had been afraid of. That his choices hurt them and forgiveness will be impossible.

CHAPTER 39

SAM

Stepping inside Sage's home is like stepping into the past. The wide foyer with wood plank flooring and an open view to the back of the house with a cushioned window seat beneath a panoramic window over the mountains is exactly what I remember. The furniture has changed, the walls are a slightly darker blue than before, and the rooms along the hallway aren't as cluttered.

I'd been in Saudi Arabia when I received the news that hired assassins burned her home. In the same phone call, Jack Sullivan assured me she was safe, and he'd be certain she was taken care of. Based on the layout of the home, which features a wide hallway with rooms on each side and an open living area in the back with a stairwell on the left side, she rebuilt using the same house plans. Photos line the section of the angled wall on the side of the stairs, and I'm drawn to the captured memories.

The photo of our family is tinged brown along the edges, and the way the brown and black hues alternate from light to drenched, it must be from fire, not age. The photo is of me, Sage, Sloane, and our parents. My father's hand rests on my shoulder, my mom is at his side, and Sloane and Sage stand before us. We're dressed in our best clothes on Easter Sunday. The photo was taken the year before I met Knox.

Another photo is of my father and me fishing beside a small pond. It's a candid photo, and you can't see my father's face, but he looms beside me, about three times taller than I am, and I'm grinning with a small perch on the hook.

Sage in a wedding dress catches my eye, and I step forward to get a better look at her simple white silk gown and the rosy glow on her cheeks. Knox stands beside her in a tux. The background is blurred, but based on the green hues, they must be outside. They're looking at each other, and Sage holds a bouquet. I should've been there. I should've been the best man, and I should've walked her down the aisle. My eyes burn unexpectedly. Unexpected because none of this is new to me. I know what I missed out on. The hurt and regret churned for years. I guess I didn't expect the hurt would intensify upon my return.

I step back from the photo, breathing through the tightness in my chest, and peruse the remaining dozen photos. There's Sloane and Max, some people I don't recognize, one of Jimmy, Sage's friend, on an inner tube holding a beer, and a recent one of Sage and Sloane in front of a Christmas tree. There are no photos of Sage in the hospital, but those were some of my favorite family photos. We had so many printed photos of us playing games, doing crafts, using the end of her bed as a table. It's not that I miss her being sick, but I miss how connected we were as a family. They weren't simple times, but looking back, we were all together, and…

I pinch the bridge of my nose and squeeze my eyes shut. This isn't the time to go overboard with sentimental thoughts.

"You okay?" Sage lightly touches my arm, and I snap to it, scanning the hallway.

It's just me and Sage out here.

"Knox is getting Lily some water."

Hearing the name Lily is going to take some getting used to. Saying it is still strange. Perhaps we should have kept her first name.

"Do you want anything?"

"No, I'm good." I pull Sage up to my side. "You were a beautiful bride." I saw photos of her, but that fact dies on my tongue.

"I have a wedding album if you want to see it."

"I'd love to." My younger self probably wouldn't have wanted to sift through wedding photos, but I want to experience what I can, and I want to hear everything I missed. "Do you still have our family albums?"

"We saved some photos. Like this one," she says, pointing out our family photo. "But a lot of the photos were destroyed in the fire. If the fire didn't get them, the water did."

"I'm so sorry, Sage." Of all of us, Sage treasured memories the most. She might not have wanted to hang photos of when she was sick, but she'd want to keep the photographs and mementos.

"That wasn't your fault," she says brightly. "The people responsible were caught, you know?"

"I know. I wasn't here, but I kept up with things." Everyone who attempted to harm my sisters is either dead or received lifetime prison sentences. It's ironic. I'd been terrified the retribution if I was discovered would put my family in danger, yet my nerdy sister nearly got them killed. "How has Sloane been doing?"

"She's been really good. Max is good for her. She's happy." Sage's expression fills with love. She's the best of the three of us. "Sloane will come around. You know how she is. Seeing you was a shock."

"It would be for anyone. I thought about the best way to do it. I could've had someone from the Navy tell you. Played it out like they found me, and I'd be coming home after a bout of amnesia, but..." I didn't want more lies. I'm done with the lying.

"You chose the right way." I side-eye my sister, amused by how much she sounds like Mom. "Knox never would've believed any story you concocted. Is he right? Is there a story we need to learn?"

"There is. There's a lot I can't tell you." Technically, I've told her too much as it is.

"But yet you got married." She beams up at me. "She's beautiful. Stunning. I bet it was her dark hair and blue eyes that caught your attention. Love at first sight."

I choke on a laugh. It had hardly been love at first sight, but I won't be the one to destroy Sage's fantasy. It hadn't been love at first sight, but mostly because she was too damn young, and I didn't have an open mind. But it is definitely love now.

There hasn't been a morning since the first one aboard *The Honey Pot* that I haven't been grateful she's by my side. I would've left her with her family. I wouldn't have taken her, but losing the best thing to happen to me in my adult life would've hurt worse than anything I've ever endured.

"You want a beer?" Knox asks from the threshold to the living area. Across the room, my wife sits on the sofa with a big dog pawing at her. She glances up, catching my eye, and shoots me a reassuring smile. She's good.

"Sure." Knox looks at Sage with concern etched in the lines around his eyes. "Why don't you sit? We'll come into the den once we get beers."

"I'm okay," she says with exasperation.

"I know that," he says. "But don't you want to get to know your sister-in-law?"

The way she smiles at him, I'm pretty sure she knows he's playing to her weakness to get what he wants. He palms her distended belly lovingly, and my chest tightens again.

"Why don't we go down to the basement? We'll grab a beer from the fridge downstairs and maybe sit outside for a bit?"

I cast a sidelong glance at my wife and sister. "Sage will take care of her," Knox says gruffly.

"Lead the way."

We pass through the living area and into a kitchen, and he opens a white-painted door. The narrow staircase descends into a cozy downstairs area that's a walkout basement. Large windows bring in light, and, looking around, it's clear this is Knox's space. There's a pool table, worn leather sofas, and a mini kitchen on one wall. On the far side is a desk with multiple monitors and a couple of whiteboards.

"I mostly work from home," he says.

"You claimed the basement?"

"Most of it. There's walk-in storage and a couple of rooms we could finish out if we ever need more room."

"You guys seem really happy."

"We are," he says, leaning into the refrigerator. "So, how old is your wife?"

I snort. I'd wondered how long it would take for Knox to comment.

"She's younger," I say with an irrepressible smirk.

Her age isn't funny to me, and neither is our age difference, but there's something about being with one of the guys that paints the humor.

"I'd ask you how that happened, but…is she at least legal?" I blink. "Over eighteen?" he clarifies.

"Yes, you fuck," I say, still grinning.

"Can I offer her a beer without getting a ticket for giving alcohol to the underaged?"

"She's over twenty-one," I say, suppressing a laugh. "And I love her. She's the best thing that's happened to me. She's probably the reason I finally got off that assignment. So watch it." The warning is coated with a grin, but Knox reads me. He always has.

He snaps the tops off the glass beer bottles using an opener screwed to the wall, and the tops fall neatly into the garbage can below. He hands me a beer and says, "Let's sit outside."

"You trust your neighbors?" I ask as we step out into the unseasonably warm fall evening.

His back yard is bigger than I would've expected. He's got a brick patio with chairs around a firepit and there's a deck that extends from the main floor. A hammock hangs on two posts from the overhead deck. And from there, the wooded area slopes downward quickly.

"Yep," he says as he takes one of the Adirondack chairs and sits, gesturing for me to take another one. "If it gets too buggy, we'll go inside. The neighbor to the side is out of town this week. Newly divorced, and he travels a lot. Neighbors to the other side are in their eighties and never come down into the back yard. Even if they did, they couldn't hear us."

A squirrel scampers through the leaves, pausing to observe us, then scurries deeper into the woods.

"This is nice back here," I say. "Feels like your house backs up to the Appalachian Trail."

"No, but it's close and accessible," he says. "House sits on two acres. It's just a deep lot. They won't develop past here because of the incline."

"Nice. It's like bordering a park."

He chugs his beer and sets it on the rim of the fire table. "What can you tell me?"

I look him directly in the eye. "First, I hate it went down the way it did. I hate what you must've gone through. I won't blame you if you can't forgive me."

"Nothing to forgive," he says. That's, of course, bullshit, and we both know it. With another sigh, he leans back and rests his elbows on the chair's arms. "Wasn't your call. I'm a big boy. I get that. And I'm also family now. Officially. I'll stand by you until the day I die. But, while the girls aren't here, what can you tell me? Foremost, is whatever operation you were on over?"

"My role is," I answer one hundred percent truthfully. "I'll give you the official spiel when we're all together, so I only have to repeat it once."

"How'd you convince them to let you come home?"

"That was always the deal. It was supposed to be a short gig."

"Extended to five years. Is that about right?"

"Yep."

"Let me guess. You had to save the world?"

"I did some good," I say, thinking more of the funds I

diverted to charities and people in need I met along the way from time to time. When you live among thieves, and especially when you don't want those thieves to trust each other too much, a little theft here and there is good for humankind.

He puts his hand to his mouth thoughtfully. "You still with the Navy?"

"No. We stopped by Coronado. Paperwork's being processed. Medical discharge. No fanfare." That's another way of saying on the down-low.

"What're your plans?"

"I'm on extended leave at the moment."

"From the CIA?"

"From everything."

He narrows his eyes. "Did you work for Arrow?"

"Officially, the operation never happened. A shell company paid me."

"Ah, one of those."

"There are people pretty high up in the US government who can't know, so yeah, one of those."

Too many politicians are bought. If some of the corrupt members on the intelligence committee got wind, I would've been eliminated years ago.

"You know what the craziest part of this is...your sister. She knew you were alive. I thought she couldn't accept the truth, but she knew. In her gut."

"She's a wise one. I'd hoped both Sage and Sloane would think about the duffels I created for them and, at the very least, hope I'd made myself disappear."

"And that woman in the bar? She was a plant."

"Not a good one. Clearly. You left her."

"I hated myself for that. For years. Thought if I'd gone with you..." He angles his head and looks away like it's too painful to look at me while he remembers.

"I'll never make that up to you," I say, knowing it's the god's honest truth. I could've trusted him. Could've broken protocol and read him in, but it felt too risky, too wrong. His reaction, everyone's reaction, needed to be believable. My allegiance had been to my country above all else.

Crunching leaves and twigs alert us of someone approaching in the woods. Knox sits up, looking down the slope, but he doesn't appear nervous. He's simply alert.

Sloane comes into view first, followed by Max. Sloane stops when she sees us, then charges forward. I stand to greet her, and brace myself. Sloane shoots straight. I deserve whatever she throws at me.

When she reaches me, her gaze falls to my feet. It's the pink around her eyes and tear-splotched skin that guts me. "You hurt us," she says. "Why?"

Agitation practically vibrates off her. She's controlling her emotions, but it's hard. I brought this on her.

"I was on a project with some people who believe in retribution. You and Sage are my only family. I didn't want them coming after you to get back at me." She says nothing, and that makes me feel like I need to say more. "I was deep undercover."

Max approaches behind her, and his fingers touch her hip.

"Do you have any idea what you did to Sage? How much you hurt her?"

"I do." Defense is on the tip of my tongue, to tell her it wasn't supposed to last so long, that what I was doing was important, that the information I gathered was critical, but I swallow it all down. "I love you, Sloaney." Her lips press into a flat line, and tears cascade down her cheeks. "I love both of you. It would've killed me if you got wrapped up in my shit. I don't expect your forgiveness, but you need to know the only reason we took that approach is because of your safety, and Sage's safety. That's the most important thing to me. Always will be."

She sniffs, and I'm not sure she's aware, but her foot taps the ground. "You were doing your job, and I understand doing your job. But we needed you, and you weren't here."

And that's the hell of it. She's absolutely right. I couldn't be in two places at once. While I was off playing secret agent, I wasn't where I should be, helping my sisters when they needed me.

She shuffles up against me, head down. I hold her as she sobs. Max stands near the Adirondack chair, appearing as helpless as I feel.

A hard punch into my side has me curving against pain. "Ow."

But she doesn't stop. She pummels my ribs. Batting me, gaze focused on my chest. Mom would shout, tell her not to hit. But she needs this. I can take it. I deserve it.

Max says, "Sloane. Babe."

His words are soft, and she lowers her fists. The recognition that he's her person now smacks a raw spot in my chest.

"I love you too." With her lower lip protruding and gaze down, it's like she's a reprimanded kid and been told to apologize. Maybe she hears Mom's voice, too.

She steps past the fire pit, away from me, but she stops at the sliding door. "I'm glad you're alive. Are you home for good, or are you going away again?"

Knox's gaze snaps up from the paver he'd been studying,

and it's clear he's got the same questions. Max stands back, hands shoved in his pockets, observing.

"I'm home for good. We're home for good."

"Don't do this again." Her voice cracks.

"You have my word. Scout's honor."

Sloane frowns. "You were never a Scout."

I half-chuckle. "I promise."

CHAPTER 40

ONE WEEK LATER

WILLOW, AKA LILY

Sam found us a rental tucked into the mountain with breathtaking views and a mere fifteen-minute drive to downtown Asheville and Sage and Knox's home. It's typically a weekly rental, but the owners recently renovated the kitchen and hadn't yet put it back on the rental market, so Sam claimed it for the next three months to allow us to use it as a base as we decide what we want to do.

The rental is unlike any I've seen before. It's round—or, well, really an octagon. Sam says in the seventies the roundhouse had its day, showing up in places all over the United States. He says that, but in our travels, we didn't come across any. But this one, with windows overlooking the mountains, feels like we're perched on a cloud. And given the wooden house is supported on stilts dug deep into the steep incline on the side of a mountain, we sort of are.

Taking in the mix of blues and grays on a misty morning, there's no question how they derived the name Blue Ridge for these mountains. It's both breathtaking and peaceful and a welcome respite.

I hear Sam before I see him. Twigs snap, and the orange splash of his baseball cap peeks through the tree canopy below.

He woke up early and headed out for a trail run. Later today, we'll go for a hike together. For me, that will be my exercise. For Sam, it'll count as a walk.

We don't get a good signal here, but we'll check our mobiles for messages when we drive into town around lunchtime to meet up with Sage and Knox. I messaged instructors from the Penland School of Craft about a glass-blowing immersion workshop. I had to tell them I had no formal training, as I had to follow the resume the CIA mapped for me, which listed me as an English major from the University of Zagreb, but I'm hopeful I can find a place within the Asheville art community and continue to grow as an artist, whether that's with paint, glass, or jewelry making.

Sam loves this area for the abundant access to nature, his sister, and his best friend, but I love it for the way the town embraces art. My father thought my desire to learn and practice art was foolish, given he believed I should only want to be a mother, but I have yet to encounter anyone with a similar philosophy. I'm sure those people are here. For that matter, I know they are. The United States has clusters of mafia and organized crime families throughout, and many of those families are as traditional as ours, but I haven't yet run into them. I hope I never do.

Sloane and Max live in Raleigh, but they plan on visiting frequently until Sage gives birth, and then for a while after, I'm sure. It's one reason Sam insisted we not take Sage up on her offer to stay with them. He said they'd need the space for guests, and we need our space too.

My face heats, thinking about the ways we've used our space. The door swings open.

"You're up," he says, sounding inordinately pleased. He shoots me a wide smile, flashing straight, pearly white teeth. His smiles are bigger out here.

"Do you want coffee?" I ask.

He bends to remove his muddy trail shoes, a cross between trainers and hiking boots. Sweat drenches the center of the back of his t-shirt, and when he rises, he lifts it from the hem, up and over his head with one tug.

My gaze immediately locks on his bare, tanned chest and ripped abdomen. He smirks, fully aware of what I'm doing.

"I'm gonna shower. I'll take that coffee after, though. Have you had breakfast?"

"No." I slowly shake my head, making a show of admiring my husband's form.

"I'll make omelets when I'm done. Can you pop the biscuits in the oven?"

I open the oven door and bend, giving him a pointed eyeful of my backside. When I rise, he stares. I lift the coffee, smiling, servant-like, gesturing to ask if he'd like some.

"Set the coffee down." His thick, syrupy voice weakens my knees.

"What?" I'm absolutely clear on why; 'what' is simply an automated response.

"Set it down."

A familiar buzz lights my body, a low hum that has my lower belly clenching. I obediently extend my arm, placing the coffee back on the burner.

He stalks toward me. My hands twitch with the desire to run them over his chest. My thighs tighten as he nears.

And then he's there, hoisting me up, walking me backward.

"You're wet," I screech, giggling.

"How about you shower with me?"

Hard kisses rain along my neck and shoulders. His hands grip my ass, and my thighs squeeze his hips as he carries me around to our bedroom.

We reach the bathroom, and my back hits the wall. His grizzly beard scratches the tender skin along my neck and ear, and I squirm against him.

"Is this all right with you, Mrs. Watson?"

"Yes," I breathe, drunk with lust.

He slows and pulls back, his dark eyes thoughtful. "You know, if you ever change your mind—"

I stop his words by pressing my finger over his lips. I wish I could stop his doubts.

"I'm not changing my mind. I love you. This is where I want to be."

My legs slowly drop to the ground, and I cup his bearded jaw in my palms.

"I love you. Don't doubt me."

He grips my wrist and places his lips against the pulse point on the inner side of my wrist.

"Don't doubt us."

His chest falls with a deep exhale. "How did I get so lucky?"

"You're a good man who helped a stranger."

"And fell in love," he says slowly, reverently.

Goose bumps sprout along my skin, and I curl my arms around him, tracing my fingers over the muscular lines of his back, secure in the knowledge I've found my home.

THE NEXT DAY

SAM

My phone vibrates in the hospital waiting room. Sloane's stern expression and her pointed gaze at the 'no cell phones' sign has me pushing up off the plastic waiting room chair and apologetically telling my wife I'll be right back after I take the call.

"We'll be here," my Lily says with a reassuring squeeze to my hand.

I don't miss the worry etched around her narrowed blue eyes. She saw the name that flashed. I don't know why he's calling, but I won't keep anything from my wife.

With a jab at the elevator button, I push the defensive thought away. Jack wouldn't expect me to hide anything from my wife. In fact, he counseled against such a strategy. It's a piece of advice he gave me on the first day we arrived at his home in San Diego.

He'd said, "I can understand the instinct to keep her in the dark. And maybe it's necessary to cloak the past. But if my one failed marriage taught me anything, it's that trust dies in darkness." I won't forget his words.

Others crowd into the elevator, and I shoot Jack a quick text that I'll call him back.

Once outside, I locate an empty bench in front of the hospital and press his name.

"Are you at the hospital?" he asks upon answering.

"I am. Sage is in labor. Knox is about to become a father."

"It's a little early, isn't it?"

"It is." I relax on the bench, as I'm more than willing to give him an update on my sister. "Doctor induced in an abundance of caution. The baby's big, I guess, thanks to Knox." It's not due to my five-foot-nothing sister.

"Sage is petite."

I smile, thinking about my littlest sister. "She's tiny, but she's fierce. I'll need to get back upstairs with the fam unless you have something else. I'll shoot you a text once my niece arrives."

"I wasn't calling about Sage."

My gut clenches in resistance. I am not doing this. "What's up?"

"Nick's in trouble."

I close my eyes, inhale deeply through my nose, and exhale through my mouth with an audible huff.

"My cover's burned. You realize that, right? A wig and colored contacts won't cut it. If anyone recognizes me, we set off—"

"That's not what we're asking. We need to strategize. I need you in the room when we do it. You know the syndicate players better than anyone we have. Hell, most of our intel came from you. You're on leave. I get that. You've put in the time and deserve a break. But we need to do some fancy footwork on this one. And your wife's cousin, Scarlet Gagliano, is in danger too."

"Did things go south with Grigi family?"

"FUBAR is the term I'd choose."

Damn Navy acronyms. Fucked up beyond all recognition. Fanfuckingtastic.

"Scarlet's working with Nick."

I look to the sky for guidance. What the hell? Why would Nick bring Scarlet into his schemes? How did that even happen?

"She's been doing the books for the Lupi Grigi," Jack says.

"Don't tell me he used her in his petty battle with them." Yes, he was pissed over Lina, but there are bigger irons in the fire.

"We'll brief you in person. But, Sam, we need you." Jack's voice is stern.

A woman with her hair wrapped in a purple scarf and tattoos along her fingers steps outside and whips out a cigarette. She glances at me as she lights it, then drops the lighter in her coat pocket and pulls out a phone.

"What do you want me to do?"

It's not like I can let anything happen to Scarlet. She's Willow's...Lily's family. And I owe Nick.

"You want me in Virginia?" I ask, hoping my nondescript word choice successfully conveys I'm no longer alone on the sidewalk.

"No. The Highlands. Not too far, not too close. You think you could be there tonight?"

The door opens, and my wife walks out, flushed with excitement. She lights up when her gaze finds me. She puts both thumbs in the air and beams.

"My niece has arrived. Gotta run. Send me the address. I'll be there."

Lily steps up next to me as I end the call. "The delivery went smoothly. For a few minutes, there, Knox thought they'd have to do a C-section, but Sage pulled through. Knox came out and told us. He looked…god, you should've seen him. He looked like he just ran three marathons." She pauses, studying me. Concern flashes, and she gently runs the pad of her thumb over my beard. "Are you okay?"

The woman with the cigarette stamps it out on the concrete and heads back inside, leaving us alone.

"I've got to go do some work tonight."

"But—"

"It's nothing to be worried about. Nick's got himself in a twist, and I'm going to go meet up with some brains to strategize."

"Is it to do with my family?"

"Probably not entirely." My fingers comb her hair, and I inhale deeply, breathing in her soothing scent. "I'll learn more tonight."

"You're not going to disappear, are you?"

I snort with amusement, but then I sense her fear. "No. I told you, I'm done with that game."

"I thought you were done, period."

"Me too, but…" I'm too young to retire completely. I'll do something, I've just spent little effort figuring out what.

"Nick's your family, too. You need to do this."

I frown, questioning if he counts as family, but I suppose in a twisted way he does. And whether or not he's my family, her family is now involved. I'll wait to tell her about that piece of it when I have more intel.

But those blue eyes peer up at me, full of trust. I let out a sigh and press her to me, kiss the top of her head, and send a Hail Mary to the sky.

"Scarlet's involved somehow, too."

I pull back, assessing. Her lips flatline, but she gives a quick nod.

"You're a good man, Sam. You'll figure it out and do what needs to be done." She pushes up on her toes and presses her lips to mine for a chaste kiss, then she stands back on her heels and reaches for my hand. "Now, come on, let's go meet our niece. I'm eager to see what our child might look like."

She steps forward, but I don't move. I scan our surroundings and, for the first time in weeks, I ache for the comfort of a handgun tucked securely on my body.

"Sam? What is it? Don't freak. I'm not pregnant, I just–"

"Babe, my thoughts did not go there. That's not…" Her brow wrinkles, puzzled.

"I promise you, if I thought…" I study her as the full weight of what she's saying and what we're talking about sinks in. "You want kids one day?"

"Well, we haven't talked about it, but I assumed. Don't you?"

For the longest time, they weren't on my radar. I tug her back against me, and she tilts her head up, expectant. "With you, I'd love nothing more. I was kind of thinking we should plan a ceremony of sorts, a renewal of vows with my family, so we have wedding photos and stuff like that." Sage's wall of photos has gotten me thinking. We don't have anything from our wedding, and one day our kids will want to see their mom in white. Besides, it's time to share life events with my family again.

"Kids, but a wedding first?" She's grinning, and there's an excited gleam in her eyes.

"Well, our wedding certificate is legal, just like all of your documents. But, I'd like to share our ceremony with my family. As for kids, I'm not in a rush. Kids can be…" I know firsthand what they can be and what can happen. "But if you want kids, yes, I want them too."

"I want them to have your brown eyes, your wavy hair, and your heart."

Grinning, I say, "Yeah, it sucks for our kids. They're gonna wish they got your blues, and it's probably not gonna happen for them."

"You never know." She beams up at me. "You can never tell what recessive genes you might be carrying." I grimace at that thought, but she soothes those worries. "Our children are going to be so lucky to have you as a father."

My chest expands, and emotion clogs my throat.

"You are a constant source of surprises. The very best kind. You know that?"

She pushes up on her toes and kisses me. The kiss is slow, and warm, and perfect. When she ends it, she runs her thumb over my lip, and I catch her wrist and press my lips into her palm. She smiles.

"Come on, Uncle Sam. Let's go meet our niece, so we have time for some mutual appreciation before you need to go play Superman."

God, I love this woman. She's my greatest blessing.

I take her hand and enter the hospital, secure in the knowledge my days of walking alone are over.

Keep reading. Nick's story continues in Scarlet Angel…

PROLOGUE TO SCARLET ANGEL

NICK

The priceless seventeenth-century map portrays boundaries that no longer align with contemporary divisions. A subtle reminder of the fluid nature of alliances. The faded compass rose yields true north.

Where the bloody hell is Ash?

Rain lashes the panes with the fury of gods, punctuated with an occasional flash of lightning reflected on the framed map. In ancient times, men might question their decisions before such a storm. A weak man might perceive lightning as Zeus's anger.

A modern man understands nature has no interest in the goings on of a singular species. Neither do the dead gods.

Faint headlights glimmer in the distance. A trick of light?

No. It's Ash.

I swing the front door open before he can knock. The man's absolutely drenched. His mop of straw-colored hair is dry, but everything from his shoulders down is soaked. Rain droplets drip from his Barbour jacket, and there's a field hat in his hand covering his middle.

"Proper nasty out there," he says, stepping inside and dutifully removing his muddy boots.

With the click of the door and one glance around the barren foyer to ensure my sister isn't lurking, I ask, "Is it done?"

Ash offers me his mobile. The screen is lit.

I press the arrow and watch as a vehicle slams into a guardrail on a two-lane bridge and careens over the edge.

A shadow crosses the road and peers over the railing.

"Let's go to my office." He follows me along the corridor. On the off chance Lina saw a vehicle approach, our conversation should continue behind closed doors. Once inside the confines of my office, the door closed and locked, I ask "Who took the video?"

"It's from his vehicle." Ash doesn't bother sitting. The fireplace is lit, but Ash doesn't step closer to the heat. He stands at my side.

"The vehicle sunk?"

"Right fast."

My part's done. Now we'll see how good these blokes are at their job.

"He's asking an additional fee," Ash says while shoving one hand in his trouser pocket.

"I beg your pardon?"

"Cohen. Said he didn't know the Lupi Grigi were a part of it."

Fucktwit. As if he cares.

"Don't tell me the bastard's saying there's extra risk involved."

Ash shrugs. "He didn't know who the girl was in the car."

I want to keep Ashraf Cohen as a resource. The man's got skills. But coming back and asking for more…it's not a good look. And it's bollocks. The assassin could take out John Wick, if the man wasn't a Hollywood creation. Cohen is not afraid of Italian thugs.

Ash takes the mobile, flicks past the video, and hands it back, set to photos.

I flick through the shots. The snapshots focus on the vehicle and pitch-black river. Can't make out the embankment from the shots.

How far away was the team?

"How's Lina going to take the news?" he asks. I slant an inquisitive eye Ash's way. "Was she close to the girl?"

"Hadn't known her long." Lina isn't one to get close to friends. She keeps them at arm's length. She's rational like that, all thanks to being raised by a clueless older brother. With an exhale, I pass the phone back to Ash. I'll miss my friend.

"We've got Andrew from Scotland Yard reporting back. With the storm, they're swamped at the moment. It's not a priority."

I step up to the window, running through logistics. "If a story develops that may need a burial…"

I let the sentence fall behind the howl of wind. Ash knows the drill.

"When you get confirmation on your end, will you let me know?"

I narrow my eyes at the head of my security. He's not one to question. "Getting soft?"

"I liked them, ya' know. She seemed nice. Leo… Good guy."

Yeah, he was. Turncoat and all.

What else?

"You didn't tell Cohen about the second part of the plan?"

Ash's right eye twitches at a rhythmic pace. It's a side-effect of a head injury when serving with the British SAS.

"Of course not." He sounds both pissed and aghast at the notion.

"These days I've got to question everyone."

He gives a quick nod of understanding. "He might question why the car drove off the bridge, given he didn't ram if off, but he gave no sign he's harboring suspicions. If anything, he might be wondering if one of his bullets caught the driver."

The instructions had been to shoot to corral, not to shoot to kill. We had a number of routes planned. Cohen believed he acted as herding dog, but he also believed that after the confrontation, he'd need to dispose of the leak.

A risky fucking plan. But the message I received forced my hand.

"How much of a fee are we talking about?"

"Cohen?"

I scowl, losing patience. *What the fuck else would I be going on about?*

"Extra hundred."

"One hundred thousand pounds?"

"He's never been cheap," Ash says, looking about like he'd like to take a seat.

"Greedy wanker. Done." I drop into my desk chair, the spot where I get my best thinking done. "Keep an ear on the case. We need word to filter."

"*London Times?*"

"No. We'll crank suspicions if it gets out through abnormal channels. Need the story kept close, then, in a couple of days, be certain the victim's names are released. If for any reason they aren't–"

"We'll leak them–" he interjects.

"We won't." Media isn't Ash's strength. "But I'll make a call. We gotta do this the right way. It's got to be natural. Believable."

The mobile flashes a flood alert.

"They're saying we might lose electricity," he says.

I won't. I have a generator.

"Why don't you head home? Check on your old man."

He nods, grabbing his coat and hat.

"When your pop's ready, say the word. We've got land. Can set you up with him out here." Ash lives in the village; a stone's throw away.

He grins. "The old man's happiest within walking distance of the pub. And while I love the man, I don't wanna live with him. But I will head on. Make sure the oaf's stumbled home."

I follow him through the house to the front, as much out of boredom as anything else.

"Think this is the end of it?" Ash asks after he's donned his boots.

Eliminating the traitor helps, but…the message I received from someone identifying himself as Prophet doesn't sit right. How did this unnamed person know Leo was the leak? What else does he know? Who is he?

The wind blows the front door back and rain paints the entry.

"Let's ratchet security up a notch."

"You expecting the Grigi boys to come after you?"

I eye my friend. "Always a possibility. Unlikely."

"Possible though," he says, a touch too argumentative for my taste. “They were after them too, you know? Might have saved yourself a mint if you let them take care of it.”

No. Leo wouldn’t leave Willow behind with an ex-Mossad assassin hunting her. And he wouldn’t confront Cohen either. The man’s skills precede him. He wouldn’t risk a loss to Cohen knowing he’d be leaving his wife unprotected. If it had only been Italian goons in a car, he might’ve walked outside and blown their brains out. Problem solved. And he’d exit following Interpol’s plan without his bride. No, I needed to act.

Besides, if I didn’t act, the so-called Prophet might have.

“What’s next?” Ash asks.

“You’re going home. Tomorrow, beef up the ranks.”

“I meant what’s next with the Italians.”

“Believe it or not, Willow was the winning sacrificial pawn.” Ash doesn’t understand, but there’s no need for his understanding tonight.

Some plans come together so perfectly, it’s tempting to believe in the gods.

GRATITUDE

To my husband and daughters, thank you for putting up with late dinners and deadline weekends as I chase my dream.

To my doodle, thank you for being my ever present office companion and home protector.

To my writing friends, thank you for serving as my sounding board and support group. To Sara Hudson, thank you for always coming through with advice from everything from this cover to my blurbs.

To Damonza, thank you for all the care you put into cover designs and marketing elements.

As always, thank you to my editors, Lori Whitwam and Karen Cimms.

To my advanced reader team, thank you so much for reading, reviewing, answering my questions, and sharing my books on the vast web and beyond. You are the loveliest! Pure gold!

To my readers, thank you for taking a chance on me. There are millions of stories out there, and I'm grateful you chose to read mine.

ALSO BY ISABEL JOLIE

Arrow Tactical Security Series

Better to See You (Wolf and Alexandria)

Sure of One (Jack and Ava)

Cloak of Red (Sophia and Fisher)

Stolen Beauty (Knox and Sage)

Savage Beauty (Max and Sloane)

Sinful Beauty (Tristan and Lucia)

Gilded Saint (Sam and Willow)

Scarlet Angel (Nick and Scarlet) - Releasing March 20th

The Twisted Vines Series

Crushed (Erik and Vivi)

Breathe (Kairi and David)

Savor (Trevor and Stella)

Haven Island Series

Rogue Wave (Tate and Luna)

Adrift (Gabe and Poppy)

First Light (Logan and Cali)

The West Side Series

Blurred Lines (Jackson and Anna)

Trust Me (Sam Duke and Olivia)

Finding Delilah (Delilah and Mason)

Forgetting Him (Jason and Maggie)

Chasing Frost (Chase and Sadie)

Misplaced Mistletoe (Ashton aka Dr. Bobby and Nora)

Standalone Romances

How to Survive a Holiday Fling (Oliver Duke and Kate)

Always Sunny (Ian Duke and Sandra)

The Romantics (Harrison and Zuri)

ABOUT THE AUTHOR

Isabel Jolie, aka Izzy, lives on a lake, loves dogs of all stripes, and if she's not working, she can be found reading, often with a glass of wine. In prior lives, Izzy worked in marketing and advertising, in a variety of industries, such as financial services, entertainment, and technology. In this life, she loves daydreaming and writing contemporary romances with real, flawed characters with inner strength.

Sign-up for Izzy's newsletter to keep up-to-date on new releases, promotions and giveaways. (**Pro-tip** - She offers a free book on her home page…just scroll down after arriving at her site.)

Buy ebooks and signed paperbacks direct from Isabel at www.isabeljoliebooks.com

Want to say hi? Email her through her website or reply to her newsletter…she loves to hear from readers.

Made in the USA
Columbia, SC
14 December 2024